MW00916029

Affliction

THE AFFLICTION TRILOGY BOOK ONE

THE AFFLICTION TRILOGY BOOK ONE

CRYSTAL J. JOHNSON

SWEET ESCAPE
publishing

Copyright © 2024 Crystal J. Johnson
All rights reserved.
Published in the United States by Crystal and Felicity, LLC
No portion of this publication may be reproduced or transmitted, in any form
or by any means, without the express written permission of the copyright
holders.
PO Box 701 White Bluff, TN 37187
www.CrystalandFelicity.com
Second Edition by Crystal and Felicity, LLC: March 2024
ISBN: 9798883276469
Names, characters, places, and incidents featured in this publication are
either the products of the author's imagination or are used fictitiously. Any
resemblance to actual persons (living or dead), events, institutions, or
locales, without satiric intent, is coincidental.

Editor: Emma Stephens
Proofreader: Isabella at Como La Flor, LLC

Cover design by Crystal J. Johnson
Images © Crystal and Felicity, LLC via Canva

Trigger and Content Warning

Affliction is a love story that just so happens to have "zombies" in it. And where there are flesh-eaters, there are horrific choices to be made. Zs and the world they live in may be fictional, but some of the subject matter the characters inside these pages face is true to life and may not be suitable for all readers.

Please cautiously step into this story if you are sensitive to any of the following:

- Gun and/or knife violence
- Attempted sexual assault
- Discussion of suicide
- Blood and gore
- Descriptions of violent death
- Loss of a loved one (parent and/or friend)
- Parental abandonment
- Child death
- Descriptive sexual scenes
- Foul language

In the world of the Affliction, characters are faced with the probability of dying every day. This includes the need to take action if they are infected with the Z virus, meaning they may need to kill a loved one or themselves to keep others safe. This topic is discussed on page and at one point a character is placed in a position where they must decide if they need to take their own life. If this topic may be triggering for you, please do not read.

If you are struggling with self-harm or suicide, help is just three digits away. Dial 988 to speak with a professional at the Suicide and Crisis Lifeline.

If you wish to continue, welcome to the world of Affliction.

Much love,
Crystal

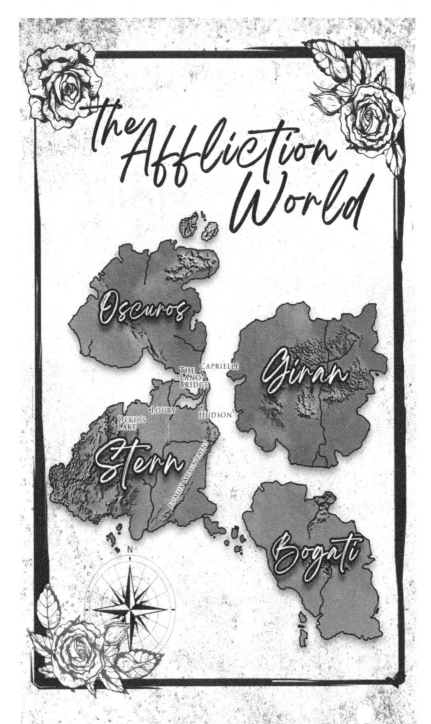

This book is dedicated to Rachel.

I will never again doubt the power of friendship.
The bond we share rivals that of sisters.
I have a lifelong friend to hold my secrets, carry my burdens, and love me unconditionally.
We can face a Z horde and probably huddle together in fear, but at least we die together.

Chapter One

The only thing normal about this Winter Solstice is the hideous thermal one-piece pajamas my cousin insisted I wear. t matches the one she's chosen from a box of our old things that belong to a life we no longer have. I should have put up a fight, told her the clothes were impractical and the holiday didn't matter without the rest of our family. Instead, I'm shimmying my damp body into the clingy material reminiscent of an ugly winter sweater. It's proof that what I would do for her has no limits.

The leg of my pajamas tangles around my foot, sending me stumbling forward and smacking my head against the towel rack.

"Dammit," I hiss, slapping the wall like it purposely moved into my way.

"You all right in there, Quinn?" River asks from the other side of the door.

I roll my eyes and rub the knot forming behind my ear. "I'd have better luck getting dressed in a coffin than in this ridiculously small bathroom."

"Just be grateful you *have* a functioning bathroom."

River is right—it doesn't matter that the bathroom contains no frills. The shower has just enough room to stand, and the toilet and sink are white, simple, and functional. The tiny space is a luxury in a time when many don't have a safe place to live or food to fill their bellies. We may live in a bunker under our childhood home, but we don't so much as go without hot water and electricity, let alone a meal. In a continent quarantined from the rest of the world and swarming with the Afflicted, we are the fortunate ones.

I fasten the countless buttons running up my torso and turn my attention to the mirror over the sink. Separating my hair down the middle, I work the wet strands into two light-brown braids on either side of my face. It's difficult not to look away from the worn-out young woman staring back at me. She's a far cry from the happy-go-lucky girl she was before the Affliction. Dark bags have taken residence under her gray eyes, her full lips are cracked, and her skin chapped and pale from the cold, dry air. But I'm not blind to the good. I've worked hard to maintain my physical strength, building lean muscle on my short frame. The universe knows I didn't look like this before I spent every day fighting to survive.

I open the bathroom door, and River jumps from the worn gray couch, clapping her hands together. Her dark golden curls bounce around her face, and her bright and toothy smile reminds me of an enthusiastic child instead of a nineteen-year-old. She takes several steps to the kitchenette, throws open a cupboard, and pulls out a package of chewy chocolate chip cookies before carrying on to the refrigerator where she removes two cans of soda.

"Are those cookies even safe to eat?" I ask, plopping down on the couch.

"I don't see why not, they've never been opened," she says, placing the snacks on the battered coffee table.

I pick up the package and look for the expiration date while she turns her attention to a dusty box on the floor. She pulls out an old digital music player and skips across the room. Opening the cabinet below the television mounted to the wall, she hooks the old music player to a small speaker.

"You do realize it's winter and we should be conserving our energy, right?"

"Live a little, Quinn. The heavens know everything is dying outside of this house. We don't have to join them," River quips.

I cross my arms over my chest, trying my best not to look amused at her antics.

Everything we do is calculated: every bite we eat, every bullet we shoot, and every bit of energy we use. My uncle took great care to ensure that our home could fully function during almost any type of catastrophe, and it's now up to us to make sure our supplies last. Still, it's hard not to get sucked into letting go when she's like this. River is an eternal light in our dark situation, and my only source of goodness in a world that is anything but.

Despite missing her parents, who also raised me, she makes the best of things. To the practical, her coping tactics may seem childish—dancing, singing, and eating an extra ration of food. To those who understand that any minute could be our last, she is the epitome of living life to its fullest. It is her refusal to be consumed by despair that reminds me I must do the same.

I shake my head and hide my smile as my cousin dances around the room, singing along to a classic Yule song we loved as children. When the verses run too long, and she can't remember the words, she gives up and returns to the box of decorations.

"Do you want to decorate the tree with me?" she asks, holding a miniature pink tinsel tree. It's the one her mom bought us when we were five and begged her to let us decorate the family tree in pink ornaments. My aunt Amara refused, but the next day, she surprised us with one of our own that included all the trimmings.

River places our childhood decorations onto the coffee table and motions me over. It doesn't take long before the tiny tree is sparkling with pink glitter and satin ribbons. She carries it to one of the side tables and plugs it into the wall. We stand together in our drab bunker, looking at the pink pine with a glowing star on top.

"Oh, wait," she says, jogging back to the cupboards along the wall. She pulls out a box wrapped in old newspapers and places it under the tree. In turn, I fetch the gift bag I put her presents in and set it on the table.

"World's Best Grandpa?" she questions after reading the block letters printed on the front of her gift.

For the first time in a while, I wholeheartedly laugh. My body doubles over, and I grasp my stomach. I try to explain it to her, but I can't hold it together long enough to get the words out. After several attempts, I say, "I'm working with limited resources. It was all I could find in the ransacked general store."

Her uncontrollable laughter joins in with mine.

It feels good to share this moment; it's almost like it used to be before Stern was overrun by those infected with the Z virus, and the continent quarantined from the rest of the world.

I reach over, pulling River into my arms and hug her tightly. "Happy Solstice, Riv."

She rests her head on my shoulder. "Happy Solstice,

Quinn."

This isn't how either of us wants to spend the holiday. We aren't supposed to be locked beneath our house, hoping the rest of our family is all right. We should be drinking hot cocoa upstairs and wrapping the gifts we waited until the last minute to buy. My uncle Josh should be sitting next to the tree, shaking every present with his name on it and correctly guessing what's inside. And Amara would have researched articles about how old household junk can be recycled into bows for the presents. We would have been up all night creating them with her, laughing and singing. Now, we have nothing but the ghost of the memories to haunt us.

"Hey, Quinn."

"Yeah?" I say, swallowing down the emotion building inside of me.

"You want to watch a movie?"

I squeeze her shoulder before letting go. "Yeah, let me go put this box back in the basement."

I press the button on the wall that releases the lock on the bunker's heavy steel door and step out onto the dark, freezing cold cement floor. We shut off all the utilities to the main house shortly after the blackout when we realized it was best if we stayed hidden. If someone happens to come across us and finds out we have running water and electricity, there's a chance they'll try and seize our home. By staying confined to the bunker, we can let our guard down a little and sleep soundly at night. It has allowed us to recapture some of the normalcy we lost to the Affliction.

I zigzag down the path of our belongings—everything we were able to carry down from the house—and place the box on top of the ones that contain the dishes from the kitchen.

Inside the bunker, River turns off the holiday music and everything goes silent—well almost. The distinct sound of footsteps and mumbling voices come from above. I hold my breath and glance at the floorboards above my head. More than one set of feet shuffle across the kitchen as they head toward the living room.

I rush back into the bunker and quickly slide my feet into my combat boots. Without a second thought, I grab my gun from the table next to the door and double-check the ammo inside of it.

"Quinn?"

"Someone's in the house."

River hurries to my side and slides on her slippers. "How do you know it's not a Z? Just wait it out until morning. They'll leave when they think there's no one to eat."

"It's people. I heard them talking. We can't take the risk of them staying until morning and wandering around in the daylight. If they were able to break into the house, they could get into the greenhouse. I'm just going to scare them away. Wait here and keep the door closed. We don't need something to happen to both of us if this goes wrong." When she doesn't reply, I glare at her and say, "Did you hear me?"

"Yeah, I hear you."

I check that the bunker locks behind me and creep up the rickety stairs of the basement. I carefully open the door to the main level and scan the area for the trespassers before slipping through and shutting it behind me. Pressing my back against the wall, I make my way to the kitchen.

The moon shines through the window, setting everything in a cerulean glow. The unused refrigerator looms like a giant in the corner and the stove is a threatening, boxy beast. Snow slowly builds outside the window above the sink. The house creaks and groans under the added weight on its room. Other than that, all is still in the kitchen.

I tiptoe through the house while my brain bombards me with thoughts of all the places the intruders can hide—the closets, the strange nooks and crannies that a house this old possesses, and behind the bigger furniture we were unable to carry to the basement, like the massive antique table and its eight chairs in the dining room. I quietly check them all but find nothing out of place.

My nerves calm a little as I step into the living room to discover it is empty as well. With my gun held firmly in both hands, I walk to the front door and stop short of grabbing the knob. Footsteps made with clumps of snow trail toward the sliding doors at the side of the living room. My breathing halts when whispering comes from Josh's study.

I shove my fear down deep within me and force my bravery to the surface. Concealing myself against the wall next to the door, I listen to the exchange between male voices. I can't quite make out what they're saying, but their tone matches the terror churning my stomach. Chancing a peek from around the door frame, I spot three guys huddle against the wall opposite from me.

"Aiden, come on man, you need to wake up," says one of the men to another who is hunched over on the floor.

I'm taken back by the sound of the speaker's voice. His accent is not from Stern—it's Giranish. In a show of good faith, the Stern president allowed for the evacuation of non-citizens before the continent was quarantined. It's hard for me to believe anyone chose to stay instead of returning to their homeland, but apparently, they did. Now, they have decided to take refuge in my house, and I can't allow them to stay.

I rest my head back on the wall and take a deep breath before making my move. With my gun firmly grasped in both of my hands, I step into the doorway and aim directly at the weakest of the three. "Don't make any sudden moves or I'll shoot him."

"Fuck," says the smaller of the two conscious men. His uneven black hair barely brushes the tops of his shoulders, and his slim face is lightly covered in hair. Filth blankets him, making his blue eyes look like they're glowing in the dark room.

The other young man is not looking any more hygienic than his friend. His warm olive face is covered with a dark brown beard, and his short hair is caked with dirt. His muscular frame is rigid and his big, brown eyes glint with worry. "Please don't shoot. Our friend is sick," he says.

My gaze falls to the fingers of the one they claim to be ill, looking for the telltale sign that he is Afflicted. There is no exposed bone or shredded tendons. Zs always try to sedate their cravings by gnawing on their own flesh first.

"What's wrong with him?" I ask.

The one with brown eyes answers, "I think it's just the flu. He's been sick for the past week, and it's gotten worse since we've had to sleep in the cold."

A pang of pity stirs in me, but I force it away. I can't take the risk of allowing them to stay, not when I don't know what they are capable of. It's River and me first, no matter how much someone needs help.

"Sorry, guys, but I need you to stand and slowly make your way out the front door." They don't move, staring at me like I'm not aiming a loaded gun at them. "I said move!"

Cold metal presses into the back of my neck. I go rigid, my next demand stuck in my throat. The man with blue eyes flashes me a quick smile, and I know I'm fucked.

"I don't think so. They're going to stay right where they are."

Chapter Two

The deep, accented voice from behind me sends chills down my spine, or maybe I'm giving him too much credit, and it's the gun poised to blow out my brain that has me frazzled. I battle through my jumbled thoughts and grasp on to one of the many survival lessons Josh taught River and me as children.

Not everything requires force, I hear my uncle say inside my head. I hope he's right because I'm outnumbered. Even if I shoot one of them, the guy behind me is going to take me out. I have no choice but to reason with them.

"How do I know you guys aren't delusional and trying to save him from a bite?" I ask the gunman.

"Because we're not."

I roll my eyes. Even he has to see how stupid his answer is. "Well, that settles it, you must be telling the truth."

The man behind me presses the gun more firmly to my head.

In response, I lock my elbows and tighten my grip

on my gun, keeping my aim steady on his friends. "Again, I'm going to have to ask you guys to leave, or I'm afraid I'm going to have to shoot your sick friend."

"Don't test me," the gunman growls.

My palms sweat, and my outstretched arms slightly tremble. This has the potential of becoming bloody, or even worse... deadly. It's a battle I'm not sure I can win.

"No, don't test *me*, or this arrow finds a new home in your lungs," says an all too familiar voice from behind us.

The gun wavers at my head and my lips lift into a cocky smile. "You never listen."

"Nope," River replies.

I step to the side, snatch the weapon from the guy behind me and point it at him. All the while, I keep my gun on the sickly one. I spare a glance at the gunman. He's a disheveled mess like the rest of them—his brown, wavy hair hits just short of his shoulders, and his five o'clock shadow does little to hide the ticking of his jaw. I meet his green eyes, and for the briefest of seconds, they speak of despair before shifting back to fierce anger.

"There is nothing in the gun," he spits, walking past me toward his friends.

"What the hell," I whisper. With one hand, I open the chamber of the revolver and let it spin—there's not a bullet in it.

River enters the room with an arrow nocked in her bow, and we watch the gunman squat in front of his sick friend, placing his hand on his forehead. "He's burning up."

And with those words, I know we're in trouble.

"What's wrong with him?" River asks. Like a moth to a flame, the girl is unable to look past those in medical need.

"The flu, I think. Aiden hasn't been able to hold

anything down for days," the gunman says, taking off his thin hoodie and wrapping it around his friend.

"Quinn," River gently warns, placing her hand on my arm and guiding me to lower my gun.

I hate that she wants me to drop my defenses. Every cell in my body is telling me not to trust these guys. But I hold my gun at my side for her.

"Can I speak to you for a second out in the living room?" I say with a fake smile.

River flashes a real grin at our unwanted guests. "If you guys will excuse us for a minute."

We step out of the room, and I leave a crack in the office door. My gaze darts between River and what I can see of the men. I harshly whisper, "They can't stay."

"But he's sick."

"Yeah, but with what?"

"He doesn't have the virus, and none of those guys are dressed to go back out there. They're wearing torn up hoodies and their shoes have holes in them. It's freezing and..."

Oh God, here it comes, I think but ask anyway. "And?"

"And it's Yule time."

Of course, she'd pull the holiday card. How am I supposed to argue with that? If I'm the bad guy that sends them on their way, River will worry about them. I can almost guarantee she will set food on the porch to feed them like stray animals. Which, in turn, will attract Zs.

I sigh and ask, "What do you suggest we do?"

"The sick boy needs to get someplace warm." She holds up her hand before I can protest. "Let's take him and one other guy with us into the bunker. I'll search the sick one for bites, so you can rest knowing he's not Afflicted, and you can search the other for weapons. We can lock the storage room, and you can sleep with your gun under your pillow."

Damn her and her tender heart, *and* her ability to make me feel guilty without even trying. "I want it on the record that I don't like this idea at all."

With a winning smile, she says, "Duly noted."

Together, we walk back into the study. All three men have now discarded their jackets and wrapped them around their sick friend who's shivering on the floor.

Up until this point, my adrenaline has kept me warm, but the cold is getting to me. Taking note of my pajamas and combat boots, I wrap my arms over my chest, hoping certain body parts have not made our visitors aware of how cold I am. Of all the nights for someone to break in, they chose this one.

The young man lying on the floor coughs and moans. If we are going to help him, it's time to get a move on it. We need to get him someplace warm.

"Here's the deal, we have an area downstairs that's heated. You—" I point to the blue-eyed man "—can stay with him and us down there for the night. And you—" again I gesture to the one with brown eyes "—can help carry him down." Lastly, I turn to the gunman. "You can wait for your friend to return at the top of the stairs."

The gunman nods in agreement. It is a testament to how desperate he is to save his friend. There is no way I would leave River's side, and I definitely wouldn't do it with strangers. But what other choice does he have?

River steps toward them, asking, "Do you mind if I look him over?"

The three men shift back with their eyes locked on her. It's not just their apprehension that has them fixated. River is beautiful, blessed with an onslaught of perfect features—full lips, big gray eyes set against smooth, light brown skin, and topped with a wild mane of curls. The stresses of the life we've lived for the past eighteen months don't show on her at all.

River checks the sick man's pulse and feels his forehead. "I'm going to do my best to help you, all right?" She needlessly assures him, brushing his blonde hair from his pale face. "His name is Aiden, correct?"

"Yes," answers the man with brown eyes.

Turning to look at each of them, she says, "I'm River Ellery, and this is my cousin, Quinnten."

"Quinn," I quickly correct her, crossing my arms.

The brown-eyed man reaches out and shakes River's hand. "Noah Oliver."

"Westin, Wes MacVey," says the man with blue eyes.

With a clipped tone, the gunman says, "Ryland Shaw."

River stands, and they follow suit, lifting their friend from the floor. When we reach the basement door, Ryland stops and watches as we descend the stairs without him. Maybe I should feel sorry for leaving him out considering their circumstance, but I'm still a little salty about him pressing his gun against my head, and I don't trust him or his friends.

Aiden's limp body is maneuvered through the maze of boxes and chairs until we reach a dead end. To the unsuspecting eye, it looks like nothing but a brick wall. I open a camouflaged panel and place my finger on a sensor pad. With a quick beep and metal sliding against metal, the wall next to us opens. The two men sigh when the warmth of the room greets their frozen skin, and my stomach turns in response. They're now completely aware of how valuable our home is, and River and I are at a disadvantage.

I force down my unease and direct them to lay Aiden on the couch. River kneels beside him and goes to work removing his clothes. Noah doesn't hesitate to abide by my rules, and with a final worried glance, he steps out of the bunker.

Turning to Wes, I say, "I need to check you for weapons."

He pulls a pocketknife from his pants and hands it to me. With a playful smile, he lifts his arms above his head. "Have at it."

I second guess my decision to frisk him; he might enjoy this way more than he should. But I have no choice, we're already treading in dangerous territory. I rapidly pat him down, finding nothing else on him. As soon as I step back empty handed, he slides in next to River and assists her in undressing Aiden.

River lifts her head, meeting my scrutinizing gaze, and says, "I'm sure those guys upstairs are hungry and cold. Why don't you grab a few of those military meal things in the storage room? There are some sweats and blankets in there as well. Stop looming over me and be useful. Wes and I are fine."

I glare at Wes, letting him feel the weight of my distrust. It clearly doesn't work because he chuckles and says, "Honestly, you're at a greater advantage here. I've got no weapons and nowhere to go. My best mate is dying and I'm not leaving his side. I won't harm you."

The sincerity in his words hit me straight in the chest. His circumstance *is* worse than mine. At one time I would have been sympathetic to his situation. Not anymore, not when it is so desperate. The things people have done for just a bite of food are unthinkable. No one is the *good guy* anymore.

"Go help them, Quinn," River snaps.

I grumble my disapproval while walking to the cabinet containing my clothes. Yanking out something more appropriate to wear, I slide through the door next to the bathroom. The storage room is lined with shelves full of nonperishable food items and our small armory of weapons and bullets—items my family collected when a zombie apocalypse simply made for a great horror story.

I change and gather the supplies for the two men upstairs, stuffing them into a duffle bag. When I step back into the living area, I find Wes sitting on the floor devouring our bag of cookies, his gaze locked on River as she sponge bathes Aiden on our couch. They seem so calm in each other's presence, so unconcerned with the unknown. I don't know if that makes them stupid, or if it makes me a bitch because I can't seem to find any reason to trust them.

With a sigh, I grab a battery-operated lantern and hesitantly leave River locked in a room with two strange men. As I approach the study, I'm met with Noah and Ryland discussing the bunker. They sit side by side on my uncle's leather couch, leaning forward with their elbows on their knees and heads close. I slow my steps and listen to Ryland's line of questions about the bunker. It is clear by his need to know the layout and what's inside that he's as uncomfortable with his friends being down there. It's good to know that at least one other person in this house has his wits about him.

"I brought you guys some supplies for the night," I say, ending their conversation as I place the duffle bag on the dark mahogany desk at the front of the room. "Are you familiar with M.R.E.s?" They shake their heads, and I open one of the tan plastic bags with the knife Wes handed over to me. "They're these ready-made meals the military uses.

This one is chicken noodle soup." I remove the lid from a water bottle and pour a bit into the pouch. "The water somehow activates this heating element, so the food should be warm in a couple of minutes."

"It's oxidation-reduction," Noah says.

"If that's what it's called when this big bag of heat warms this small bag of food inside it, then sure," I say, preparing the second M.R.E. I set it aside to warm before pulling out the rest of the supplies. "I brought you both some sweats to wear while your clothes are drying. You can use the bathroom next to the stairs to get dressed. There's no running water so please don't use the toilet. You'll have to go outside for that."

I don't even finish what I'm saying before Noah jumps from the couch collecting the folded gray sweatpants and shirt from me. I hold out the lantern to him, and he takes it before quickly rushing from the room, saying *thank you* over his shoulder. Regret washes over me as I realize I'm alone with the man who held a gun to my head earlier.

With a long exhale, I return my gaze to Ryland. His hands are clasped together with his index fingers pressed against his lips. He stares at me like he's devising a plan to murder me in my sleep, and the hairs on the back of my neck rise. I look away, uncomfortable with his intense scrutiny. As I busy myself with finishing their meals, I can feel him watching my every move.

I get it, I really do. If I were in his position, I'd be doing the same. He's at a disadvantage. River and I know every nook and cranny of this house. We have weapons stashed here and a room to lock ourselves inside. Ryland and his friends are at our mercy. And that is exactly why I believe he is devising a plan to take us out if he must. He hasn't remained alive without knowing he always needs to find a way to gain the upper hand.

When the soup is warm, I give it to him along with a plastic spoon and a bottle of water.

He mumbles a *thank you* and digs in.

I sit on the edge of the desk as he devours his meal. Greasy waves fall across his face when he leans over the bag to keep the food from dropping on him and the floor. He takes bite after bite, hardly chewing before swallowing.

The sneakers he wears are muddy with holes worn on the side, terrible for trekking the snow. His thin, black t-shirt reveals a collection of tattoos covering his arms. They're mostly traditional nautical artwork tied together with subtle waves. The most beautiful piece is the antique compass inked in black with shades in gray on his right forearm. He wears a couple of pieces of jewelry—a silver ring and a necklace swinging back and forth from his neck. Hanging from the chain is a pendant—a sharp pointed crescent moon. It is the symbol of the continent Bangoti. I find that strange since his accent suggests he is from Giran. This all opens a new slew of questions.

The creaking of the door opening down the hall has me abandoning my assessment of Ryland. Noah returns with a bright smile on his bearded face. He tosses his dirty clothes on top of a backpack, and we exchange the lantern for the other bag of food. He digs in to eat before he sits next to Ryland.

Seeing how famished they both are, I prepare another packet. I'd intended for their second M.R.E. to be their breakfast, but I don't like the idea of them having empty stomachs. For tonight, I want them to be full and have a warm, safe place to sleep, even if I'm uncomfortable with our arrangement. Tomorrow, they can leave rested and well-fed, and my duty to the less fortunate will be complete.

I'm not surprised by my weakness toward their hunger. For as long as I can remember, my summer vacations were humanitarian projects with my aunt and uncle. During our journeys to remote villages, I witnessed the pure pain on someone's face when they're starving. I hate the thought of people going hungry, especially when all four continents were close to eradicating the problem. That's not the case anymore, at least not in Stern. Mass production farms and factories are extinct, and survivors of the Affliction are left scavenging for food while trying not to be the next meal for a Z.

If it were not for River's and my safety, I might not have been hesitant to help these guys. I may have invited them into my home, cooked them a meal, and played a board game as we got to know each other. We could have become friends. That's not how it is now though, and every move I make must take both River and me into consideration. Nothing is going to distract me from that, especially the four men now taking refuge in our house.

Chapter Three

I'm cranky this morning, and I don't mean like give-me-a-few-minutes-to-wake-up-and-have-a-cup-of-coffee cranky. I'm legitimately annoyed-by-everything-I-might-take-out-my-gun-and-shoot-someone cranky.

When I returned to the bunker after situating Noah and Ryland last night, I found Aiden in clean clothes and soundly sleeping on the couch. On the floor, next to him was his guardian freshly showered and cocooned in a pile of blankets. River sat on her top bunk, using a battery-powered light to skim through the medical book she never got to use at university, looking to diagnose Aiden's ailment. I silently crept through the room and slipped into my lower bunk, facing the two men. Wrapping my hand around my gun under my pillow, I tried to relax. I dozed off a couple of times but woke up from the bed shaking as River climbed down to check on her patient. It was a rough night to put it kindly.

Everyone is still sleeping when I tuck my gun into my jeans and tiptoe to the kitchenette. I take the coffee carafe out of the cupboard, preparing it to brew on the stove before moving on to an economy-sized box of pancake mix.

Across the room, River checks Aiden's temperature before plugging in our little Yule tree. With our gifts to each other in tow, she joins me in the kitchen and hands me mine. With a bright smile, she digs into her bag and holds up a large tube. "Oh my God, face scrub, and it's a good brand!"

I grin at her excitement for the product we used to take for granted and watch as she pulls out a box of tea. "I used to drink this all the time in grade school. I forgot how much I loved it." River bats away tears with the back of her hand. "Thanks, Quinn. I love them."

I nod, too emotional to speak.

"Open yours," she urges.

I tear the newspaper from around a small box, revealing a picture of a gaudy ring labeled *Mood Ring*.

"This should be good," I say, pulling out the ring and slipping it onto my finger.

River removes a folded piece of paper from inside the packaging. It's a chart explaining what mood corresponds to the color of the stone.

"It's black. You're stressed," she declares.

A humorless chuckle escapes me. "That sounds about right."

She frowns and continues to study the meaning of the other colors. "I wish it were pink, or at least light blue."

I look over her shoulder at the chart. "Happy or relaxed? Riv, I'm not even going to bother with happy, but relaxed, are you kidding me? There are four grown men in our house, three of which could probably overpower us. I'll feel more relaxed once they leave today."

She walks away from me, folding the paper and

placing it back into the box. "They're not leaving today."

"Oh, yes, they are," I say through clenched teeth, trying to keep my voice down.

"I think I know what's wrong with Aiden. His breathing is strained and crackly like he has fluid on his lungs. I think he has pneumonia. He can't go back out there, or he'll die."

Blowing out a puff of air, I pace the kitchen. Damn, I hate the feeling of being torn between what my mind says to do and what my heart knows is right. We've done more than what's necessary to help these guys out. I can't help my thoughts from roaming in the seedier territory. They could be trying to break us with the sad story of their pneumonia-ridden friend, hoping to throw us off so we're unsuspecting when they execute the hostile takeover of our home. The blond boy hasn't even woken up. Who's to say they didn't find him on the street dying and think they could play a sympathy card with him?

I sigh and close my eyes.

It's a far-fetched idea, and last night, every single one of the men had a clear moment of panic. Aiden is someone they care about immensely, and no matter how I try to spin it, I can't deny that.

There's no way they will survive the world beyond these walls. Ryland didn't even have a bullet in his gun, and someone would need to carry Aiden. They would never make it through a Z attack, and if the Afflicted don't kill them, the sub-freezing temperatures very well could. Can I honestly live with myself if I send them out to die?

"Quinnten, you're taking longer than usual to come to the right answer," River says over her shoulder as she flips a pancake in the skillet.

I stop moving, lean against the wall, and examine

Aiden's and Wes's sleeping forms. I think about what it would take for me to sleep in a room with people I don't know. They must have been through hell to be so exhausted that they'd risk death at the hands of strangers for a few hours of rest.

My brows furrow as I catch a drop of sweat traveling down Aiden's cheek; his fever has spiked again. "What's it going to take to get him well?" I ask.

She places a plate stacked with pancakes on the table and starts another batch. "We have some medication, but it's expired. It won't be as potent as it should be, but even then, I need him to wake up, so he can take it. Thankfully, he's still sweating, so there's still some fluid in his body, but I have to get him to push water. If he dehydrates, it won't be good."

"How long do you think it will take for the medication to kick in?"

The spatula in her hand hits the pan and her shoulders slouch. "I don't know, it just depends on how bad it is and if it spreads anymore."

I push away from the wall and fill my coffee mug. "Is he contagious?"

"I don't think so. For as long as they say he's been sick, the other boys would be showing signs by now. My biggest hurdle is figuring out whether he has contracted a bacteria or a virus."

I shudder at the mention of a virus and remind myself that Z is just one of the thousands. "All right. Have Wes help you move Aiden to my bed, and then he can sleep in yours. You and I will share the sofa's pullout-bed," I say and take a sip of the hot black sludge in my cup.

After preparing the food and moving Aiden, we invite Wes to sit at the table and eat a plate of pancakes. I take one cake, slather it with homemade strawberry jam, and roll it up as a meal to go. I grab two dishes, a dozen pancakes, and a jar of grape jam and take them with me upstairs.

The sun hides behind gray clouds, but the house is much brighter than it was last night. I find Noah and Ryland standing at my uncle's desk, leaning over a map sprawled out on the top. Noah looks comfortable in his clean sweats, but Ryland is still in his filthy jeans, t-shirt, and has put on his hoodie again.

I clear my throat, walking closer.

"Morning, Quinn." Noah smiles.

"Good morning. I brought you breakfast," I say, setting the plates beside the map.

Ryland doesn't bother to address me and remains busy examining the northern regions of Stern. He runs his fingers through his hair, pulling it away from his eyes. "I don't know, Noah. That route puts us hiking through major cities. It's best if we avoid populous areas to get to the land bridge."

Noah spreads jam on several pancakes as he listens to his friend. I quietly stand to the side, nibbling on my food. In deep concentration, Ryland runs his finger along a route leading from here to the land bridge joining Stern to the content just north of it, Oscuros. Every time he reaches a well-known city, he curses under his breath and starts the path again.

Noah cuts into his stack of cakes and takes an enormous bite. "You're right. With our luck, we need to steer clear of anywhere we know is crawling with the Afflicted." With a shake of his head, he picks up his plate and glances at me. "These are good. Did you make them?"

"River did," I say.

"Tell her I said thanks," he says, sitting on the couch.

Ryland gives up on the map and prepares the leftover pancakes.

My curiosity gets the best of me, and I finally ask, "Why would you guys want to go to the land bridge? Rumor has it that Oscuros built a huge wall and placed a military presence there to keep the people of Stern out."

Ryland stops mid-motion with a fork full of grape jam hovering over his breakfast. His gaze meets mine, and I cease breathing for a moment. His eyes are a vibrant jade, but the harshness of his stare takes away from their beauty. With an intense glare, he studies me, and I can't find the strength to look away. My chest tightens as my mind races to make sense of his baffling demeanor. Finally, he rips his eyes from mine, freeing me from his hold when Noah answers my question.

"We're hoping the land crossing is still open. Hopefully, our passports will get us into Oscuros and from there, back to the Giran." Noah furrows his brow in response to Ryland's apparent disapproval. "Well, she asked."

"But why didn't you guys leave during—"

"Noah, get your shoes on. I'm going to need your help outside," Ryland orders, folding the map and placing it in his bag. He waits for his friend at the doorway while Noah stuffs the last of his food into his mouth.

Before they exit the room, Noah gives me an apologetic grin. "Thanks again, Quinn."

The plate Ryland was preparing is left untouched on the desk, and I want to scream at him for being an asshole, but I think better of it. He doesn't trust me, and I can hardly blame him. In all honesty, he's the only one in their group showing any caution when it comes to us. I admire him for looking out for his friends when the others seem to be a bit careless, but that's the extent of my admiration. The guy is an inconsiderate jerk. I didn't have to give him two M.R.E.s last night, and I surely didn't have to bring him breakfast. Just because civilization is in shambles doesn't mean he needs to act uncivilized.

I stroll over to the dusty window looking out over the front yard. Ryland looms over Noah at the bottom of the porch steps. His face contorts as he points to the house. He's clearly not happy I was told about their plan to get home. I don't see what the big deal is; I'm a Stern citizen, and it's not like they're going to let me mosey across the continental line.

Before the blackout happened, the news was reporting that Oscuros was building a massive wall at their end of the land bridge to keep people from Stern from entering. They were erecting the barrier quickly, and by now, the only way to leave Stern is by sea—that is if nobody is still patrolling the waters. And even if they're not watching the water, it would be difficult for someone to find all the provisions needed for a long sea voyage. If these guys have a plan to get home, then more power to them. I'd take the opportunity to leave if I could too.

The question still remains—if they want to go home so badly, why didn't they leave when they had the chance?

I discard my curiosity and come to terms with the fact that my house guests are a complete mystery. Moving away from the window, I pick up Noah's empty plate. Since he was ungrateful, I think about taking Ryland's meal away but stop myself. He might change his mind after he's done scolding his friend, and I can't bring myself to waste the food.

When I return to the bunker, Wes and River are crowded around a conscious but lethargic Aiden. Wes holds him in a sitting position while River brushes his hair back from his face. She tries to coax him into drinking some water, but instead, his head rolls in my direction. His eyes are a dim, lifeless blue and light blond stubble covers his gaunt face, but it's not enough to cover the dimple in the middle of his chin. Underneath his sickly façade is a handsome young man.

As I stand at his bedside, he gives me a broad smile and says, "Hey."

"Hey." I laugh through my response.

Something tells me he's the friend that nobody can get mad at. The one everyone runs to for a good laugh and a little ray of sunshine when things feel too bleak.

Wes turns to me with a worry-line between his eyes. "Quinn, do you mind getting Ry, please?"

I shift side to side before nodding and heading back out.

Ryland is sitting on the couch in the study with one leg crossed over the other. The plate of food I left behind rests on his thigh as he eats his breakfast. Noah stands on the opposite side of the room, folding the blankets he used the night before. It's dead silent, with thick tension lingering in the air.

"Aiden's awake, and Wes asked me to get you, Ryland." I don't bother to wait for an answer, and instead tell Noah, "You can come too."

Both men leave behind what they're doing and rush to follow me into the bunker. As soon as I open the door, Ryland breezes past me, walking straight to his friend's side. "How are you feeling?"

Aiden weakly shrugs. With a brogue from the west coast of Giran, he says, "You know, I could go for a pint about now."

"Yeah, me too," Ryland replies with a smirk.

River hands Ryland a pill and a cup of water. "I need

him to take these."

With a quick nod, he turns back to his friend. "Do you think you could take a sip of water for me?"

Aiden's head barely moves from one side to the other. "I don't believe so."

Placing his hands on each side of Aiden's face, Ryland forces him to look at him. His long fingers twitch at the feel of the heated skin under them—a reminder of the critical condition of his friend's health. "You have to take this pill. Do you hear me?"

"I hear you, but I don't want to be sick anymore," Aiden whines. His attitude is reminiscent of a child who doesn't want to eat the vegetables on his plate or wishes to stay up after his bedtime. He doesn't seem to comprehend that taking the medication will make him better. The right choice is overshadowed by the unwanted feeling of throwing up.

Ryland moves in closer and drops his voice. "I can't lose you, too. We made an oath. You promised us you would uphold it, Aiden. Take the damn pill so you can get better, and we can go home."

The ill man's eyes turn glassy and his lip trembles, but finally, he opens his mouth wide. Ryland lays the pill on his tongue and presses the cup to his lips until every drop is gone.

Aiden immediately gags. His body violently contracts, and it takes both Ryland and Wes to keep him on the bed and from hitting his head against the wall. A small noise escapes me, and a gentle hand rests on my shoulder. I give Noah a strained grin, thankful for the small gesture of reassurance.

Wes lays Aiden's head on the pillow. "Hold it down, mate. Deep breaths."

Aiden does as he asks, taking several laboring breaths until his body stops convulsing. It's not until he relaxes and starts to drift to sleep that everyone steps away from his bedside and joins Noah and me across the room.

Ryland turns to River and asks, "What did you give him?"

"Antibiotics. I believe he has pneumonia. The rattling sound of his breathing suggests fluid is in his lungs."

"How long before it starts to work?" he asks, desperately pressing for answers.

"I don't know. It expired over three years ago, so it will take longer than if it were brand new. Plus, I'm not sure what type of pneumonia he has. This is going to be a process of elimination. It will be weeks before he's well enough to travel."

Ryland gathers the hair on the top of his head into his fist. "Weeks?"

"Yes, weeks." She allows her words to sink in before continuing, "I suggest you let Quinn take the three of you into town. You need warmer clothes, and she knows the areas that have a higher probability of finding necessities. Maybe you'll run into some newer medication in one of the houses; I'll give you a list of what I need."

Part of me wants to strangle River for offering me as a tour guide, and the other wants to hug her with pride. While I've been on edge and hesitant to help these men, she's kept a cool head. Her collected demeanor and her studious nature are why she was accepted into one of the most prestigious pre-med programs in Stern. One day, she'll make an excellent doctor.

With a quick nod, Ryland gives in to her suggestion. I've not seen someone this determined in a long time. He has the same look I have when I think about reuniting with our family, and all the steps I need to take to make it happen. There's not one damn thing on this planet I'll let stand in my way. Ryland might be the only person in this room who can relate to the sentiment.

"We're ready to go when you are," he says, pulling me away from my thoughts.

I match his firm look—squared shoulders, straightened spine, and a refusal to look away. Yep, he's as resolute as I am about protecting those he cares about. My admiration for him increases a little. We stare each other down, neither of so much as blinking, waiting to see who will fold first. The side of Ryland's mouth slightly turns upward before he turns on his heels. I glare at his back as he weaves through the maze of boxes in the basement.

I question if that hint of a smile was just a figment of my imagination. It has to be. There is no way his hard exterior cracked. If I've learned anything in the past few hours, it is that Ryland Shaw is a complete asshole.

Chapter Four

The dark gray snow clouds that have blocked the sun for days have finally broken. I close the house door behind me and pause to take in the billions if not trillions of tiny snowflakes unite to create a thick white blanket as far as the eye can see. It's blinding the way the sun's rays reflect off the snow. I squint to take in the way nature has adorned our old country style house with long pointed icicles hanging from the eves. On the outskirts of the property, a slight breeze catches the powdery snow weighing down the branches of the pine trees, creating a fog of icy dust. The Ellery estate is the perfect picture of a winter wonderland.

I adjust the strap of the duffel bag over my shoulder and descend the porch's wooden steps. As soon as Ryland said he was ready to venture into town, I prepared to go. We need to get this over with since waiting will do more harm than good. Sleeping soundly through the night when the next day brings a chance of imminent danger is next to impossible, and lack of sleep is a recipe for disaster. Our safest bet is to find what the guys need and quickly return home. Procrastination holds no comfort when there's the chance of dying at the hands of hungry, flesh-eating ex-humans.

The snow crunches beneath my black boots, and inside my pocket, a knife taps against my leg with each step. I opted to forego my usual heavy coat and fleece-lined gloves for a sleeker look—a tight black thermal shirt topped with a thin black jacket. My unruly brown hair is pulled into a ponytail at my nape and topped with my favorite gray beanie. I don't give much thought to what I wear these days, but this is my badass take-no-prisoners look. Even in a world full of Zs, a girl sometimes has to dress the part in order to feel it.

I step from around the house and find everyone waiting for me in front of the garage. Our uninvited guests have all returned to wearing the clothes they had on last night, and their backpacks hang loosely from their shoulders, waiting to be restocked during today's outing. Each of them has an anxious energy that they seem eager to unleash. I understand the feeling. Sometimes I feel like I can take on a whole slew of Zs, all the while I'm a nervous wreck.

I've walked the property and driven into town by myself a time or two since the quarantine, but never have I left River behind with someone else. Granted, I'm overreacting a bit, the chances of Aiden finding enough energy to attack my cousin is like one in a million, but it doesn't stop me from worrying. It's all I seem to do these days.

I lift the panel to the garage's security pad and enter the pin with trembling fingers. The jig's about to be up on one of our most carefully guarded secrets.

River steps beside me, and together, we raise the

door. Our routine is like a choreographed dance—I crawl under the front of the old blue truck and unplug it from the charger while she looks under the hood and checks all the fluids.

Noah stands next to River, examining the internal workings. In complete awe, he says, "It's electrical."

I stand and find River smiling at his childlike fascination. Her cheeks brighten with a hint of pink, and her eyes lock onto his hands fidgeting around with the wiring.

"It's pretty amazing, right? My dad is an engineer who specializes in alternative energy. The truck is electrical, but also has the capability to run off ethanol gas, which he used to make here."

"The fact that he converted an automobile this old into an energy-efficient machine while keeping so many of its original parts is remarkable," he gushes, leaning in to examine the engine closer.

The pride River shows at this moment tells of how much she loves and admires her father. Not that I blame her, but my respect for Josh is for an entirely different reason. It's not every day you hear of a brother taking on the task of raising his sister's child, but that's what he did. He's not only my uncle, but the only father I've ever known.

River doesn't bother with downplaying her dad's greatness. "If you think this is amazing, you should see all the upgrades to the house. It's powered by solar and wind energy, and it filters the water from the lake on the edge of the property. It is completely self-sufficient—off the grid."

My body buzzes with nervous tension as she gives away our secrets one by one. "All right, that's enough nerdy flirting from you two," I say. "We need to get on the road, so we can be back before dark."

They take a step back and I close the hood with a

bang.

Noah's face reddens as our gazes meet. "We weren't... I wasn't flirting."

Wes opens the truck door, saying, "As painful as it was to watch, you were flirting. Honestly, your game is a bit shit."

The mortified young man steps away from River with a strained smile. He scurries behind the front seat to join Wes on the bench in the back, and immediately, the two exchange heated whispers.

River closes the space between us and pulls me into a hug. She presses her cheek to mine and quietly says, "Well, he is cute."

The lack of social interaction in our current situation is bound to make anyone hypersensitive to any attention given to them. Also, it doesn't hurt that Noah is handsome, despite the unkempt facial hair and the filthy strands on the top of his head. It's strange. Just yesterday, the idea of having a crush on someone would have been absurd, but here River stands smitten with a boy.

I roll my eyes. "Promise me you'll stay in the bunker until we get back."

She reaches up to my beanie and rights it on my head with both of her hands. "First, admit Noah's cute."

The light gray color of her eyes reflects humor and a hint of lightheartedness. She's held steadfast to a piece of her innocence in spite of a deadly disease, estranged parents, and ravenous people-eaters. Our eye color is the only physical trait that can attest to the fact we are related. Yet, it's also the telltale sign that we are so vastly different.

Lightly squeezing her hands, I move them away from my face. "Stay out of trouble, Riv."

Without further delay, I jump into the driver's seat

and start the engine. The truck is deceitfully quiet, disguising its real power.

Ryland opens the passenger's side door and slides in next to me. I spare him a sideways glance while he focuses straight ahead. His fingers curl into fists and his jaw flexes. He reminds me of a fighter who refuses to let his opponent see his weakness. Just like those who have trained to fight in the ring, I have a feeling his downfalls are limited. He'll do whatever it takes to win.

I back out of the garage and wait for River to close the door before I pull onto the rustic dirt road. My attention is divided between steering through the trees and Noah. He cranes his neck as we pass two critical structures on the property—Amara's greenhouse and Josh's workshop. His curiosity for either building makes me uncomfortable. Next to the bunker, they're our safety nets. One is the major supplier of our food, and the other protects a small fleet of energy-efficient vehicles like the truck. Both resources are worth more than their weight in gold in a society that no longer produces such luxuries.

I'm preparing a story to stifle his curiosity when he asks, "Is that a cell phone tower?"

"Yes," I slowly answer.

His question about the tall tower disguised as a massive pine tree is unexpected. One of the major cell phone companies paid my uncle a load of money to build it on the property. Amara wasn't fond of the idea and only agreed once they promised to dress it up as one of the surrounding trees. Even with its fake branches and faux brown bark, it's never quite fit in.

Leaning forward to get a better view, Noah asks, "Does it work?"

I shrug. "It did before the blackout."

With a hum, he sits back and falls silent with the

rest of the passengers.

I find it hard to keep my concentration on the road. It's been a year and a half since I last spent an extended amount of time with someone other than my cousin. There was a time when I looked forward to making new friends, trying new things, and living outside of my comfort zone. Now, the presence of strangers unsettles me. I question if I'll ever get used to having anyone but River within arm's length. If the nerves I feel right now are any indication, the answer is no.

We turn onto the main road leading to town, and I take in the familiar sights that are at the same time unrecognizable to me. The mom-and-pop store with its awning over the storefront flapping in the freezing wind, the gas station with its pumps rendered useless, and the movie theater where half of the letters on its marquee are missing. Devil's Lake is a shell of the cozy small town it used to be.

"What's your plan?" Ryland asks, pulling me from my thoughts.

I gather my wits and with as much authority as possible say, "There's a middle-class neighborhood east of downtown, and the homes are abandoned. If people are hanging around here, my guess is they've moved north to the more expensive houses. Hopefully, we'll find everything we need without any trouble."

A motion in my peripheral vision catches my attention. Ryland pulls the pendant hanging from the chain around his neck in between his fingers and rubs the smooth surface. It's the first sign of a nervous habit he's shown since I met him. The tiny gesture may betray him, but his deep voice doesn't. "Give me the worst-case scenario. What kind of trouble might we run into?"

"We hardly ever encounter people; it's mostly Zs and one or two at the most," I say.

"You mean someone with the Z virus?"

"Sorry, yeah, one of the Afflicted." I roll my eyes. I hate the humanizing term, but I also laugh every time someone says zombies. The countless creatures I've killed don't possess an ounce of humanity and they're not reanimated corpses, moaning about eating brains. So Zs it is.

I steer the truck away from the road and park it in a thicket of high brush covered in snow. "We're going to walk the rest of the way. I don't want to risk there being anyone around that might try to steal the truck. It's only about two blocks to the neighborhood," I say, exiting the vehicle.

I pull my duffel bag from under my seat. Inside is a small medical kit, two bottles of water, and five guns—one of which is the revolver Ryland pointed at me last night. Reaching over the seat, I hold it out to him. "Try not to aim it at my head now that it has bullets in it."

Ryland takes my offering while biting the inside of his cheek to keep from smiling. Opening the revolving chamber, he lets it spin once before saying *thank you*.

I raise the front of my shirt and slide a semiautomatic handgun into my waistband at my hip. "Five shots isn't a lot," I state, referring to the bullet capacity of his gun.

"No," he says.

Wes moves beside me and says, "Ry only takes clear shots."

Waiting for a clear shot must be nerve-wracking. River and I always do our best not to waste our ammunition, but there are times when adrenaline and panic drive us. Rapidly firing while a Z runs at superhuman speed to eat our faces off doesn't leave a chance to contemplate if we're using ammo responsibly. We shoot until we hit a vital organ, and they fall dead.

Taking an extra gun from the bag, I hand it to Ryland. "Just in case you get more than five clear shots today."

"Thanks," he mumbles, placing the revolver in the back of his pants and leaving the semi-automatic out.

The remaining two weapons I give to Noah and Wes, who proceed to check them for ammo.

I say a silent prayer that I don't regret arming these guys. Every minute I'm with them, they learn something new about how River and I made it this far. It's information they could use against us. Even if they don't intend to physically harm us, they could take advantage by stealing or perhaps overpower us for rule of the house. Every day they're in our home is a chance to take a jar of jam or to sneak into our bags and confiscate a box of bullets. They can gradually build up their resources until Aiden gets better, and when they're ready, they'll take the truck in the middle of the night and be long gone without us knowing any better.

I couldn't hold it against them if they double-crossed us. We live in a world where good old-fashioned morals are pushed aside for survival. Still, I don't want to feel like a fool for giving them the guns they use to rob us.

I sling my duffel bag across my torso and lock the vehicle. With weapons in hand, Noah and Wes move to either side of me, and Ryland takes the lead. I pick up my pace, matching his long strides while shooting him a side-long glare. It's noble that they want to protect the girl, but they're blocking my view of what's coming for us. I've gotten this far holding my own, and I'm not letting that change today.

It's eerily quiet when we approach the homes we plan to ransack. There is no sound of traffic or dogs barking in the distance, just the crunching of our steps in the snow. Trees line the street, and white picket fences border the two-story homes. The windows are dark, and some homes sit with their front doors wide open. All signs of life have vanished, leaving behind a ghost town haunted by Zs.

As if we are making a house call, Noah knocks on the first door. We wait to see if anyone answers before Ryland steps to the side and moves me behind him. I gasp at his audacity, and he gives me a sharp glare. I bite my tongue, knowing this isn't the time to argue, and shoot him a death glare. With a shake of his head and his mouth quirked, he reaches for the door handle and finds it unlocked. He swings it open, keeping against the outer wall.

"Hello? Is there anyone here?" he shouts. When no one answers, he turns to us, blocking our entry. "Wes and Noah, you search downstairs for any medicine or food. Quinn, stay with me, and we'll take the upstairs. We enter each house as a group and exit as a group. Eyes on your partner at all times."

Wes and Noah agree, and Ryland lets them pass. Before I can slide through, he puts his hand on the door frame and leans in until we are eye to eye. "Quinn, do *not* leave my sight for *any* reason at *any* time. Do you understand me?"

The same electric green gaze that caught my attention earlier bores into me. An irrevocable perseverance radiating from him, and I must admit—it has me intimidated, and therefore, defensive.

"I know what to do," I spit, ducking under his arm.

"I'm sure you do," he mumbles, taking the lead

again.

The house is dusty, but neat. Blankets lay folded on the back of the couch and chairs. Knickknacks line the fireplace mantle and a stack of magazines rests on the coffee table. Other than the banging of cupboards closing as Noah and Wes rummage through them, everything is normal.

We climb the stairs and Ryland points to a family picture on the wall. "Hopefully, we find most of the clothes we need here."

I study the color-coordinated outfits and smiling faces in the portrait. The mom and dad sit next to one another on green grass with three young men kneeling behind them. They look so happy. I wonder if they're all still alive and together, or if tragedies managed to get the better of them. If I was forced to guess, I'd say it's most likely the latter.

We enter the first room, and Ryland goes directly to the closet. He shuffles through the clothes with his backpack at his feet, filling it with whatever he deems a necessity. I, on the other hand, am at a loss. If I were gathering clothes for River or me, there would be no problem, but I'm trying to help clothe four men I don't know.

I open the first drawer and ask, "Do you guys need underwear or boxers or whatever?"

He looks at me from over his shoulder. "I'm not wearing another man's underwear."

"Are you sure? It is not like we can stop and buy you a brand-new designer set."

A sly grin pulls at the side of his mouth. "I can manage just fine without underwear, love."

My cheeks burn red hot, and I reply with a quick

"oh." It's all I can manage as my brain races with images of Ryland's lack of underwear. He has me blushing like an idiot. I feel utterly incompetent... and did he call me *love*?

I slam the drawer filled with boxers closed, brush off our exchange, and submerge myself in the task at hand. Opening drawers of t-shirts and jeans, I gather what I think will fit my male companions.

At the next couple of houses, the words between Ryland and I are all business. I ask a question, and he barks orders. The system works. We acquired several articles of clothing, multiple food items, and some essential medications. But we haven't found what we truly need—the antibiotic that will heal Aiden.

It's not until the final house that Ryland and I hit the jackpot. We're inside a gigantic walk-in closet, rummaging through an endless array of practical men's clothing. I'm on the floor going through drawer after drawer of t-shirts in all colors and styles, and Ryland sifts through the clothes on the hangers.

"Do you guys live in Stern?" I ask. The muscles in Ryland's shoulders and back tense, and I pause for a moment, treading lightly. "I don't understand why you didn't go back to Giran or wherever you are from when you had the chance."

Taking the beanie off his head, Ryland ruffles his greasy, brown waves which are in dire need of a shampoo, rinse, and repeat. He leans back against the wall and slides down until he sits on the floor. Pulling his overflowing backpack between his long, bent legs, he situates the items inside. There's no trace of confidence or authority, only a sense of defeat and an unwillingness to talk about this topic.

"Sorry, it's none of my business," I say, returning to the contents of an open drawer. Asking questions was a stupid move on my part. Just because we've spent a couple of hours rummaging through houses doesn't mean we're friends, or even acquaintances, for that matter. I should have known better than to pry.

"We were on holiday, backpacking through a canyon."

I whip around at the sound of Ryland's voice. He concentrates on folding the clothes in front of him and continues speaking. "I had this brilliant idea that we should disconnect from the world. I convinced everyone to leave their phones in the car. We wandered from the trails in search of this waterfall I'd heard about. It took us hours to find, but it was worth it. We spent four days camped next to a blue oasis surrounded by red rocks, and it was incredible. By the time we found out about the evacuation, it was too late."

My chest aches with empathy. I'm too aware of what it's like to be stuck here when you should be somewhere else. I curse myself every day for trading safety and being with loved ones for an Afflicted war zone and despair. It's a fate I wouldn't wish upon another soul no matter how terrible their sins.

"You shouldn't be here," I say.

He tugs the zipper to his backpack closed and stands. "No one should be here, Quinn. Not one damn person, Stern citizen or otherwise."

He scoops up a pile of winter coats with one arm and towers over me. "That's good enough. I'll come back for the shoes."

He extends his hand, and I accept his help getting to my feet. Hand engulfs mine in a firm and sure grip. It radiates a warmth that shoots up my arm. It's surprisingly comforting, and a feeling I didn't know I missed until this moment.

As I hold his hand, I admire the intricate tattoos woven together and crawling up his toned arm. Each symbol is a beautiful piece of art. From the anchor to the compass, I can't help but feel they all have a story behind them. It's like his body was the blank page and written on it are stories of friendship, self-discovery, and love. An entire life that existed outside of the world we now know.

"Hey, Ryland."

He stops and turns with my hand still in his.

"I hope you all make it home." I give his fingers a gentle squeeze before letting them go.

His eyes fill with gut-wrenching sadness as he says, "Unfortunately, it will never happen."

There's an undeniable truth behind his words that make my heart ache. He believes he will never make it home. Yet, I don't understand why he bothers giving the others that hope. Just this morning, he was studying the bridge that is the only land crossing into Oscuros. It's not like the outcome will change if he's honest with his friends. In fact, they might agree with him, and together, they can come up with a more realistic plan that doesn't rely on hoping a border crossing is still open.

I can't recall ever meeting anyone as complex as Ryland.

We enter the kitchen where several items line the counter, mostly cases of water and non-perishable foods. Wes and Noah stand next to each other, holding multiple prescription bottles, carefully reading the labels.

"It doesn't hurt to take it all, just toss them into a bag and River can determine if any of it will be useful," Ryland says.

We've found so much in this one location. I feel like we have barely scratched the surface of what this house has to offer. I'm set on searching as much of it as I can before we leave. I open the pantry and pull out three boxes of mac and cheese and an unopened jar of peanut butter. Several cloth shopping bags hang from a hook on the back of the door, and I take them and stuff them full.

"I don't want to walk back to the truck with our hands full. Even though it's been quiet, we still need to be able to defend ourselves. Why don't you both take a small load to the truck now?" Ryland says to Wes and Noah.

They agree, gathering cases of water and leaving the house.

"I'm going to grab the shoes. Will you be all right?" he asks.

"Go, I'm fine. I'm just going to pack this and make sure we're taking everything we can." I dismiss him with a flick of my wrist and listen to the stomping of his shoes as he climbs the stairs.

I finish organizing the bags and turn to the tiny hallway leading to the back of the house. I take no more than two steps when I notice the door to the basement. The smile that takes residence on my face is uncontrollable. Most people keep their hunting supplies safely locked beneath their house. With all the treasures we found here, I doubt I'll turn up empty handed.

I return to the kitchen, grab one of the cloth bags from the counter, and take out my flashlight before making my way down the stairs into the pitch-black basement. My light hits three aisles of industrial-style shelving units. They're filled with boxes of ammunition and an array of weapons—guns, crossbows, and knives.

"So predictable," I say to myself, moving to the row farthest from the entrance. Boxes neatly display the description of their contents. Bullets. Never in my life did I think I would get giddy about bullets. I wasn't excited about shooting a gun as a kid. They're loud and the kickback from the discharge makes them hard to control. The power they hold at a moral level is something I never wanted. It's too great of a responsibility. But Josh was adamant that we learn to handle a firearm. It was a lost cause to argue with him. He would lecture me all night long on the necessity of being able to protect myself from humans and animals. I learned about gun safety and how to aim and fire to appease him. Living in the woods, I always thought I was most likely to shoot a bear. Oh, how wrong I was.

River, on the other hand, was born wielding a weapon. She's always seen beyond the devastation they can cause to enjoy the sport behind them. She's not out shooting at animals for fun, but she knows how to hunt. Where I feel bile rise from the depths of my stomach at the thought of killing and skinning an animal, she can concentrate purely on the necessity of it. I don't know how she does it, but thankfully, she's able to gut a fish and pluck a bird. My protein intake would be nonexistent without her.

Placing the flashlight on a shelf, I open the bag and fill it with ammo. It has been a while since River and I have practiced shooting a gun. We haven't wanted to waste bullets on a harmless target, but we know we can't perfect our shots if we don't. It's vital that we stay comfortable with what a gun can do, and this is going to give us the opportunity to do that.

I move from shelf to shelf only taking what we can use when the sticky sound of rubber-soled shoes stops me. I turn my attention to the entrance of the aisle, dimly illuminated by the open door of the basement. A hefty figure cast in shadows stands at the end, blocking my way out. I freeze at the outline of the gun pointed at me.

"Look what we have here," says a gruff voice, taking a step closer.

I slowly bend to set the bag of bullets on the floor as my free hand inches to the back of my jeans. "I'm so sorry, I didn't realize anyone lived here," I say, distracting him as I wrap my trembling fingers around my loaded weapon.

He steps into the beam of my abandoned flashlight. The lower half of his face is covered with a long scraggly beard, and his long hair is matted. His beady eyes examine me, and his crooked teeth gleam with a sinister smile. With no intention of slowing his pace, he closes in on me. Never have I wished for a run in with a Z the way I do now.

I yank my gun out and aim it at him. "Stop where you are, or I'll shoot."

"You're going to put up a fight. I like that."

The distance between us is dwindling, and I'm running out of time to decide on my best course of action. I've never shot anyone who wasn't Afflicted. This is a human life, and even with my well-being at stake, I'm not sure if I can kill him. It's different from a Z. I'm able to reason that I'm putting someone out of their misery. Nobody in their right mind would be happy knowing they've lost all consciousness and exist with nothing but a desire to eat people. A human being, even an evil one, is a whole other story.

The man snatches my gun from my hand and slides it on the floor behind him. Thick meaty fingers clasp over my mouth as he presses his massive body against me, sandwiching me between him and a brick wall. His gun presses to my jaw as he drags his nose over the other side of my face.

"You think you want my bullets, pretty little girl, but

I have what you need." He finishes by kissing my cheek. His breath is rancid, and his grip on me is painful. The mixture makes my stomach churn.

I know how I should respond, all the actions I should take, but they are a jumbled mess in my brain. I'm paralyzed. It's not until the musty air of the basement meets the tears sliding down my face that I come to my senses. I struggle, but he firmly pins in place. My arm presses against my hunting knife in the pocket of my pants, and I scramble to open the button and slide my hand around the hilt. He buries his face into my neck, his beard scratching my skin. I fight harder to pull away, refusing to let this go any further. Without removing the knife from my pocket, I plunge it through the material of my pants and into his leg.

He jumps back holding the stab wound, and I try to maneuver past him, but he is enormous. He releases a groan and charges at me. I slam into the wall, knocking the air out my lungs. His bloody hand grasps my jaw as he spits, "You have no idea how much I'm going to enjoy watching you cry and beg."

He slams down his gun on a high shelf, out of my reach, and his hand moves between us as he yanks on his belt.

Tears blur my vision as I try to scream for help. Fear has my voice trapped inside my throat. Every movement of his hand and satisfied grunt as he comes closer to taking what he wants renders me useless. I surrender to my helplessness, squeeze my eyes shut, and will my brain to transport me to the happiest times in my life. I have to protect some part of me... any part of me.

A deafening bang rings in my ears, and my attacker falls upon me. I only pause for a second before my brain jumpstarts again. I push back as hard as I can, and he topples to the ground like a tree axed down in the middle of the woods.

Ryland stands silhouetted at the end of the row with his gun pointed at the man on the floor. His voice booms throughout the basement as he says, "Move, and I swear, I'll put a bullet in your fucking head." He turns his attention to me, scanning me from head to toe. "Are you all right?"

"Yeah," I whisper and reach for the bag on the floor.

"Quinn, come on. Let's get the hell out of here," he orders.

I'm obsessed with the bullets. My brain is stuck in a single thought as I sweep my arm over the shelf and fill the bag. We'll never be able to survive without these. I must stop anyone who wishes us harm. We must protect each other, and we can't do it without ammo.

"Quinn," Ryland yells.

I stop and look at him. He stands over the man, who wails on the ground, holding onto his knee. Ryland extends his hand, and with a gentler tone says, "Quinn, let's go, love."

It takes a second for my body to follow the commands of my brain, but I eventually wrap my fingers around his. He pulls me over the wounded man and maneuvers me behind him as he walks backward. Not taking his eyes from his target, he gathers my gun from the floor before yanking me up the stairs. We rush to the kitchen as Wes and Noah come running in.

"We heard a gunshot," Noah says between labored breaths.

"Grab everything and let's get out of here," Ryland says, taking the bag filled with boxes of bullets from my hand and giving me my gun.

The four of us run from the house to the truck, and the cold winter air nips at my face, bringing me back to reality. Everything happened so fast. I forgot the cardinal rule of survival—never go alone. Stupid mistake. I'd been careless. What would've happened to River if Ryland wasn't there to rescue me? I can't stand contemplating the possibility.

Once we reach the truck and are sheltered from plain view, Ryland turns to me. "What the hell was that? I told you not to leave my sight."

Frustration, fear, and anger become rioting emotions within me. "You left to go upstairs!"

"That wasn't an invitation for you to go roaming through the rest of the house by yourself!"

"I don't need an invitation. I'm a big girl who's fully capable of making my own decisions. I'm not in need of a dictator who controls my every move. I can handle myself!"

He releases a cynical laugh. "Please correct me if I'm wrong, but wasn't your gun lying on the ground across the room and some sick fuck pinning you against a wall, or was it just my imagination?"

My body shakes, and my stomach flips at the thought. I bite my lips, blinking back tears. I hate how I allowed myself to become helpless, and if it weren't for someone else, terrible things would be happening to me right now. Everything I was taught about defending myself had failed me. *I* failed me.

"Ry, that's enough," Noah says. "Quinn, why don't you let me drive, sweetheart?" He holds his hand out.

I blankly stare at the creases in his palm. They're cracked, the pads of his fingers calloused, and dirt is embedded under his fingernails. They've worked hard and look incapable of harming someone. His fingers appear skillful and gentle, and for inexplicable reasons, it makes me trust him.

"Okay." I nod, giving him the keys.

My bones feel brittle like my heavy muscles and flesh will shatter them into splintered pieces. The step I must make to pull my body into the passenger seat appears higher than usual, and I don't think I can lift my leg to do it. Thankfully, I don't have to.

Wes patiently places his hands on my waist and lifts me into the truck. "Up you go."

I slide across the bench seat toward Noah, allowing Wes to pull my side forward and crawl behind it. With the supplies packed in the bed of the truck and all of us accounted for, we pull onto the road.

For the longest time, I stare straight ahead. My mind is bombarded with thoughts. They mesh together like they are creating a sticky goop. In the end, it's like I'm thinking of nothing at all.

I catch my image in the mirror extending from the truck door. Blood, that isn't my own, is smeared across the lower half of my face, and the sight of it makes me want to gag. I rub my hand vigorously over the dried stain, but I can't get it off. Tears well in my eyes as the dreadful reminder of what happened marks my skin.

A dark-gray hoodie presses against the side of my arm. Behind me, Ryland leans forward, presenting me with his dirty jacket. A faint spot where he used a bottle of water to dampen the material sits on the top. I hesitate at first, wanting to stand my ground and prove I don't need his offering. It's now my sole purpose in life to be strong, and the last thing I want is to admit my weakness. But I didn't have anything under control. If he hadn't come looking for me—it's a thought I can't finish. He'd been the reasonable one when I gave in to the panic. As much as I try to be a protector, it was me who needed saving today.

With a hushed thanks, I take his hoodie.

I owe him an apology and a word of gratitude, but it will have to come later. My heart isn't in the mood for appreciation or forgiveness, and I'm not going to say something I don't really mean. For now, I want to try to wash away the remnants of one of the worst days of my life.

Chapter Five

I shuffle into the house from the garage with Ryland, Noah, and Wes close behind. We don't make it far when I come to a sudden stop. Tilting my head to the side and holding my breath, I listen as a constant vibration flows through the wall. The dead silence which is always prevalent on the first floor has vanished, and in its place is a sound I've not heard in over a year—water running through pipes.

"Quinn?" Wes whispers.

Ignoring him, I toss my duffle bag to the ground. My hands shake and my jaw clenches as I march down the dimly lit hallway to the bathroom.

River stands at the sink, holding her hands under the flowing water.

I enter and slam the door shut, leaving us in the buttery glow of her flashlight. "What are you doing?" I ask.

She glances at me from the corner of her eyes and continues to wiggle her fingers under the faucet. "Cleaning out the pipes and making sure the solar water heater still works."

"Are you kidding me? You went outside alone?"

"I very well couldn't take Aiden with me, so yes, I went alone. I can fend for myself."

"I realize that, but what if something happened?"

She shakes her head and releases a long sigh. "This will make things easier for the boys."

I place my hands on my hips. "Easier for *the boys*? Are you offering turn-down service and mints on their pillows as well?"

With her focus still on the sink, she raises an eyebrow and says, "No, but I did chop them some wood for the fireplace."

I can't believe she would be so reckless. She literally risked her life to give strangers a flushing toilet. It infuriates me. I told her to stay safe inside. She knows we shouldn't go off by ourselves. The risk is too high. She made all the same terrible decisions I made today, except mine almost cost me my life.

I push the sickening thought away and focus all my rage on the issue at hand. Throwing my hands in the air, I pace back and forth. "I got an idea, why don't I go hang a big neon sign on the road, advertising that we're a damn bed and breakfast now? Running water, cozy sleeping arrangements, I'm sure some Zs would like to get in on the deal, too."

River turns off the faucet and leans against the sink. She wears a deadpan expression, blinking several times before saying, "They're not going anywhere any time soon, so we might as well make sure everyone is comfortable and has what they need."

"That's not your job! You get Aiden well enough to stand on his own, and they leave. End of story."

"You know this is the right thing to do."

I scoff, rolling my eyes. "This is ridiculous!"

River's cheeks burn red, and her hands ball into fists. "No, what's ridiculous is that you're choosing not to show compassion to four men in need!"

"I'm choosing to protect us!"

"You're choosing to play it safe, and disregard everything Mom and Dad taught us, and you know it." She presses her fingertips to her eyes, and the volume of her voice drops as she says, "The Affliction has torn so much apart. Don't let it do the same to you. You're better than this, Quinn."

River's words mixed with my earlier trauma crash down on me. Holding back the tears that so desperately want to streak down my face, I concede. "It's done, just don't go outside without me again."

"I won't."

I nod and leave the bathroom.

"Quinn," she calls after me, but I can't turn around. Nobody knows me like she does, and she'll see there's more behind my outburst than just her recklessness. I can't face the truth, and I don't want her to see it either.

The following days pass in a haze. I keep my distance from everyone, especially River. It's only a matter of time before she discovers that my anger was hypocritical, and my stupidity outweighed hers. I just need a little more time to gather my thoughts before I confess to it.

I lie awake staring at the ceiling, watching the subtle orange glow coming from the wood-burning heater dance in the dark. After a night filled with coughing fits from Aiden, the room is finally quiet with only the occasional shifting of sheets or the creaking of the bunk bed frame. My cousin has stolen all the blankets we're supposed to share on the sleeper sofa. I'd usually put up a fight to keep my half, but she's been tending to our sick guest most of the night. She's optimistic that one of the medications we brought back will work for him, but so far, there's only been a minor change in his condition. Her mission has been non-stop as she frantically looks through outdated medical journals while taking care of Aiden, and I'm glad she finally has a moment of peace. Unfortunately, the same can't be said for me.

It would be easy to blame my inability to succumb to my fatigue on sleeping in a bed that isn't mine or sharing a room with strangers. But I'm my own worst enemy in this case. My mind continuously replays the events from the supply run. Days are consumed by cursing myself for everything I did wrong, and at night behind closed eyes, I see vivid images of my attacker pinning me to the wall. On a subconscious level, I believe I'm trying to accept what happened by over-analyzing it, but if that were possible, I'd have been fast asleep hours ago.

I roll out of bed, grab my clothes, and head to the tiny bathroom to get dressed for the day. As I finish washing my face, a gentle knock sounds at the door.

"Give me just a second, I'm almost done," I say.

"It's just me," River whispers from the other side.

I let her in, and she relocks the door before taking a seat on the toilet lid. For several seconds, she quietly watches me buckle my belt. When I don't make any attempt to speak first, she says, "What's going on with you? I know you can't still be mad at me for going out without you."

Knowing my voice will fail me, I simply shake my head.

"Did one of the boys do or say something to you?"

"No. They're fine."

"Did something happen on the supply run the other day? You've not really spoken to me since then."

"It's nothing, Riv."

She stands in front of me and takes my cheeks into her hands. Her eyes roam over my face, examining every detail which betrays my words. "Talk to me," she says, gently coaxing me.

I step away from her and run my palms over my eyes. "I was so stupid."

"It's okay. Tell me what happened." She glides her hand up and down my arm.

Unable to hold back any longer, I allow my tears to flow and recount what happened in that basement. She pulls me into her arms and brushes my hair with her fingers while whispering comforting words. I cling to her until I'm incapable of shedding another tear.

"I wish I could've been there to protect you," River says, kissing the top of my head. "I would have shot him in the balls with an arrow."

Chuckling, I pull away from her hold and dry my eyes. "I know you would have."

The unspeakable acts we've committed since the virus took over are countless. We've killed former classmates and neighbors who wanted to eat us alive. I never envisioned us raiding local stores for supplies or searching dead bodies for ammunition. Every moral lesson we were taught was thrown away like trash the minute we were living just to make it to the next day. I don't regret it, and River doesn't either. We will continue to do whatever it takes to keep the other safe. That's why I don't doubt that she would have killed the man who attacked me.

The sound of coughing interrupts our moment. River stares at the door, waiting to see if the hacking will subside.

"Go, he needs you," I say, with a weak smile.

"No more keeping secrets. If you need to talk, I'm here for you," she says, giving my arm a gentle squeeze before rushing out.

While River tends to Aiden, I pack my satchel with my gun and a box of the stolen ammo that got me in trouble. I take a protein bar from the cupboard in the kitchenette, not in the mood for anything heavy sitting in my upset stomach. With one last look at my cousin, I head out of the bunker.

On the first floor of the house, the sun shines brightly through the windows, causing me to squint against its assault on my eyes. There's a calm crackle coming from the fireplace in the study, and the comforting smell of burning wood resonates in the air. Without paying any mind to whether Ryland and Noah are awake, I exit through the front door.

My boots make a squishy sound as they meet the sludge caking the ground. I walk around the house, heading toward the far end of the property where Josh installed two shooting targets—one for guns and the other for archery. I unwrap my breakfast and take a bite while approaching the wooden snow-coated slabs. Brushing away the ice, I reveal the silhouette of a human painted dark blue—my opponent for the day.

At a decent distance from the target, I drop my satchel to the ground. With half of the protein bar hanging from my mouth, I squat next to my supplies, load my gun, and place a silencer over the barrel.

Half of my sleep deprivation comes from my irritation with myself. For over a year, I've considered myself the protector of what's left of my family, yet I was unable to shoot a man when my life depended on it. The seconds I used to deliberate his humanity overrode my natural survival instincts, and it almost cost me. I refuse to let myself fall victim like that ever again.

I finish my food before standing and aligning my body with the mark. I imagine the face of the sick pervert who tried to harm me. His massive form is three times as big as mine, and his eyes are glued to me while he wears a wicked grin. This time when he approaches, I don't falter. I fire the first shot and a pop echoes through the tranquil morning.

The initial kick of the gun startles me, but I shake it off and quickly unload the entire clip into the target. I aim for all his vital organs—lungs, heart, and brain. It's crucial that I forgo my reasoning and let my instincts take over. The next time I hesitate to shoot someone, it could be River who ends up hurt. I focus on the distant sound of Josh's firm words in my mind. *Don't close your eyes. Keep your shoulders square and stand tall. It's you or them, Q-Bean, so make sure it's them. Take control and don't let them back you into a situation you can't get out of.*

Every shot I take is within centimeters of my intended mark; it's almost flawless. Still, my conscience is a conflicted place, holding me back. I need to override the internal setting that has me questioning right from wrong. It doesn't matter how many times I'm spot-on with landing a bullet if I can't find the courage to fire my weapon in the first place. I swear, never again will I question myself like I did in that basement.

The world is no longer as it was two years ago. The line separating good from evil and right from wrong is blurred. My optimistic view of humanity has shifted to that of a realist. People are a product of their environment, and our surroundings are hostile and ruled by unmitigated evil. Those who haven't mutated into flesh-eaters are self-serving. They live with the knowledge that every day could be their last, and so they stop at nothing—not murder, rape, lying, or stealing. They're out for one more gratifying moment before their life is taken. The inherently beautiful traits I once believed to be the foundation of the human race have met their match in the face of the Affliction, and they're losing the fight.

My new outlook on humanity mixed with my guilt and self-loathing creates a toxic emotion within me. It demolishes the core of my being and guts me of the compassionate and fun-loving girl I used to be. I'm fashioning into someone hardened and calculated, and I hate that this is who I have to become. It goes against everything my family taught me to be.

The price of River's and my survival very well could be the sacrificial offering of my soul. It's going to take the both of us to make it through this, and one day reunite with our parents. I owe it to them to make it happen. Josh and Amara sacrificed so much for me, and now, it's my turn to repay them. The only way I know how to make that happen is to kill the old me and build a new pragmatic me.

A metallic click and absence of a blast jar me from my thoughts.

"I think he's dead," says a low whisper as warm breath contradicts the ice-cold shell of my ear.

I turn on my heels with my gun held firmly, shoulders squared, and arms straight. I'm ready to fight and resolute to win. The barrel of my weapon collides with a chest, but my finger waivers over the trigger.

Ryland doesn't even flinch as I hold him at gunpoint. In fact, he seems completely indifferent. His eyes are void of any signs of emotion, looking directly into mine. Brown feathery waves frame his clean-shaven face, and the scent of soap and deodorant linger in the cold breeze. Gone are the grungy clothes he wore when he first arrived at my home, and in their place is a red flannel shirt bundled under a thick winter coat. His long fingers wrap around the gun, and calmly, he guides it away from him.

The magnitude of my impulse reaction weighs heavily on me. I flipped to autopilot and abandoned my self-control. I was lost in thoughts of being more reactive and less mindful. As I stand face to face with Ryland, my idea to discard all rationale is reduced to a terrible idea. I risk taking an innocent life if I live only by instinct. Although my conscience can be a limitation, I must learn to incorporate it into my tactics. If by some miracle, we make it out of this mess alive, I don't think I can live with myself if I'm not confident that any life I take intends to harm us.

It feels like tiny ice cubes are being pressed under my eyes and frozen streaks run down my cheeks. It's not until Ryland lifts his hand that I realize what I'm feeling. I beat him to it, using the sleeve of my jacket to wipe away my tears.

His hand retreats, and he pushes it into his hair. "What are you doing out here?"

I take a step back, needing to put some space between us. "I was just practicing."

He looks over my shoulder at the target. "I think he would have been down after the first shot."

I turn to assess the damage—a single bullet to the head, two to the chest, and the rest of the clip emptied into the groin area. My subconscious took a sadistic turn, and it's a little embarrassing.

"Well, you can never be too sure, and you should hit 'em where it hurts, right?" I say, playing down the turmoil raging inside of me.

He laughs. "True, and *that* would've properly done the job." He steps in front of me, removing the gun I gave him from the back of his pants. "You're going for the kill, and it's why you're reluctant to pull the trigger. If you don't want to overthink it, you're going to have to aim for smaller targets on the body. Injure them enough so they stop and possibly have a chance to live." With little effort, Ryland shoots the target in the knee, hand, and shoulder.

The three precise shots and the smug grin on his face pull me in two different directions. With such accuracy in his aim, I wonder if he went to sharpshooter training or maybe took serial killer 101 classes. He's shown he has advanced skills when it comes to firearms, and it's a little scary. Yet as he smiles, I'm transfixed by the perfect dimples on his cheeks. The indentations change his whole appearance—they soften the harsh edges of his face and give him a boyish charm. My confusion raises hundreds of questions regarding him. I'm trusting him to help maintain River's and my security, and I don't know the most basic facts about him.

I release the clip from my gun and kneel next to my satchel to reload it. "How old are you, Ryland?"

He secures his gun and stuffs his hands in the pockets of his coat. "Twenty-two."

His answer is shocking. He carries himself with such command and certainty; I thought he was older. Nobody questions his authority. It's like his judgment is backed by years of experience. But now that I'm really looking at him, I see a young man. His life, like mine, was only beginning when everything changed.

"What about you?" he asks.

I stand and slide the clip back into my gun. "I'm nineteen."

A line forms in between his eyes. "You've been on

your own since you were seventeen or eighteen, I can't imagine."

"You're not much older than me."

"I didn't mean it like—"

"It's all right," I say, moving into position and aiming for the outlined body.

Releasing a deep breath, I do my best to mimic his movements, but I don't possess the same grace in my technique. There's a pause before each of the three shots as I try to line my sight on the smaller, less vital marks. Each bullet is off from where it should enter, and my posture slumps with defeat.

Ryland walks up behind me. "You need to stop thinking about it." He gently kicks one of my feet with his. "Your stance is too wide and not natural. If you're in danger, you're not going to have time to get into position before you fire. Relax and just keep your eyes on where you want to hit." He shakes my shoulders. "Even if it feels sloppy, I want you to lift your gun and pull the trigger."

The air I hold in my lungs burns before I gradually release it. I'm not used to having someone so close to me. It's nerve-wracking. Part of me is grateful for the barriers of our clothing and another is aching to feel skin to skin contact. I like his touch. I shouldn't, but I do. He makes me feel desire and need, emotions I have not experienced in over a year.

I shake the thought before I take it too far and focus on Ryland's instructions. Pulling the trigger in quick succession, I hit two out of three targets.

"Better," he says.

"Thanks." I clear my throat and step away from him. "Are your friends the same age as you?"

Kicking the tip of his boot into the snow, he

answers, "Yeah, we're twenty-two to twenty-four. What about River?"

"She's just a couple of months older than me."

I release three more bullets into the target and carry on with my interrogation. "Were you in school before coming to Stern?"

"Don't get too sloppy, just stand comfortably." He places a hand on my hip to turn it slightly before returning to my question. "Yes, I was preparing to start my final year at university. I was studying photography."

I raise an eyebrow. "Really? I would've guessed combat training."

He laughs for the second time. It's not a hard belly laugh, but a quick, deep chuckle, and I like the sound of it. "With the current state of the world, I might have to consider it. I don't think majestic landscapes are in high demand. What about you, were you going to university?"

I shake my head. "I was going to study psychology, but then everything went to hell, and I never made it to university."

I fire a final round and receive a nod from Ryland. "Good job."

Placing my gun in the back of my pants, I lean down to gather my satchel and drape it across my body.

Surprisingly, I've learned something from Ryland today. I can be hard-headed and get caught up in my old habits. Mutual respect is a must between me and someone before I'm open to their criticism, and Ryland earned my respect when he saved me. I hadn't so much as said a thank you for what he had done. It's time I rectify that and show my gratitude.

"About the other day—"

"I wanted to say—"

We give each other coy smiles as we reach the steps

of the front porch.

"You go first," Ryland says.

I pick at the white chipped paint on the stair's railing. "I was going to say you were right—I made about a hundred stupid mistakes, and I had no control over what was happening the other day. Thank you. If it weren't for you, I could be dead right now." I finish with a tight smile and ask, "What were you going to say?"

His eyes soften as he looks at me, and I seize the moment and study the imperfections of his face—the dark brown beauty marks, the scar above his eyebrow, and the signs that prove he's not been sleeping well. Each blemish compliments him and does little to lessen how handsome he is. I could get carried away studying him for hours.

I break his silent hold on me and busy myself by fidgeting with the mood ring on my finger. The stone is a nervous red, confirmed by the swift beating of my heart. I take a couple of deep breaths until the crimson fades to the unsettled shade of amber. When I finally turn back to Ryland, I find that his eyes have gradually hardened to a dark, dingy green. His body is rigid, and his face expressionless. I suck in a lungful of cold air and brace myself.

"I was going to say that I hope you learned something new today, because the next time I might not be there to save your ass," he says.

My jaw falls open like it's connected to a broken hinge. The nerve, and after we just had a little moment getting to know each other. And I apologized! Sarcastic comebacks flood my mind—comments about his mother teaching him manners and observations about his douchebag attitude, but it's the least harsh remark that spews from my mouth. "Got it. Next time, I won't hesitate to shoot him in the knee."

Disgusted with my weak retort, I turn to leave, but he grabs my arm and spins me back around. Ryland closes the distance between us, forcing me against the steps' railing. It digs into my lower back as I lean away from him. His angry stare bores into me, and his breath is warm against my lips as he speaks. "No, Quinn. The next time you shoot the bastard in the head. You were too close, and I wouldn't take the risk of the bullet going straight through him and hitting you. Have no doubt, I would have killed him. I wanted to kill him. You were the only thing that saved his worthless life."

He stomps up the steps, and I jump at the sound of the front door slamming behind him.

What the hell am I supposed to do with that? His mood swings are unpredictable—he goes left and then he makes a sharp right. His inconsistency has me twirling in circles and is throwing off my equilibrium. I feel like I'm stumbling in a world that is wobbling as it spins, but it's only my mind playing tricks on me. Everything is as it should be. It's only me who is going in circles.

He wants me off-kilter when it comes to him, and in some ways, I am. He exhibits intelligence, valor, and determination—all traits I envy. He's also overbearing and rude. It's like he's setting me up just to knock me down, and I can't fathom what purpose there is for his contradictions.

Unfortunately for him, I'm not the kind of girl who lets people walk all over her and goes down without a fight. He's sorely mistaken if he thinks I won't stand my ground, even if I fear I'm no match for my opponent.

Chapter Six

As quietly as possible, I slide into the house. There's a discussion happening in the study, and I don't want to be drawn into it. After my exchange with Ryland out on the porch, I'm not in a social frame of mind.

"It will be such a relief to have extra hands to help in the greenhouse," River says. She goes on to explain the solar climate control system and the daunting tasks of keeping our organic food supply healthy.

I roll my eyes as she gives away our last survival secret. It really shouldn't matter. If they want to figure out how we've made it to this point with minimal physical damage and full bellies, they will.

When I reach the basement, I find the heavy metal door to the bunker wide open—a new habit to accommodate our guests. The guys can't use the fingerprint scanner, and I refuse to give them the pin code, so we agreed to leave the door open during the times when everyone is awake. I stop at the doorway and find the main reason for the change sitting up in my bed.

Aiden.

Since he's been with us, he's only awake to take his medicine and force down a couple of bites of food. Most of his day is spent in a fitful sleep as his body tries to recuperate. He's been so weak that he hasn't sat up without the support of one of his friends, so to find him alone and leaning against the headboard is a vast improvement.

I enter the bunker, and his blue eyes glint with a bit of mischief. "So, it wasn't all a dream?" he says in a raspy voice.

I remove my satchel and fight not to smile. "Nope, welcome to paradise."

He laughs, sending him into a coughing fit. I rush into the kitchenette for a cup of water and hold it out to him. His hands shake as he reaches for it. I sit on the edge of the bed and keep a light grip on the cup as he tilts it to his mouth. He downs it all before letting out a big, satisfied breath.

"Do you want me to get one of your friends?" I ask.

"Nah, it's kind of nice without them hovering."

I can't blame him; there's someone by his side almost every minute of the day. Even if he slightly opens his eyes, they ask about his comfort and rearrange his pillows. His temperature is checked at least a dozen times a day, followed by constantly trying to coax him to drink some fluids. I'm sure he's thankful for their concern, but I understand how it would become overwhelming after a while.

"I don't think we've been formally introduced, I'm Aiden Donnelly." He extends his hand, and we shake.

"Quinn Ellery. And just for the record, I don't usually let boys sleep in my bed if I don't know their name," I quip.

"I'll have to make it up to you once I'm feeling

better. How does a candle-lit dinner sound? I'll even let you pick the restaurant, anywhere you want."

Even in his fragility, Aiden is the charmer I guessed him to be. It's obvious why the other three men are overprotective of him. His demeanor is good-natured, and his smile is effortless. In times like these, it's a rare person who doesn't let the severity of the situation squelch who they are. Just as River is a source of happiness in my life, he's the same for them.

"I'm not a picky girl, any place where our waiter doesn't want to eat me as the main course sounds good."

"So, the zombie thing didn't work itself out, huh?"

"I'm afraid not."

Together, we erupt into laughter. If only eradicating Zs were so simple.

"Well, look who's finally awake!"

I turn at the chipper sound of River's voice. She enters the room with Ryland close behind her, and the sight of him dampens my mood. Just when the memories from this morning slipped my mind, here he is to remind me of them all over again.

With no regard to me sitting on the bed, River wedges herself between Aiden and me and lays her palm on his face. "You still have a little fever, but you don't feel as clammy."

Aiden glances at me with a pleading look, begging me to rescue him from the constant coddling.

"It could be worse, it could be him who's making a fuss over you, and not her," I say with a quick jerk of my head in Ryland's direction.

Aiden looks at River and back at me. "She is prettier to look at than Ry."

"You're hurting my ego," Ryland says, walking to

the side of the bed.

"I doubt it's possible," I mumble.

He shoots me a glare while Aiden's laughter resonates throughout the bunker. "You've already upset her. I remember when you had girls lining up to be with you."

Ryland smirks and says, "If I didn't start pissing them off, there would've never been a chance of you getting a date."

Again, Aiden falls into another fit of laughter, but this time it ends with his entire body rattling from uncontrollable coughing. It's harsh and wet sounding as if he has water in his airway. I'm unsure if he has gotten any better over the past few days.

River pats his back until the outburst subsides. "Why don't you lie down?"

"I'm fine," he says through haggard breaths. "I actually need to use the toilet."

River and I move out of the way, and Aiden pushes the blankets down his body. He turns to the edge of the bed and lets his socked feet fall to the ground. His legs shake as he tries to stand, and Ryland moves to his side and wraps an arm around him. They shuffle to the tiny bathroom, and I give a fleeting thought as to how it's going to work with two grown men in the space. They must make it work because minutes later, they return with Aiden a little more stable on his feet.

"I'd like to hang out with the rest of the lads," he says.

River shakes her head. "You're going to have a hell of a time getting up the basement stairs."

His eyes reflect his desperation. It's like he's suffering from the worst case of cabin fever ever. I'd go mad too if I were stuck for several days in a room without windows.

"He's just going upstairs. I'm sure he'll be fine, Riv," I say.

She gnaws on her bottom lip for a moment before sighing. "Just to the study."

Aiden nods. "Will you lend me a hand, Ry?"

"Of course," he says, escorting him out of the room.

River and I listen as they move at a snail's pace through the boxes and struggle up the stairs leading to the main level.

"Why don't you go with them, and I'll start dinner for everyone?" I suggest.

"What happened between you and Ry? He looks like he wants to strangle you."

"Ry? You are on a nickname basis with him. Cute," I say, pulling pans out of the kitchen drawers. "And nothing happened. He's an ass."

She stands behind me, wraps her arms around my waist, and rests her head on my shoulder. River has always been the more affectionate one out of the two of us. Not to say I don't like to be touched or to touch someone else. It's just that she's more in tune with the exact moment when someone is in need of a hug.

"Are you sure you don't want me to stay and help you?" she asks.

"Yeah, go make sure *Ry* doesn't let Aiden tumble down those stairs."

With a quick squeeze, she lets me go and joins the men.

Cooking has never been my thing. I don't get the gratification some do when feeding others. It's another chore, but I'm thankful for the solace it offers tonight. More than ever, I feel like I need time to work through my thoughts. The arrival of Aiden, Noah, Wes, and Ryland has my whole world discombobulated. Our regular routines are derailed, and an entirely new series of anxiety has been released. But after speaking with Aiden, I feel a little better. I like him as well as Noah and Wes. They've been appreciative of our hospitality and eager to help in any way they can. The three are slowly becoming a welcome addition despite my reservations.

On the other hand, there's Ryland—a complete enigma. I can do no right by him. Just when I think we're making some progress, he pulls the rug out from under me. I'm left starting all over, and for what? A fleeting friendship at best. I'm wasting my time trying to peg him down. I'd have a better chance of ridding the world of Zs.

I finish the veggies, rice, and bean dish for dinner and prep the meal to go upstairs. When I reach the study, I find River sitting on the couch, sandwiched between Aiden and Noah. Across the room, Ryland sits on my uncle's desk while Wes tends the fire. They continue their conversation as I prepare to serve the food.

"If it works, I don't know how long we'll have, but my guess is five minutes at the most," Noah says.

"Why only five minutes?" River asks.

Noah rubs the side of his face and looks at the ceiling. "It will be a direct uplink to the tower. That's if we can get enough electricity to it. The amount of power it's going to transmit can't be sustained for long by the phone, and there is a fair chance it will overheat since we have to directly wire it in. Once the phone overheats, all chances for communication will be lost."

I take Aiden and River a plate of food. "What are you guys talking about?"

"Noah thinks he can use the cell tower to get Dylan's mobile phone to work," Wes explains, prodding the fire.

Three sets of eyes quickly narrow in on him, and he shies away from the glares.

"Who's Dylan?" I ask.

Ryland shakes his head while preparing his own plate. "A friend."

Before I can ask more questions, Noah continues where Wes left off. "We would have to charge the tower using one of the solar panels, but once we do, I think I can bypass the mainframe and establish a connection with the phone's mobile carrier. There's no reason to believe the phones in Giran don't work, so it's possible we could place a quick call."

After everyone has their food, I make my plate, sit on the ground, and jump back into the conversation. "So, you guys call Giran and then what? The chances of them sending help are slim unless one of you is the President's son."

"It doesn't hurt to try, Quinnten." River shoots me a glare that says *don't kill their hope* and places her hand on Noah's knee, giving it a reassuring squeeze.

I open my mouth to give a smart-ass rebuttal, but fall short when Aiden points his fork at his plate and says, "This is good, like really good. This might be the best meal I've ever had."

I release River and Noah from my stare and smile at Aiden's enthusiasm for my cooking. Granted, he hasn't eaten in a week, therefore his opinion may be skewed, but it's nice to see him feeding himself and not putting up a fuss about the pain it causes to swallow. Hopefully, he's on the mend.

After dinner, my cousin disappears for a moment and returns with a box in her hand. "Who's up for a game?" she announces and sits next to me on the floor.

Leave it to River to turn the disintegration of our continent due to a deadly virus into a party. I wholeheartedly believe nothing can bring this girl down. If there is a good time to be had, she will make it happen.

We form a circle on the floor with Aiden on the couch. River quickly goes over the rules for the silly game. It is simple: a question card is drawn, and everyone must answer it with one of the cards in their hand. The person with the most ridiculous answer wins. After she deals us in, we set to work picking a card we believe will make the others laugh. Our answers are horrible, and the house is filled with nonstop cackling. The whole game is out of control, but it's the most fun I've had in a long time.

We set up for our sixth round of the game when a muffled thump comes from the kitchen.

I go rigid and gesture for everyone to quiet down. "Did you hear that?"

A louder thud echoes through the house, and the room instantly falls into a dead silence.

The hairs on my arm stand straight up and my heart rapidly beats in my chest. I scurry to my feet and head for the window where the thick, floor-length drapes are shut to minimize our exposure to the outside world. Pressing my body to the wall, I slide the fabric to the side. Everything looks normal out in the yard, but my view is limited. I take a closer look, stepping in front of the glass. If someone or something is out there, they'll disrupt the snow, and I need a better vantage point. I shift slightly to glance the other way and come face to face with the intruder. Its feet away from the glass with pasty, paper-thin skin, molting hair, and razor-sharp teeth. I quickly bounce back, closing the curtains and spin around to find Ryland hovering over me.

"It's a Z," I tell him.

"How many?"

"I just saw the one."

"Noah and Wes, you're with me," he orders and turns back to me. "You and River get Aiden to the bunker. Don't open the door unless you hear a patterned knock."

"But—"

"Quinn, just do as I say," he commands, before leaving with the two men.

River and I help Aiden to his feet and guide him down the stairs to the basement.

"I hate that they're out there without me," he says through labored breaths.

"Me too," I confess.

The battle has come to my front door, and I'm forced to hide. I'm not some helpless girl who needs the protection of a boy. I guarded this house for a year and a half with my cousin. It feels wrong to hide. I want to fight for what's mine.

As soon as we settle Aiden into my bed, I rummage through my drawer until I find a hoodie. I toss it on, and as I'm zipping it, I grab my bag full of ammo. I secure my hunting knife to my hip, and with a final check of my gun, I turn to River. "Don't let anyone in."

"Quinn, I don't want you to go without me. We've never faced Zs alone if we didn't have to. The boys have got this," she says.

She isn't asking anything that I wouldn't ask of her. I should give in to her request, but I can't. Not when danger lurks on our doorstep. "I'll be damned if I sit here and do nothing while those disgusting things roam our property. This is *our* home, not theirs. Aiden doesn't need both of us."

She shakes her head. "I know, but... Please be careful."

"I promise I will," I say with a curt nod before shutting the door and locking River and Aiden inside.

Chapter Seven

I run up the stairs two at a time and dash across the house to the study. My first objective—protect our home. I slide the heavy mahogany doors shut, blocking out the glow from the fire and casting the house into darkness. Before I ease through the front door, I stop at one of the windows to make sure nothing decrepit is hanging around. With the coast clear, I ease out onto the porch. It's unnervingly quiet, and each step is like ringing the feeding bell for any nearby Zs. I move into the snow and keep my back to the house, heading in the direction where I saw the Z from the study window. As I come around the corner, I find it lying in a puddle of infected, purple blood with a bullet wound to the head. The guys must have fired on it when I was in the bunker.

The sound of shouting in the far corner of the property draws my attention. I'm eager to join the fight, but first, I have to make sure nothing else is trying to get inside the house. As I reach the back, a young man steps out from the other side.

"Quinn," he says in a low gravelly voice.

I pause as does the tall figure. I take in his sandy blond tousled hair and his unzipped Devil's Lake High School jacket.

"Luke, what are you doing here?" The hairs on my arms raise on end and chill runs down my spine. Luke Aims and I were never close, but he did graduate with River and me. I've seen him around town, and we would wave hello. He was just another familiar face in town.

He takes a sluggish step forward, looking at me with a longing in his eyes. "I need your help."

I sharply inhale as he reaches out. Several of his fingers are bleeding and so disfigured that the bone is exposed down to the first knuckle. I pull my gaze away from his hand and recognize the need in his eyes—hunger.

A low growl rumbles through him, and he sprints forward inhumanly fast. I line my gun with his head and pull the trigger. The bullet misses and hits him in the shoulder, but his nervous system doesn't register the oozing, gaping hole. He rebounds within seconds, controlled by his desire for human flesh.

I fire again, and this time, his head whips back and dark purple surges from the center of his forehead. Luke crashes face-first into the snow. I brace my hands on my knees, catching my breath and fighting against my churning stomach.

Luke was in the first stage of the infection; it's rare to come across a Z like him. Hours after he was bitten and exposed to the virus that lives in the Afflicted's saliva, he began eating his fingers. When they lost their appeal, he went on the hunt for the flesh of others. Within the next two weeks, he would have lost his ability to speak and see. His nervous system would have shut down, and his sense of smell and hearing would have heightened. The teeth and fingernails of the Afflicted grow and sharpen at a rapid pace, helping them to become the ultimate predator.

After I finish my check on the house, I rush in the direction of Josh's workshop. I slip into the shadows of the metal building, following along its walls toward the male voices. The Z groans grow louder the closer I get, warning me of the battle that lies ahead.

"Shaw, let it go," someone yells, followed immediately by, "Goddammit, he never listens."

I use their distraction to my advantage and move in next to Noah and Wes. We crouch in a line against the wall, trying to make ourselves as small as possible.

"Speaking of people who never listen," Wes says, cocking a dark eyebrow and shooting his blue gaze my way.

I flash a feisty grin. "It's my house, and I don't have to listen to your dictator."

"Ten o'clock," Noah says, pointing his gun and releasing a shot.

Wes waits for the Z to drop before addressing me. "He's only a dictator if he makes all the rules. We have a say."

I pick off a Z bolting across a clearing of trees. "Sure you do, just keep telling yourself that. Where's your fearless leader anyway?"

"He chased after one of them into the woods," Noah says.

I scan the snow for Ryland's tracks. Of course, he went through one of the worst areas. The forest is dense beyond the human-made trails, and with so much snow on the ground, there is no way he can follow the paths. If he gets lost, he won't be able to find his way back until the sun rises. As a child, I spent hours lost amongst the trees and piles of snow. It was the perfect maze for Hide-n-Seek. But tonight, the woods are a Z funhouse with Ryland trapped inside.

I drop my satchel on the ground and grab a fistful of bullets and cram them into the pocket of my jeans. "Try not to shoot us when we come back through," I say and dart across the yard.

"Quinn," Noah yells, but I ignore him.

I take my time, listening for the sound of footsteps and sliding from tree to tree for cover. Zs are typically in a hurry when they smell flesh. Their one-track minds want to get to the food source as quickly as possible, but occasionally, they take their time and calculate their hunt. They play games and enjoy the chase before it's over. I never know what kind of demented monster I'm up against, so I have to be always on high alert.

A gunshot goes off close by, echoing through the tall pine trees. It's impossible to determine what direction it came from. I walk in circles, focusing on the snow to get a fix on Ryland's tracks, but the trees are blocking any light the night sky may provide. I'm left with no choice but to head back in the direction I came and work through a plan with Noah and Wes to lure the Zs out of the trees.

Again, rapid gunfire blasts through the woods. Without reservations, I bolt toward the loud popping. My head whips back and forth as I frantically search for Ryland while anticipating a Z attack. I have no clue where I'm going until I come upon a small clearing. I skid to a stop just short of the open space. Ryland crouches against the trunk of a tree, using it for cover. In his haste to fight the Afflicted, he forgot to grab a jacket, and I can make out the dark lines of his tattoos on his arms. His head leans on the tree trunk, and his eyes are open to the sky above. All the while, four Zs slowly creep up on him like wild cats ready to pounce. With a huff, he tosses his gun on the ground between his legs. He's out of bullets. He gnaws on his bottom lip, and I can almost see the thoughts swirling inside his head as he tries to find a way out of his dilemma.

My first instinct is to shoot, but if I do, we have no chance. The Zs will rush Ryland and me, and I'm not fast enough to clip off four of them and save us both. I need to get his attention without drawing theirs. If he knows I'm coming in, I can give him my gun and hope he fires right away while fending for myself with my knife.

I reach for a pinecone on the branch above my head and pick it off. The rustling of the pine needles sounds like a siren in my ears, filling me with dread. I swiftly toss the pinecone at Ryland, hitting him in the leg. He turns to me, and I hold up the gun. He discreetly shakes his head, and I counter with a nod. Without giving him the chance to object again, I race toward him. I close the last couple of feet by diving to his side and transferring my gun to him while unsheathing my hunting knife.

The Zs go wild and rush us.

Ryland fires two shots, but it's not enough to stop the Z coming around my side of the tree. I wrinkle my nose at the smell of it—a rotten mixture of vomit, body odor, and human waste. I try to dodge away, but it grabs my arm. Long nails sink through the sleeve of my jacket and rake over my skin with burning pain. The only reason I can resist the urge to pull away is because I know the wound isn't fatal. As long as the Z's saliva doesn't make contact with my blood, I'm safe. So, I wait for the perfect opening. With snapping teeth, it leans down to bite into my arm. When it comes closer, I plunge my blade into its eye socket. Dark blood oozes over my hand, and with a fast twist, I turn my weapon inside its head. Yanking on the knife, I kick its lifeless body to the ground.

The final standing Z picks up speed.

Ryland places his hand on my shoulder to hold me back as he steps out from the cover of the tree and shoots it in the chest. It staggers backward, but the blow is not enough. Again, it presses ahead, and Ryland fires, hitting it in the head. It tumbles lifelessly to the ground.

I slide down the rough bark of the tree and reach for my injured arm. I silently thank the stars that I was merely scratched. I would have been a goner if it sank its teeth into my flesh, directly exposing my blood to the virus.

Ryland kneels next to me. "Are you all right?"

"Yeah. What about you?"

"Dammit, Quinn. I told you to stay with River and Aiden."

I shake my head. "Don't start in on me. I just saved your life. Now, we're even."

Reaching into my pocket, I pull out a handful of bullets, pick up the gun Ryland discarded on the ground, and reload it.

His frustration is exactly how I feel when River does whatever the hell she wants when I'm trying to protect her, but this is different. She's my family and my best friend. What's transpiring between Ryland and me is a power struggle. He's used to everyone following his orders without question, and I'm accustomed to only fighting River to get my way.

"We don't need to be even," he says in a solemn tone.

I push the clip back into the firearm and offer him the remaining ammo. "I don't want to give you anything to hold over my head. You've made your feelings toward me abundantly clear."

"Have I?" He sighs, taking the bullets from my hand.

I give him a sideways glance and quickly brush off

the confusion written on his face. "Besides, this is my home, and I'm not standing by while someone else defends it."

"You're so fucking stubborn."

I shrug and wait for him to finish loading his gun.

He stands and brushes the snow from his pants. "We'll do this together, but you can't go rogue on me. You have to stay with me, do you understand?" For the first time since I met him, he talks to me as if he wants to fight beside me and not with me.

I get to my feet. "Sure, but don't be a misogynist and ignore my input. I know what I'm doing."

Towering over me, he counters, "I'm not a misogynist or chauvinistic. I know you're capable of taking care of yourself, but I want to help. You don't have to do this alone. It's called being chivalrous."

I roll my eyes. "Well, let's forget the chivalry. This isn't a date, Prince Charming."

He chuckles and takes the lead. "You have to admit that if it was, this would be one hell of a date."

"Yeah, yeah." I smile, jogging in front of him. "Incoming Z, straight ahead."

Chapter Eight

Ryland and I work together to take out the Afflicted for most of the night. We wander through the woods for what seems like hours picking off Zs one at a time. When my nerves are shot and I'm on the verge of cardiac arrest, we finally step out of the trees and join the others.

The four of us spread out along the edge of the property, hoping to lure the Zs from the cover of the trees. The boys talk back and forth, not bothering to lower their voices, and I keep a vigilant eye on our surroundings. The body count steadily increases throughout the night, and the battle is called in our favor shortly before the sun breaks over the horizon.

Victory is a double-edged sword. I wish we could bury the dead. They were, after all, once human, but it's impossible with countless bodies. The guys believe if we leave them in the open it will only attract hungrier Zs as they rot in the sunlight. My experience with an attack this size is nonexistent, so I have no choice but to take their advice.

We cover the bloody tracks of our battle and gather

the dead into a pile to be burned. Wes and Ryland toss the last body on the stack of remains, and Noah squeezes an old bottle of lighter fluid onto the mound. Never in a million years did I think I'd be cremating bodies, yet here I am tossing the match.

We step back as the fire blazes toward the morning sky. The sound of flesh sizzling and the putrid smell of the Zs makes me sick. None of these monsters look as if they're at peace with their deaths. Most of them wear tortured expressions with their mouths gaping, and their blank stares watch us as they smolder. My entire body shakes from the gruesome sight, and I struggle against the bile rising in my throat. The adrenaline from fighting all night has worn off, and shock and fatigue have taken over.

"Quinn."

With my arms wrapped around my waist, I look at Ryland on the other side of the bonfire.

"You're shivering. Why don't you go inside and clean up? We will watch over the fire," he says, with his hands shoved deep into the pockets of his pants. Like the rest of us, his clothes are wet and covered in dirt and blood. His hair is matted with a variety of filth, and his face is streaked with Z blood. He is exhausted and cold too.

"I'm okay," I reply.

He closes his eyes and takes a deep breath. "Don't fight me and go... please."

If it weren't for his plea and our physical state, I'd stay just to defy him, but we're both too tired to go back and forth. With a sigh, I meet the gazes of the three men who helped defend my home. "Thank you, guys."

It's a simple form of my gratitude taking into account I could write an entire book about the magnitude of the sacrifices they made last night. Without a second thought, they put themselves in harm's way to protect my house, my cousin, and myself. They didn't have to and could have suggested we barricaded ourselves in the bunker. Instead, they faced the danger head-on, proving how brave and selfless they are. My *thank you* will never compare to their heroic acts, but it's all I have to give.

Wes squeezes my shoulder as I pass by him. "It's what we do. We take care of each other."

It's what River and I have done alone for too long. I imagine what it would be like to add the boys to our twosome and make it permanently six. Extra eyes to look out for trouble, hands to hold guns, and able bodies to help with the day-to-day chores. Their addition would alleviate some of our stress. It's not just the strength in numbers that appeals to me, but the idea of a multi-person unit like a family. Since they've been here, their presence has monopolized my thoughts, allowing me little time to reflect on the past and for depression to consume me. They have helped in so many ways.

I walk into the house and head to the study to pick up the dishes we abandoned last night. I'm not surprised to see them gone and the cards from the game neatly placed in their box. With aching muscles, I inch my way into the basement and scan my finger to unlock the bunker door. Aiden is fast asleep on my bed while River sits with her legs crossed on the couch. Her tight curls are a mess, and her eyes are void of their customary sparkle. She may not have battled Zs all night, but she looks just as sleep deprived.

She gives me a weary smile. "You look like hell."

"Ditto."

She looks at her fingernails and says, "I'd ask how it went, but I already know."

I kick my shoes off and drop my soiled satchel onto

the ground outside of the door. "Yeah, I saw you cleaned up the study."

"I just thought the food might attract the Zs into the house."

"They eat flesh, not vegetarian dishes," I sarcastically state as I shut the door.

"You never know, maybe one of them is having second thoughts about eating people. Besides, you guys had been gone for hours, and I needed to know you were all okay. I saw you piling up the Zs."

"Yeah, they wanted to burn them, so they're still out there keeping an eye on things until the bodies disintegrate." I hold myself back from shaking at the memory of the dead blankly staring at me from their fiery grave.

"You should go upstairs and take a hot shower," she suggests.

"This bathroom is fine."

River crosses her arms over her chest. "No, it's not, and I don't want to take care of another sick person. I turned on the hot water, and you should use it. Now, go upstairs."

Send me out to battle a handful of Zs, and I have a chance of prevailing, but going head-to-head with River when she's made up her mind is a losing battle.

I grab all the items I need to wash away the remnants of last night and head to the second-floor bathroom. As tempting as it has been over the last year to move back upstairs and partake in the comforts it provides, self-preservation has overruled the notion. We knew it was a gamble to live in a space where we could be discovered, and after last night, I have to ask if we were always right. Perhaps the reason for the attack was that we spent days unguarded and in the open. Our living situation with the boys might need reevaluating.

The bathroom is void of its accessories, no toothbrush holder, tumbler, or trash can, just a dusty blue shower curtain. The entire space is covered in light grime and not the most sanitary, but the room to move freely makes up for it.

I let the water run for a couple of minutes to wash out the unused pipes and remove the dirt from inside the tub. When the mirrors fog up, I disrobe from my disgusting clothes. The fleece from my hoodie has fused with the deep Z scratch on my arm. I whimper as the scab rips away and ignore the blood running down my forearm as I climb into the shower.

My pain vanishes when the hot water pelts down on me. I'm convinced this is a perfect representation of heaven. Reveling in the heat of the water, I take my time and clean my hair twice, rub every inch of my body with soap, and shave all the unwanted hair. I almost feel like the old me again, and it makes me want to stay in the bathroom forever.

In here, I can pretend my world is how it should be. River is in her room, talking on her phone with music playing in the background. Josh is in his workshop concocting a great invention that will save the planet from imploding, and Amara is picking vegetables in her greenhouse for tonight's dinner. We're all safe, happy, and life is moving forward in perfect harmony. But the water turns to a cold stream, harshly reminding me it isn't so.

I should feel sorry for using all the hot water, but I don't. This luxury is long overdue, and I'm happy I took advantage of it. I leisurely dry my body, comb my hair until it's smooth, and dress. With my soiled clothes wrapped in my towel, I return to the bunker. As I pass my satchel and shoes outside of the door, I scrunch my nose at how awful they smell and drop the rest of my reeking laundry on top of the pile.

I enter the underground haven to find Noah sitting in one of the chairs in the kitchen with River standing behind him. She uses her father's hair clippers to buzz off his hair. His eyes are closed like it's the most delightful experience of his entire life. Across the room, Wes sits next to Aiden on my bed, deep in discussion. My hot shower must have lasted forever, considering Wes and Noah are clean and my cousin had time to find the clippers.

Wrapping a blanket around my shoulders, I curl up on the couch. I focus on all the events going on in the room. It's these little things I miss the most, like deep conversations and basic tasks. I close my eyes and bask in normal sounds, praying they will consume my wayward imagination and guide me to sleep.

The door to the bunker bathroom opens, and I crack open my eyes. Ryland holds a towel in one hand to dry his hair and a t-shirt in the other. He's perfect. Every inch of him is defined, lean muscles and tan skin. My wandering eyes skim over the artwork on his body. The smoky swirls that interlock the tattoos on his arms trail over his shoulders and under his collarbone, arching over a large, embellished hourglass inked onto his sternum. His low-riding jeans allow for a full view of the only colored pieces of artwork on his body—two red roses, one on each hip bone. Their thorned vines peek over the waist of his pants before plunging downward again. I wonder just how far they reach.

"What would you like me to do with my dirty clothes?" Ryland asks, pulling his shirt over his head.

I snap my jaw closed and quickly divert my eyes.

"You can set them outside the door with my stuff. I'll see if I can salvage them later."

He opens the door and sets his soiled clothes with mine as River turns off the hair clippers.

"Not bad for never going to beauty school," she declares, rubbing the top of Noah's head.

He leaps from the chair and runs his hands through his short hair. "Thanks, babe," he says before kissing her on the cheek and sitting opposite me on the couch.

I look at my cousin and silently mouth, "*Babe*?"

She flashes me a coy smile and grabs the broom to sweep up the hair.

"Do you think you can give me a trim, River?" Ryland asks.

"I can only shave it all off. If you want an actual cut, you need to ask Quinn. She's spent *years* working on her hairstyling skills."

I roll my eyes as she pokes fun at my teenage experimentation with cutting my hair. I've never been able to live down the one time my hair adventures went awry, and I had to make an emergency appointment with a professional hairdresser. Clearly, my explorations into the art of hairstyling paid off since it's now my responsibility.

Ryland clenches his jaw, moving to the other side of the bunker.

Is he serious? We spent all night relying on each other, but he can't request a simple favor from me.

With a sigh, I stand and move to the drawer where we keep a pair of scissors and a comb. "I'll do it."

"No. You need to sleep," Ryland replies.

I smile and pat the chair in front of me. "It's all right, come and sit."

Ryland does as I ask and sits his long, tense frame on the dining table chair. I run my hand through his wet hair like a comb. It curls when it's wet and the coiled strands wrap around my fingers like they don't want me to pull away. After a few more brushes, I take my nails and playfully scratch his scalp to help him relax.

"Don't worry. I've only stabbed someone with the scissors once, and it bled just a little. Right, Riv?"

"Yeah, as soon as the doctor took out the stitches, the hair started to grow over the scar."

"Funny," Ryland scoffs.

River scoots in next to Noah on the couch and rubs his head. She attempts to make the act look innocent by complimenting her handy work, but there's a tenderness to her actions. With a yawn, Noah leans into her touch until his head falls into her lap, and she covers him with a blanket.

I'm torn between focusing on Ryland's haircut and the two of them. Things are getting too comfortable, and I'm not sure I like it. Perhaps I'm jealous of their blatant affection, or maybe it's that River has someone other than me to dote on. It might be a little of both.

When Noah closes his eyes, I turn my attention entirely to Ryland.

"Something isn't sitting well with me about last night's attack," I tell him.

He moves to cross his arms, but I give a gentle tug on the strands of hair between my fingers, reminding him to remain still. He opts to sit straight and says, "It was a horde-attack. They happen."

"I know, but not here, not in Devil's Lake, and not on this property. I just find it strange that we've only had a stray Z here and there, and last night was out of control."

"What are you thinking?"

"Maybe with so many people in the house, we

attracted them. Is it possible?"

Ryland purses his lips and shrugs. "It's possible, but why would they show up now when you and River have been in and out of here for over a year?"

"We have limited our trips into town and spent almost all of our time down here," I say before combing out a piece of hair and cutting it.

"Until we showed up."

"Yes."

We both fall silent, thinking about the possibility. Ryland is a lot like me when it comes to walking on the side of caution. I appreciate that he's taking my concerns seriously. It's better to inconvenience ourselves by entertaining assumptions than risking the lives of our loved ones by disregarding a gut feeling.

"All finished," I say after trimming the last section of hair.

He looks at me over his shoulder. "We'll take shifts guarding the house tonight and be prepared if it happens again."

I give him a tight smile and nod. "Thank you. Now stand so I can make sure the front is all right."

He gets to his feet and faces me. My fingers barely touch the curls framing his face when he takes my arm and turns it. "What happened?"

I glance at the angry, red scratch and try to pull away, but he firmly holds on. "The Z I stabbed grabbed me and dug its nails in."

"It looks horrible. I have antiseptic cream in my bag in the study. I can wrap it for you."

My cousin's head snaps in our direction, and she chimes in, "Yeah, you should let Ry take care of it for you. Z nails are gross, and it can get infected."

I gently pry my arm from his grip and shoot a glare

at her. We have a first aid kit, and she's very capable of tending to my wounds, but if I decline his offer, I stand to make a big deal out of nothing. Also, I'm exhausted and all sleeping space in the bunker is claimed. I might as well go with him, and afterward, I can sleep on my old mattress upstairs.

"Let me put everything away and we can head up," I say.

When Ryland and I reach the study, he retrieves the first aid kit from his backpack. With a red pack in hand, he sits on the couch and motions me over. I take a seat beside him and fidget with the mood ring on my finger as I watch him remove a tube of ointment, gauze, and bandage. He sets the items on his thigh and gently rests my arm on his lap before applying the antiseptic cream to my skin.

I shut my eyes against the initial sting, but relax as his cool fingertips lull away the pain.

"I'm sorry for my outburst yesterday. My words were harsh and absolutely uncalled for," he says, his voice raspy with emotion.

I open my eyes to find him staring at me. There's kindness, goodness, and most of all, unadulterated beauty in the depths of his jade eyes. It would be easy to be consumed by a universe shaded in green. But reality is relentless, reminding me that my daydreams can never be any more than what they are. I don't have time to chase after a mysterious boy and waste away the days with thoughts of him.

I silently urge the butterflies in my stomach to calm and try to focus my thoughts. "Thank you for apologizing."

My heart aches as he swallows and pulls his gaze from mine with a nod. For the slightest fraction of time, there was something between us. An omniscient presence tying us together and opening me up to the types of emotions I abandoned long ago. It's not enough to stifle out my lingering fear—the terror of letting someone slide past the defenses that I put in place to minimize the pain of losing them. In a world like this one, my best chance of avoiding a broken heart is to hold tightly to that fear.

Ryland places the gauze over the scratches before wrapping my arm in a white bandage. He stands, reaches for the blanket on the back of the couch, and shakes it out.

Realizing what he's doing, I say, "You can sleep here. I'm going upstairs to my old bed."

He ignores my words and proceeds to lean in and cover me with the blanket, forcing me to lie back to keep space between us. After he tucks me in, he smooths the hair on the top of my head and says, "Please, Quinn. After everything that happened last night, I'll sleep better knowing you're here and not in danger."

My cheeks heat in response to his touch, and I turn on my side to hide their redness. He takes a folded blanket and pillow from the top of the desk and throws them on the floor in front of the fire. Carefully, he removes his gun and places it under the pillow before lying down so we face each other.

We remain in awkward silence until I build up my courage and say, "Is your family still in Giran?"

"Yes. They live in a small village outside of the capital."

"Will you tell me about them?"

He takes a deep breath and says, "My parents divorced when I was young, and I spent most of my time with my mother and older sister. My mother remarried a man who is like my second father. But I worry about my dad. He lives alone and I never saw him as much as I planned on. I was busy being young and spending time with my friends."

"What's your sister's name?"

He smiles. "Avery. Do you have any siblings?"

I shake my head. "River is more like my sister than my cousin."

"If you don't mind me asking, where is your family?"

I consider where this conversation is heading and if I want to engage in it. Every tidbit Ryland learns about me will give him leverage to wiggle his way into my life, and I can't afford to have another person I care for. I need to have a single focus, and it must be River and me. Any thought I give to another person takes from our safety. Then again, Ryland is biding his time until Aiden is well enough to travel. Once that happens, he will be on his way. He's not meant to be a permanent fixture around here. Maybe his temporary presence isn't such a bad thing. If he doesn't stay, I'm free to be open with him with no strings attached. Besides, I can use a little therapy, and good therapists are nonexistent these days.

"I was raised by my aunt and uncle, River's parents. Every summer, we go on an aid trip to Bogati. My aunt and uncle had already left for the village we were to be stationed in. Normally, River and I would have gone with them, but I wanted to stay behind for a couple of weeks. It was our last summer at home before going off to university on opposite sides of the continent, and I just wanted some time alone with her. We were scheduled to leave the day after the quarantine was announced. Needless to say, we never made it."

"You blame yourself for River being here."

He has me pegged, and there's no reason to deny the truth. "She would've been just as happy leaving with her parents as she was staying back with me. I talked her into it."

He doesn't say anything as he processes what I've said. I want to pull the blanket over my head and hide from his analytic gaze. I worry he is affirming my self-hatred due to my stupid decision. As much as I dislike myself for the choice I made, I don't want him to feel the same.

"What if you're wrong and she wanted to stay behind with you? What if that summer was the best of her life?"

It's something I've never taken into consideration. I have always been accountable for the part I played in the separation of our family. "It was my idea. I initiated it. I put it into action, and if it was the best summer for her, that's great, but it's still my fault we're here."

"I can respect that." He doesn't flash a reassuring smile or shake his head in disapproval. He remains neutral as he sizes me up. It's a bit uncomfortable to be under such scrutiny, and I finally have to look away.

River and I have only spoken once about my feelings toward being stuck here. It was a month into the Affliction, and I broke down into a tearful apology. In true River form, she told me I was ridiculous, and it wasn't my fault. I hate how she has never gotten angry with me about our predicament and tries to brush it off as something I didn't play a part in. I don't want her to make the best of a shitty situation. I want us to be safe with our family.

After a few long minutes, I look in Ryland's direction again. His steely gaze is still fixated on me, his forehead crinkled in concentration. In a hushed voice, he asks, "When was the last time you spoke to your aunt and uncle?"

This is the one subject I try my hardest not to think about. It's not just that I miss them terribly, but I can't help reflecting on their state of worry. Every morning they must wake up and wonder if we're all right, and every night, I'm sure they pray we've lived through another day. Josh has probably worn through several pairs of shoes pacing back and forth, trying to reassure himself that he taught us everything we need to know to pull through this. Amara is a light sleeper, and I guess she's not slept through the night in almost two years. Perhaps they've given up hope on ever being reunited with us. They could believe we're dead. I can't imagine the toll not knowing has taken on them.

Although I dislike thinking about it, I answer, "A couple of days before the blackout. My aunt, Amara, is from Western Bogati, and they were going to leave the village and go stay with her family until they could come and get us. Being in the middle of nowhere, they didn't know how bad things were. They just knew millions of people in Stern had died and the continent went into self-isolation to protect the rest of the world. I don't think they fully comprehended how the virus had changed after the quarantine and what it was turning people into, and we couldn't bring ourselves to tell them. We thought there would be a chance to talk about it later, but again, we were wrong."

"What about your biological parents?" he asks.

Looking at the ceiling, I bite my lip. Now, he has crossed into an area of my life which I'm in no hurry to divulge. I pull the blankets under my chin and avoid looking at him. "That's a story for another time."

"I'm sorry. I didn't—"

"Please, don't apologize. You did nothing wrong. I'm just really tired."

"All right," he says, forcing a smile before turning his back to me.

I stifle down the ugly, raw emotions rising inside of

me. I have to keep them buried. They're the reason for every insecurity I've ever felt. It doesn't matter how many times I'm told I'm loved and wanted, the doubt is always there, whispering the opposite. I've worked hard to move past it, but it waits for a moment like this to get the better of me.

Chapter Nine

My eyes flutter open, taking in a simple palette of deep brown. Without moving my head, I gaze back and forth. It's a moment before my brain registers that I'm looking at the back of the couch in the study. Glancing at the thick drapes, I take in the soft glow of orange light seeping through a crack. I slept away the entire day.

"Did you sleep well?"

I roll to my side and find Ryland sitting against the wall. His legs are bent, and a book hangs loosely from his hands resting on top of his knees.

I brush away the damp strands of hair clinging to the side of my face and say, "I did once I fell asleep. Did you?"

"Surprisingly, yes. Dinner is ready if you're hungry."

I sit up, letting the blanket slide away from me. My head falls back as I stretch my arms to work out all the kinks. "Did you eat?"

When Ryland doesn't answer, my gaze darts his way, following his line of sight. I quickly grab the hem of my t-shirt and pull it back into place. When I turn back to him, there's a sly grin on his face, and my cheeks burn. It would appear that I'm not the only one who sneaks a peek when I think someone isn't watching.

He stands, places his book on Josh's desk, and finally answers my question. "No, I haven't eaten. I asked everyone to let you sleep and eat their dinner in the bunker."

"You didn't need to do that. You should have gone."

"I didn't want to leave you alone. Besides, I didn't mind. It gave me a chance to catch up on some reading." He leans against the side of the desk and taps the top of it with the book in his hand.

"What are you reading?"

"It's a classic about the last man in the world and his attempts to end his life so he can join his family and friends in paradise."

"Morbid," I mutter. "How many times have you read it?"

He looks down and thumbs the pages. "I'm not sure. It's the only book I have."

I walk over and pick up the item in question. The pages are dog-eared, and the cover is dirty and torn. I wouldn't doubt that he's read it at least twenty times.

"Maybe after dinner, I can find the box with all our old books, and you can pick a couple," I say.

"I'd like that."

Something about his tone makes me want to fall to my knees and weep for him. He sounds forlorn, but at the same time, appreciative of my offering.

Throughout the Affliction, I've been surrounded by what's familiar to me. Little odds and ends help to conjure memories of my past. There are moments when I walk through the basement and see a picture or a piece of furniture that sparks a memory. Ryland is limited to the items in his backpack, and perhaps the pieces of jewelry he wears. I hope he still remembers the faces of his loved ones and all of the treasured memories he made with them. It's those little flashbacks that motivate me during my darkest days, and I can't imagine being stripped of them.

We enter the bunker to find everyone gathered around the television with plates of desserts in their hands. Yet again, River has gone above and beyond making dinner and added homemade pie to the menu.

Ryland and I join them, sitting on opposite sides of the room. I take a seat next to River's legs where she's curled up on the couch with her arms around Noah. She and I are going to have to talk about what is going on between them. As much as she would like to believe shooting me an innocent smile while wrapped around him will stifle my concern, it won't. I'm afraid she'll get in over her head and be hurt in the end.

After the movie, Ryland stands and collects the dirty dishes. "We need to figure out how we're going to work patrols tonight. I don't want anyone outside alone after the sun goes down."

I cross my ankles and lean back on my hands, looking up at him. "I don't think anybody needs to be outside. All the Zs came from the woods on the northwest side of the property last night. The primary bedroom on the second floor has a balcony facing in that direction. If the Zs follow the same path, we will see them coming and have an advantage over them."

"I still want two people patrolling, even if it's inside. One person will be stationed in the primary bedroom, and the other will move throughout the house just in case the Zs change it up."

"I'll take the first watch," Aiden says before erupting into a series of coughs.

"You're absolutely hilarious, Donnelly. You and River are exempt from patrolling until you're better." Ryland goes on to explain the scheduling for each shift and turns to Wes. "It's you and me in ten minutes. I'll meet you in the study."

Everyone gathers their dishes and takes them to the sink.

Noah moves behind River and places a kiss on her temple, saying, "I'll be back to help clean up after I talk to Ry."

The men walk out of the room, leaving Aiden behind with River and me. I'm dying to find out what's going on between Noah and her. I catch her attention and jerk my head to the storage room.

Playing dumb, she says, "What?"

I fake a smile. "Can I talk to you for a minute... in *private*?"

From the other side of the couch, Aiden's head pivots between us, watching as we speak.

"I'm good right here," River says.

I do my best to keep any altercation between us quiet, and the storage room is ideal for what I need to say to her. But if she wants to have this discussion with an audience, it won't stop me.

"Aiden, do you mind pretending like you can't hear us and putting on earmuffs?" I demonstrate by placing my hands over my ears.

He smiles, doing as I ask.

I flip my attention to my cousin. "What are you doing? You've only known Noah for a week, and the two of you have pet names and are cuddling. He's kissing you goodbye!"

She pulls her thick, curly hair from the back of her neck, twisting it into a bun. "He's so sweet. The two of us can just sit and talk about anything," she explains, securing the knot on the top of her head.

I throw up my hands and shrug. "I'm sweet, and the two of us talk about everything."

"You're jealous."

I twist the string on my hoodie around my finger and pace the room. "I'm not." The lie feels thick on my tongue, and I hurry to replace it with the truth. "I just think it's ridiculous. The two of you are..." I shake my head and try again. "Is this a good idea when you know he's going to leave?"

River crosses the room and grabs my arm to stop me from moving. "Time is not on our side, Quinn. I don't have the luxury of going out on dates and taking it slow with someone. I like Noah a lot, and I won't stand down because you want me to follow irrelevant dating protocol. Even if he goes, and I never see him again, I need you to let me do this without judgment. Let me throw some fucking caution to the wind and open myself up to what might be my last opportunity to fall in love."

I vigorously shake my head. "This isn't going to be your last opportunity, Riv. I swear to God, it won't."

She wraps her slender hands around my neck and uses her thumbs on my jaw to hold me in place. "I trust you with my whole heart, but your promises are too big this time. Our lives are unpredictable and you trying to guarantee my future is absurd."

I hate that she feels like time isn't on her side, and she must seize the moment. It rips me apart to admit that she is right. I can't promise her a future, and she deserves to fall in love and have a bit of normalcy. We both do.

I jerk my head from her grip and use my sleeves to dry my eyes. "Okay, you're right. If he makes you happy, I'll be happy for you."

"Thank you."

"But—" I point at her "—if he breaks your heart, I'll take my hunting knife and castrate him and feed his balls to the Zs."

A huge smile brightens her face. "Understood."

"As his friend, I do feel obligated to warn him," Aiden says, with his hands still over his ears.

"Earmuffs never work." River grins.

Aiden laughs, but abruptly stops when the hacking begins.

River rushes to him. "All right, you've had too much excitement for the last couple of days. You need your rest." She helps him to his feet and walks him to my bed.

I start cleaning the kitchen, and shortly after, Noah appears at my side. I give him a sideways glance and keep scrubbing the plate in my hand.

"Are you always going to look at me like you're planning my death?" he asks.

River clears her throat from behind us—a wordless warning to watch my words.

It's not that I don't like Noah. He was the first one in their group who showed any sign of manners. Despite my hang-ups about how quickly they're moving, I have to admit that he's a sweet guy. There is no denying that he is just as hung up on my cousin as she is for him.

I release a sigh and say, "I'll stop planning your demise if you help me with laundry tonight."

If I'm going to have to be nice, I might as well get something out of it, and scrubbing Z blood out of clothes is the worst. The extra help will make the daunting task go by quicker.

"Just tell me what you need me to do," he says, with an eager smile.

Four pairs of shoes line the kitchen counter, and our clothes are in the process of being hand-washed. Noah helped me connect the makeshift clothesline from one end of the main floor kitchen to the other, and a couple of shirts hang from wooden clothespins. In the morning, enough sunlight should come through the window to dry the laundry.

I use the time with Noah to grill him on all aspects of his life. I learn about his parents who are still happily married, his two sisters, the city he grew up in, and that he was studying to be a mechatronics engineer. He comes from a good family, is smart, helpful, and finding his faults is extremely hard.

He talks nonstop about my cousin, asking questions and sharing his new insights. In all my years with River, I don't ever think I've discussed her this much. My only saving grace is the moments when Ryland passes by on patrol. The two of us exchange glances and roll our eyes as Noah goes on about River. We make a game out of it. Ryland passes by and makes a face behind his friend's back while I do my best to look like he has my undivided attention. Even though Ryland and I have a good laugh at Noah's expense, I can't deny that he seems genuinely smitten with River.

We return to the bunker to find Aiden asleep and River sitting on our sofa-bed, reading a book in the light of a lantern. I consider for a split second taking the upper bunk and letting Noah sleep with her, but I'm not ready to be in a room where they're giggling and whispering all night long. Plus, he has his first shift in a couple of hours and needs his sleep.

I may have wasted most of the day sleeping, but my body is quick to subside to it again. When I wake up, I look at the top bunk to find Noah is gone. The battery-operated clock River set to go off every three hours shows I still have over thirty minutes until I'm due for my shift. Knowing I won't be able to fall back to sleep, I slip on my combat boots before placing my weapons in their usual spots on my body. Tiptoeing to the refrigerator, I pull out the coffee carafe containing the leftovers from yesterday morning and pour the liquid into a cup. I grab a shot glass and a bottle of whiskey from the back of the cupboard and slip out of the bunker.

As I pass Noah in the living room, I nod in the way of a greeting before he returns to looking out the front window. The old wooden stairs creak under my weight as I move to the landing and veer to the side toward the primary bedroom. The double doors are wide open, and as I enter, I slow my steps, allowing my eyes to adjust to the darkness consuming the room. There in the light of the moon, I find the person I'm looking for. He sits in a high-back chair in front of the glass double doors leading to the balcony. His legs stretched out before him, crossed at the ankles, and his gun resting on his lap. He looks peaceful almost like he's drifted off to sleep, but he turns in my direction as I move closer.

"I brought you a nightcap before you head off to bed," I say, raising the coffee in one hand and the shot glass and bottle of amber liquid in the other.

Ryland returns his attention to the landscape outside the doors. "Do you think it's a good idea for you to drink before your watch?"

I sit on the bed next to his chair and hold up my already filled cup. "Don't worry, mine is straight espresso.

I brought the good stuff just for you. I figured you could use a little help unwinding."

I set my drink on the floor, pour the whiskey into the glass, and hand it to him. Grabbing my cup, I hold it up in a salute, and we both kick back the liquids.

Ryland holds his glass out to me, and I fill it again. He clears his throat against the burn of the whiskey and asks, "Why aren't you asleep?"

"I slept all day and then another five hours. That's a lot for me."

He nods as he scours the lawn for intruders. "Did Noah end up winning you over?"

I shrug. "I don't get it, but I guess if this is what they want, who am I to stand in their way?"

Ryland leans forward in the chair and rests his elbows on the tops of his legs. "Noah will make a great boyfriend."

"Whoa, now you're jumping the gun."

He smirks and shakes his head. "I'm just saying he'll do anything for her."

"Sure, until it's time for him to leave."

Ryland sinks into the chair again and focuses on what lies beyond the balcony. He can sing Noah's praises all night, but there's no way he can deny the truth. They have a plan, and it is not to stay here.

I move back on the mattress and lean against the massive wooden headboard of the four-poster bed. All of the room's personal artifacts are packed away. The walls are bare, as are the dresser tops that used to display family photos. The small walk-in closet is open with nothing remaining inside but a few hangers. River and I erased any sign of my aunt and uncle ever being here. The room they once shared is a vacant tomb.

My mind drifts back to River and Noah, and what's transpiring between them. "It's weird, the love at first sight thing."

"You don't believe in love at first sight?" Ryland asks.

I bite my lip as I contemplate my answer. It's a bizarre notion that the minute you see someone, the stars align, and you instantaneously know you've found your soulmate. That fate has pre-selected the person you're meant to spend the rest of your life with, and your free will has absolutely nothing to do with your decision. I can't wrap my head around it.

"Attraction or lust at first sight, sure, but love?" I say, before taking a sip of my expresso. "Being in love the minute you meet someone... no. Love is so complex, yet we have simplified it to apply to everyday things. I'm in love with this song, or I'm in love with these shoes, but when you're truly in love, there's an unbreakable connection. Whether someone you love is near or far, they're still part of you. They consume you and the choices you make bear them in mind. Simply loving or profoundly caring for someone will deplete when you believe what you're giving is not being returned in the same way. I mean think about it, people say they're *madly in love,* and then something changes. One of them feels like the relationship can't be salvaged, so they give up and walk away. The one who's left heartbroken comes to realize over time, and with newer and stronger relationships, it wasn't that they were *in* love, but simply loved the person. When someone is in love and that connection is severed, their heart is forever scarred. They approach the next relationship with hesitation because they never want to feel pain like that again. The bond isn't meant to be broken. Ever." When I look up after my rant, I find Ryland staring at me.

"Are you talking from experience?" he asks.

I fidget with the ring on my finger. "Not in the way you might think. My experience with love outside of the family dynamic is zero. I was supposed to gain all those relationship experiences at university." I cock an eyebrow. "I'm limited, but observant. What about you, have you been in love?"

His eyes are glassy, and it's hard to tell if it's from emotion or if the alcohol is taking hold. "I've loved, but never been in love."

"So, there's no girlfriend at home waiting for you to find your way across the Oscuros border?" I pull my knees to my chest and wrap my arms around my legs.

"No."

The whole subject of love and having someone to love seems to hit a chord with him. I wonder if he feels the same as River. Does he believe he will never have the chance to become familiar with the inner workings of being in love? Does he look back on his life and kick himself for not trying harder, or not being brave enough to take a leap that would make him vulnerable to others? To be as young as we are and give up on the chance to be a part of the most complex and yet fundamental of human emotions is heartbreaking. It's difficult not to feel like you're missing out on something amazing, and that you're forced to forgo love and fight for your life instead.

"Ry, times up," Noah says from the doorway.

Ryland stands and reaches for the bottle of whiskey. "May I?"

"Sure," I say, motioning for him to take it.

Ryland pats his friend on the shoulder as he wishes Noah a good night and exits the room.

When the sound of his steps fades, Noah moves

across from me. He keeps his voice quiet as he says, "Tread lightly."

I furrow my brow. "What does that mean?"

"I know he comes off as sort of a badass, but he's just as fragile as the rest of us."

I'm not sure how to respond. Fragile is not a word I'd use to describe Ryland. Whenever I catch a glimpse of his vulnerability, it never lasts long. He's quick to stifle the emotion and replace it with a brave face. It's hard to imagine him crumbling under the pressure of anything. Then again, that's what he wants me to see. Ryland's friends know that side of him that he keeps hidden.

"I'll keep that in mind," I say, scooting off the bed.

Noah removes a watch from his wrist and gives it to me. "When Wes comes to trade places with you for the foot patrol, hand it off to him."

"All right." I slip on the watch, and it dangles from my wrist like a bracelet.

Noah slides into the chair where Ryland sat and says, "Just yell if you see anything."

"I will."

The night carries on without incident, giving me hours to reflect on all areas of my life that seem questionable at the moment. The appearance of the four men living with us, Noah and River, whether the horde of Zs was a coincidence or not, and Ryland are a few of the topics I fixate on. Of course, Ryland consumes my thoughts the most. No matter how hard I try to push him out of my mind, he wiggles his way back in.

When my shift ends, I return to the bunker, seeking a couple of hours of sleep. I press my finger to the door scanner and enter the room. I barely make it inside before I notice River sitting on the edge of Aiden's bed, and in her hand is a cloth covered with red liquid.

"We have a huge problem," she says.

Right on cue, Aiden coughs, and she presses the soiled fabric to his mouth. I watch as what is left of the white washcloth is saturated in bright red blood. When she pulls it away, the remnants of the coughing fit are still around his lips. His eyes are sunken into his skull and outlined in dark purple bruises. She gently dabs the blood away, removing the only thing coloring his pale lips.

My voice hitches with dread as I say, "I'll wake up the guys."

There are thousands of things that can go wrong, but for me, the most disturbing is knowing Aiden could die. He's wiggled his way past my defenses and coaxed me into caring for him. I like him and the idea that our friendship may soon come to an end is heartbreaking. I'm not sure what can be done to save him, but I'm willing to do whatever it takes.

Chapter Ten

"Camden and Rogers are the nearest large cities to us, but they also house military installations, meaning the chances of soldiers still being in those areas are good. They would have raided the hospitals right away, and if they haven't, we have no chance against people with military-grade weapons. I think we take too big of a risk going to either of those places," I say.

For the past hour, Ryland, Noah, Wes, and I have sat around the small table in the bunker, staring at a map of the central-northern region of Stern. This part of the continent wasn't populated like the cities along the coasts before the Affliction. Around here, metropolitan areas are far and few between. It's the reason people had chosen to live in a place like Devil's Lake. They wanted to avoid the crowds, traffic, and overall busy life that those in the city love. It also means that trips to major hospitals are a lengthy drive.

The debate over where we should go to find the medication that could save Aiden's life has been extensive. We not only have to take into consideration the Zs, but the type of people we might run into. Then there's the question of how far the truck can take us with enough fuel to get us home. Every suggestion is met with a scenario to counter it, making forming a solid plan impossible.

"Explain to me again why you can't go to the hospital in town?" River asks from her new permanent station at Aiden's bedside. A medical book is open on her lap as she tries to diagnose him for the second time. She believes his lungs have become so inflamed and riddled with an infection that they're failing and causing him to cough up blood. She prescribed him steroids with the hope they'll strengthen his lungs. Unfortunately, it's a medication we don't have.

Ryland sighs before answering her question. "Because of the increased Z sightings around the house since we got here. I worry if we continue to make our presence known, they will only get worse. It's best to lay low and stay out of town for now. Besides, you and Quinn have said it yourselves, everything has been thoroughly ransacked around here. We're going to be hard-pressed to find what we need."

Noah's brow lowers and the glare he shoots Ryland feels like it can set the room on fire. Someone is clearly not pleased with the way his friend speaks to my cousin. To defuse the situation before it explodes, I lean forward and point at the map.

"I'm sticking with Blythe. It's our best bet. It's big enough that we'll have multiple medical facilities nearby, there are no major military bases in the area, and we can get there by avoiding those places that do. Also, it's close enough that the truck will still have enough battery life to make it home if we have to take a slight detour."

River stands with a bowl of bloody, pink water and

a soaking dish towel, and takes it to the kitchen sink. "With Blythe being the capital of this region, you don't think the city will still be crowded?"

"Most likely, but it is our safest and best bet. If we can't find the medicine there, we won't find it," I say.

She glances at me over her shoulder before voicing her next concern. "You can't take the truck all the way to the city, it will draw too much attention. You're looking at five hours of travel time, including walking to Blythe."

Wes chimes in, "Plus, scavenging for the right steroids, that's at least another four hours if we're lucky."

All of this meticulous planning to get a drug that used to be readily available through a doctor is frustrating. Every movement we make needs to be charted out, and every possible scenario that could go wrong must have a contingency plan. Try as we might to cover all our bases, there's going to come a moment when we give up on playing it safe and come to terms with the fact that we're bound to run into trouble. Going into a city is dangerous, there's no way around it.

Ryland pulls his hair back from his face, running his fingers through it. "Driving at night is risky, and I don't want to do it unless we have to. It's too difficult to see when you're being hunted in the dark. If something were to happen to the truck, we're sitting targets. We're going to have to stay the night. Hopefully, we find a safe place to park the truck and camp out on our way there."

"After that horde attack, I'm not leaving River overnight by herself. She needs backup," I say.

"That's fine, you can stay behind with her," he counters with indifference.

What the hell? They can use all the support they can get. I was expecting Ryland to devise a plan to have us back before nightfall, not forgo my help. I understand I've only had the privilege of knowing Aiden for a few days, but this isn't just about his well-being. We all have something at stake here. If this mission fails, the outcome will affect all of us. I'm a strong player on this team, and my skills are better served in Blythe and not in the bunker. If someone has to stay behind, it won't be me.

"I think Noah should stay," I suggest. "If he thinks he can finagle the cell phone to connect with the tower, then he needs to get to work. If we fail to get the drugs, at least, there's a chance of getting Aiden home."

Ryland raises an eyebrow and points a finger at Noah and River. "Do you honestly think either of them is going to concentrate on what they should when they're left here alone?"

I lean back in my chair, cross my arms, and stare straight into his eyes. "I think you better hope they do because I'm coming with you. Besides, I know what to do if something minor goes wrong with the truck."

Ryland mimics my posture and with an equally feisty tone says, "You forget, Noah's studying to be a mechanical engineer. I'm fairly confident he can handle a minor malfunction, love."

"This is a dead issue, Shaw. It's my truck, and I'm going."

Wes bursts into laughter. "You know it's a pissing-match when last names are dropped."

Ryland shoots his friend a glare which promises pain if he doesn't shut up before turning back to me. "Why do you have to make everything so damn complicated?"

"It wouldn't be difficult if you'd agree with me for once and stop putting up a fight every time I offer to help. I know the roads better than you, and I've proven over and over again that I can hang with the *big boys* when it comes to holding my own against Zs."

Kicking his chair back, Ryland stands and pounds both hands on the table. Leaning in toward me, he yells, "This isn't about you not being able to handle yourself, Quinn!"

I jump to my feet and close the distance between us. My stare bores into his as the tips of our fingers meet in the middle of the table. "You're being ridiculous! If I stay, I'm useless in trying to improve this situation. I'll sit here with River doing nothing, but Noah can work on the cell phone link, and perhaps we'll have a feasible backup plan if this mission doesn't work. You said he'd do anything for my cousin, so I'm taking you at your word. He'll keep her safe while we're gone."

Ryland pushes away from the table, his rage brightening his face to a heated red. "Fuck it, Quinn! No matter what I say you're going to override me. So go on and plan this the way you want and tell me what you need me to do."

I close my eyes and bite my lip. Each angry stomp of his boots is like an explosion echoing in my ears as he walks out. When the basement door slams, I sink back down into my chair and cover my face with my hands. This isn't what I wanted to happen. I just wanted him to agree to my help, to find me valuable to this mission.

Aiden's raspy voice pulls me from my misery. "Ry doesn't know what to do with someone quite so independent, Quinn. The lads and I can all hold our own, but he's one of the main reasons we're still alive. You have to understand that he's scared and doing his best to fix a bad situation while trying to keep all of us safe, including you."

I rest my cheek in my palm and look at my sick friend. He's propped up on a few pillows, saving him from choking on his own blood during a coughing fit. His eyes are still bright blue, but have sunken in and are encircled by dark bags. The luster of his skin has dimmed to a sickly gray. He looks terrible, and I feel sorry for taking part in the heated argument that woke him. The mere sight of him has me on the verge of tears. The last thing he needs is to stress and not get any sleep. We fight every day against the Affliction, and now, he's battling a sickness that used to be easily curable. Out of all of us, he currently has the rottenest deal.

"What do you suggest I do, Aiden?" If he tells me to not go on this mission, I'll do it for him. I'll hate it, but I'll do it and not add to his worries.

"Go talk to him and figure it out together," he says with a faint smile.

"He refuses to listen to reason."

Wes scoots his chair closer to mine and rests his hand on my shoulder. "You're going to hate hearing this, but the two of you are a lot alike. I've come to notice you don't do well with being told what to do either, but you're a bit more willing if you're asked. Just like you, a polite please goes a long way with Ry."

Am I acting pigheaded if I don't ask nicely to come along? Maybe. But it's not like they can set off to get the medicine Aiden needs without my truck. It seems unreasonable to me that I should have to ask. Perhaps it's a stubborn take on my part. I can recognize a time and place to give in to do what's best for everyone. As much as I hate that Ryland won't meet me in the middle, Wes is right—it's me who should compromise first.

I pat Wes on the leg and stand. The people in this room mean more to me than maintaining my ego. Besides, I'm not asking Ryland to make me queen, just a respected part of our tiny democracy. How hard can that be?

I find Ryland sitting on the couch in the study. He's leaning forward with his face in his hands like he's trying to hide from the world. I sit beside him and rest my elbows on my knees, so we're in the same position. He doesn't move away, but doesn't acknowledge me either. This is going to take a little finagling on my part to get through to him.

"It's not my intention to frustrate you. Believe it or not, I do care about Aiden, and I just want to help."

Ryland rubs his hands over his face, and I question if I'm worsening the situation. Maybe there's no amicable way to settle our differences. Wes said Ryland is just as stubborn as me. If that's so, the only solution he's going to be content with is if I give up on pleading my case. It would be easier to do just that and go with him to Blythe without his blessing. But the hard feelings it will create will only add to the difficult task we have ahead of us.

He finally clasps his hands together, resting his chin on top of them. Seconds tick by as he watches the flames consume the log in the fireplace. Finally, he says, "Have you been outside of this town since the quarantine?"

"No," I whisper.

There's no reason for River and me to go beyond the borders of Devil's Lake. We have everything we need here. Also, survival 101 says, if there's a possibility of someone looking for us, then we should stay put. Even though the chance of Josh and Amara gaining entrance to Stern is slim to none, there's this eternal hope that they will return. We want to be where they can find us if they arrive. So yes, my experience with the new society around us is minimal at best.

"Everywhere is different, Quinn." Ryland scrunches his face like the images running through his head are painful. "What we encountered with that guy during the supply run or even the Afflicted the other night, it's not a fraction of the violence I've seen. As this sickness spread, it consumed the decency in people. I've seen mobs of the Afflicted surround children and the elderly, slaughtering them in the most gruesome ways. Men who used to be upstanding citizens now capture young girls and force them into serving them in repulsive acts. There's no rhyme or reason to their self-serving motives, and I'm scared to death I won't be able to protect you from any of them."

"I'm not asking you to," I say, thankful my nerves don't betray me. Hearing him confirm my worst fears has me on edge, but I'm unwavering. I won't let anything stop me from doing what is right.

Lifting his head, he faces me. "I understand that you're not asking me to, but it's impossible for me not to. I know you're capable of defending yourself, and you managed just fine before I arrived. I see your bravery, resilience, and strength, but it doesn't change this unrelenting need I have to keep you safe."

Ryland reaches out and tucks a piece of my hair behind my ear. His touch lingers, moving to a strand resting on my shoulder. My heart speeds up and warmth pools in my lower stomach. I press my thighs together as I watch him rub the tendril between his fingers.

The feeling vanishes when a sad smile plays on his lips and he says, "The other night in the clearing, when I was surrounded, I panicked when I saw you. Then I realized you were going to give me your gun and make yourself known to the Afflicted. I was going to run and lure them away from you. I couldn't stomach the thought of them killing or turning you. The only thing stopping me was knowing if they followed and killed me, you would be on your own. I had to stay alive and fight with you."

His confession is unexpected. I honestly believed his qualms with me accompanying him on the trip to Blythe were because he didn't think I was as capable as he and the others are. It never occurred to me that he fears for my safety.

For so long, it's only been River and me. There's no question as to where the two of us stand when it comes to the safety of the other. Sacrificing ourselves to save the other is always a lingering possibility. It's that, or we go down together. I stay alive, so she stays alive, and vice versa. But Ryland is another side of this apocalyptic coin. There's no reason for him to have even considered sacrificing his life for mine.

"I don't know what to say," I finally admit.

His long fingers slide around the side of my neck, and his thumb brushes back and forth over my jaw. His callused skin is rough against my face and a welcome touch. It triggers thousands of small prickles as every one of my nerve endings spark to life. They remind me that I'm still someone who is easily excited by the attention of a handsome man.

Ryland's forehead creases, and he softly pleads, "Say you'll stay. I'm begging you to give me some peace in knowing you'll be alright."

His expression is pained, and his words convey his torment. I don't want to contribute to his worry. In fact, there's nothing more I want right now than to relieve him of his unwarranted concern, but he's asking me to save my own ass while he and others risk theirs. I can't do it.

"I'm sorry, Ryland."

He closes his eyes, and his chest expands with a deep intake of air. I brace myself for his rebuttal, but it never comes. "I knew you would say that, but I had to try."

"If it's any consolation, I promise to not wander off without you. I'll follow your directions. I really don't want to get myself killed." I finish with a small smile and pray it soothes him.

His eyes dance across my face as his thumb brushes back and forth over my cheek. I'm struggling not to lean into his touch, to close the distance between our lips. It's been ages since I've felt the warm press of lips to mine. I miss the tiny fluttering in my stomach as my hands grip the hair on the back of my partner's neck, pulling him closer. The feeling of fingertips digging into the small of my back as he tries to use his body to feel every curve of mine. I long for the slow exhale of his breath and the feel of it fanning against my lips as we draw closer to one another. That last second before my world is dancing with stars and the room spins as our lips move as one. I miss the simple complexities of things like a first kiss so very much. And I want to experience them with Ryland.

His knee skims mine, and the small spark inside of me ignites into a blazing flame. I fist his shirt and draw him closer. My eyes flutter shut as I anticipate what's sure to be one of the most earth-shattering kisses I've ever experienced. They say things get better with time, and my last kiss was over two years ago, so this is poised to be off the charts.

"I guess the two of you worked out your differences."

Ryland and I quickly push away from each other, and I jump to my feet.

River leans against the doorframe with her arms crossed. She doesn't bother to hide her amusement, her eyes sparkling with delight. She can't wait to corner me and extract what she believes are juicy details about

Ryland and me. I wish I could be upset with her for disrupting our moment, but it's too damn hard when she has a mischievous look on her face.

Ryland flashes a lopsided grin and says, "We're okay. I think we can have a tentative plan mapped out before the end of the night."

With her index finger, she points between Ryland and me, saying, "And how was that going to work into the plan?"

"It wasn't—I mean, nothing was happening. We're just talking." I walk past her and out of the study. "Do you need help with dinner?"

Turning on her heels, she follows me with Ryland behind her. "No, I was coming to tell you dinner is made, so if you need to continue talking—"

"Nope, we're good," I answer, followed by River's laughter.

After everyone finishes eating, we sprawl out across the living space in the bunker and continue planning. The framework to execute the medical supply run is already in place. There are only small loose ends to tie up and minor complications to work through. All in all, it's as solid as we can make it.

It would be a lie to say I'm entirely at ease with what tomorrow will bring. After all, this will be the first time I've left Devil's Lake since the quarantine. In the beginning, there were still newscasts and ways to connect with others across the continent. Now, I'm isolated and genuinely oblivious to the conditions outside of our small town. Come morning, that will all change.

Chapter Eleven

Two hours into our journey on the back roads leading from Devil's Lake to Blythe, and all is calm. The snow-covered, flat land spreads out on both sides of the paved road as far as the eye can see. The occasional animal scurries away as the truck approaches, and at one point, a herd of buffalo grazes in the distance. If I didn't know any better, I'd think someone played a dirty trick on me, and nothing ever changed. Maybe I'm on a hidden camera show, and the whole world is enthralled with how ridiculously naive I am to believe Stern has been annihilated by a zombie-like takeover. If it's true, I'll be so relieved that I'll forgive the idiot who set me up in a heartbeat.

Wes begged me to let him drive the truck. He went on a rant about how long it had been since he'd driven a vehicle and promised to be forever in my debt. With a sigh, I handed over the keys, and it has been worth it. His excitement is the best payment I could receive. For the first few miles, he reverted to a child—smiling brightly while he played with the big toy. He even rolled down his window, so the freezing winter wind blew through his ebony hair. Even as I freeze to death, I don't regret my decision. How can I when he is so ecstatic? I've given him a little happiness in a place where joy sometimes feels obsolete.

I reap my own benefits from not having to drive. I sit with my back against the sidewall of the truck, and my legs stretched across the small bench seat. From my position, I can appreciate the sight of the countryside. The repetitiveness of the flat land contains a beauty I've neglected to admire until now. When I was younger, my family and I would take local exploration trips, and I must've passed this scenery hundreds of times. Never once do I remember it being this striking. Then again, I was probably too busy trying to get in my last hours with my phone before I was forced to abandon it and spend quality time with my loved ones. If I had any inkling that this would be my life, I'd never have taken those long car trips for granted.

My position behind the driver's seat also gives me the perfect view of Ryland's profile as he studies the passing landscape. His eyes are in constant motion, sweeping over the land, and his chiseled jaw flexes, giving away how focused he is. His gun rests upon his thigh with his index finger ready beside the trigger. The heightened concentration he displays is fascinating, but even more captivating is the way his chestnut waves curl around his ear, creating tiny peek-a-boo openings. My fingertips tingle with the desire to pull on the soft strand and let go, watching as it coils back up against his skin.

I shake my head, trying to expel the daydream from my mind. I can't get rid of the giddy schoolgirl feelings I have when Ryland is near. Ever since last night, it's as if a filter has shaded my vision, making every one of his features and movements even more attractive. I'm completely distracted by him, and it's both good and bad. I've not given much thought to the danger that awaits us in Blythe, and therefore, I'm at ease. Of course, I'm not as focused as I should be, making me a possible liability on today's run. I've got to get over this and concentrate on what matters.

"Slow down." Ryland's voice breaks the silence. "Do you see that?" He points past an empty field with deserted farm equipment left to rust in the snow.

I squint toward the building in the distance and say, "It looks like a barn."

He spreads a map on the dash and glides his finger from our location to Blythe. "We're almost to the edge of the city; I'd say less than five miles. If the barn isn't occupied, we can store the truck in there, return before nightfall, and take shelter inside until dawn."

"It looks like the road to the barn is up there." I point to a crude turn-off.

Wes pulls onto the narrow side road and slowly maneuvers the truck to the barn. When we reach the weathered building, Ryland and I step out into the cold, scanning the land for any sign of life. Before we move to the barn's wooden double doors, Ryland pulls me to his side. "You take the rear and keep me in your sight at all times. Don't hesitate. At the first sign of aggression, you shoot."

"I got it," I say without a second thought. I won't willingly be the victim again.

I skim the tree line and field for any sign of movement as Ryland uses his boot to chip away the ice piled against the door. It takes a couple of tries, but he finally pries the door open, and we slip inside. The interior doesn't contain any great hiding places, just four walls constructed of wooden slats and a loft. The ground is sprinkled with hay, and an array of farming tools hang from rusted nails on the walls. In the back, a wooden ladder leads to the hayloft where I can make out a couple of bales. Ryland scales the ladder and disappears above me. Moments later, he returns to the ledge and says, "I think this will work. There are no signs that anyone has been here for quite some time."

I cross my arms and turn in a slow circle. "So far, so good, which I don't like. I'd rather get any trouble out of the way now. Things never go this smoothly."

"I agree," he says, descending the ladder. "But we'll take every break we can get until then."

Together, we push the doors open and motion Wes to back the truck in. After we're secured inside, we take a short break to eat and warm up the best we can before heading out into the cold on foot. We're about to become a slower moving target without the truck and will be at the mercy of anything or anyone who is familiar with the area. They'll have the upper hand, making us an easy three-course meal or perhaps long-range shooting targets. If it weren't for Aiden's rapidly diminishing health, staying in the barn and solidifying our plan further would be a no-brainer.

I tuck my hair into my black beanie and zip my jacket. Other than a fruit bar and a couple of water bottles, my backpack holds mostly ammo—two extra clips and a pouch of bullets. My hunting knife is strapped to the outside of my leg, another smaller blade is at my ankle inside my boot, and my gun is tucked into the back of my pants.

On the other side of the truck, Wes and Ryland follow a similar routine. They check their packs to make sure they take only what we'll need and strategically place their weapons on their bodies. Before we leave the barn, Ryland kicks the snow back into place around the door, securely shutting it.

We follow the truck tracks back to the highway. The neglected farmland is unnaturally quiet. The crunch of dirt under our shoes is a resounding gong, proclaiming our vulnerability and making me cringe. It doesn't get any better when we reach the main road. It too is covered in ice and sludge and is slippery to walk on, but it's better than being knee-deep in snow.

It doesn't take long before the skyline of the city comes into view. For some reason, I had it in my mind that it would be in shambles. Buildings would be skeletons of their former glory with smoke smoldering from windows. Fires burning in the distance as a dark gray cloud looms over what was the northern region's capital, but it's not the case. Other than a lack of traffic, all seems to be well. It's as I remember it from my childhood.

We stroll along the highway until reaching the suburban areas. Ryland doesn't want to stay on the main street for fear we'll be noticed, so we move along the side roads. Row after row of cookie-cutter homes fend for themselves against the elements. Some are boarded up, awaiting the return of their owners, but most sit with their doors wide open. There's a chance the medications we need are in one of these houses, but we can't afford to be frivolous with the daylight, so we head for a more definite location. The execution of our plan must be precise and swift. Every wrong move or unexpected hurdle prolongs our mission and puts Aiden and our safety on the line.

After over an hour of walking, the scenery evolves into precisely placed trees throughout a park, surrounding a tall business building. I've been to this very spot on a school field trip, and it, like so many other things I've seen today, has not changed.

Ryland stops short of stepping foot onto the capitol building's grounds and turns to Wes and me. "We need to be alert and stick together. If we weren't short on time, I'd avoid this area, but it's a direct route to the street the hospital is on."

"You think some Zs are playing government in there?" I say with a smartass smirk.

"No, I think people are using these buildings as shelter. Think about it, government buildings are made to protect the officials inside. These are some of the most secure places in the city. Generally, we would avoid the capitals, but at your suggestion, I made an exception."

It hadn't occurred to me that people would be here. I assume everyone is like River and me and wants to stay in their homes. It was a silly suggestion now that I think about it. We're safe because of the bunker, but the best that most homes have is a furnished basement or cellar. Both will do little to keep a hungry Z out. This was my plan, and if something goes wrong and Wes or Ryland gets hurt, it will be my fault.

We fall into formation with me in the middle and march across the property to the backside of the capitol grounds. Before us stands two buildings—a rectangular single-level and a tower at least twenty stories high.

Without warning, Ryland pulls me to his side behind a tree, and Wes effortlessly follows his lead.

"Guards," Wes whispers from behind me.

I peek around the trunk of the tree. Two armed men walk the perimeter next to the sidewalk.

"We'll wait for them to walk away and then move in next to the building and use it for cover," Ryland says, and

Wes and I nod.

As soon as the coast is clear, we briskly walk to the side of the capitol building. No sooner do we reach the wall and the bellowing voice of a man resounds throughout the grounds. I flinch, fearing that we've been caught. Ryland snaps his head in my direction, placing his finger over his lips. He points to the front of the building and looks around the corner. I nervously await his next command and listen to the speaker carry on over the hushed murmurings of others. Finally, Ryland straightens and motions for us to follow him.

Hundreds of people face the steps of the capitol. We casually walk to them and melt into the crowd. Before us sits three high back leather chairs in the middle of the platform with two men dressed in black robes seated on each end. Standing center stage, a man whose robe is adorned with a red sash across the front and a golden broach. His wrinkled skin sags on his slender face, and his salt and pepper hair blows in the breeze as he speaks to the crowd.

"I wish to remind the members of our society that talk of the Sanctuary is strictly prohibited," the man says. "Family-heads are free to make the decision to leave with those in their charge, and with nothing more than the clothing on their backs. We will not stop them. We are people who care for our own, and anyone who chooses to disavow our community will not take with them what has been given by our graces." His shoulders square as he holds up a bright orange flyer and switches to a hostile tone. "But talk of the Sanctuary within our walls will not be tolerated. We will not have our impressionable youth brainwashed. Following a ridiculous set of riddles will not lead them to a hidden community that promises our old way of life. Our job is to protect the most vulnerable among us and to teach them to fend for themselves. I have mandated unannounced sweeps of all living quarters. If Sanctuary propaganda is found, the holder will be stripped of their possessions and sentenced accordingly."

The man crumples the paper in what is no doubt a metaphor of what will happen to those found with the flyers. His words about propaganda for a hidden community and being stripped of possessions doesn't sit well with me, but the crowd isn't the slightest bit upset. To my surprise, they cheer and yell derogatory things about this Sanctuary. It appears these adults—mostly men— have done some brainwashing themselves. What happened to personal property and freedom of speech? These were fundamental rights before the quarantine.

"Our next order of business is today's trial," says the man, lowering himself into his chair.

A girl no older than me is dragged onto the steps. Her blue dress is filthy and tangled around her legs, but it doesn't stop her from struggling against the two men restraining each of her arms. Through a mess of matted red hair, her shoulders shake as she sobs.

Another man in a brown robe stands to the side of the steps and unrolls a page of white paper. "Justice Fowler and his honorable counsel." He nods to the three seated men. "This woman, Madison Lane, is a charge of the Henderson household. Director Henderson has staked a claim on her to be his third wife come this spring. Ms. Lane was caught in the act of having relations with a charge of the region."

The man seated furthest to the right calls out to the crowd, "Director Henderson, how do you wish for punishment to be administered to your charge?"

A man, who is old enough to be the girl's

grandfather, steps onto the stage. He's well dressed in clean slacks and a button-up shirt and strikes me as a person of importance. The man nods respectfully to the panel of judges and says, "If it pleases the court, I wish to resume the responsibility of my charge."

The girl collapses to her knees and yells, "I'd rather you kill me!"

Director Henderson shoots her a menacing glare with his beady eyes and continues. "I ask that the man who stole from me be brought to justice, and that my charge is also punished for her crimes. I request she receives twenty public lashings tomorrow at dawn."

The judge on the left says, "May I ask why you wish to delay her punishment?"

Again, the old man turns his attention to Madison and says, "Because I don't want the pain of her lashings to distract her from the memories of what happens here today. For at least one night, I want her to wallow in the grief of knowing she will never see her lover again, and at the same time, fear her impending punishment."

I bite the inside of my cheek, stifling down the fear bubbling inside me. These people have reverted to a barbaric way of governing. It makes me sick to be a silent bystander, like I'm condoning their hideous system of so-called justice.

The judges exchange curt nods before Justice Fowler states, "Your request has been granted, Director Henderson." He turns to the man in brown. "Bring forth the accused."

The announcer steps forward again and reads, "Justin Reims has not been claimed by a citizen's household and therefore is a charge of the Northern Region of Stern. He is accused of defiling the property belonging to Director Henderson and conspiring to rob him of said property."

A shackled young man in tattered clothing is led to the platform. He's worse for wear with his black hair clumped in knots, and his face swollen from being used as a punching bag. Despite the fact that he should be carried up the steps in his condition, he holds his head high.

"Mr. Reims, how do you plead to the charges brought against you?" Justice Fowler asks.

"As seen by the region, I'm guilty," he says in an unwavering voice.

Madison thrashes from side to side and wails, "No, Justin!"

My heart breaks at her desperate plea and her efforts to fight off the two massive guards holding her in place.

"Then this court hereby sentences you to death for your crimes. That is, unless a house will speak on your behalf and sway the court otherwise."

I frantically look around for someone to intervene. Surely all of these people wouldn't let this boy die because he simply fell in love with a girl? Since when did messing around become a crime punishable by death? I'm sure a vast majority of adults in this crowd should also be victims of capital punishment if it were the case. Yet the silence from those around me is loudly sentencing this young man to death.

"Ry?" His name escapes my lips in a quiet plea for him to reassure me this will not end badly. I turn to face him, and he wraps his arm around me, pulling me to his side. He has nothing to offer but this weak attempt to comfort me.

"I want to go," I whisper against his chest.

He leans down and speaks into my hair. "We have

to wait for everyone to disperse, so we don't draw attention. I'm so sorry, love." The same helplessness and sadness I feel are evident in his voice. He's a mastermind who can plot his way out of almost anything. Even the night I found him in the clearing surrounded by Zs, he hadn't fully surrendered. As hopeless as he looked, his mind was shuffling through hundreds of ideas of how he would turn the outcome in his favor. This time he's giving up.

"Mr. Reims, your sentence stands," the head judge states in an emotionless tone.

Madison loses control, fighting against her captors to break free and reach the boy she loves. Tears stream down her pale face, and her hair wildly whips around her. "Take me instead. Please, kill me in his place," she screams.

Justice Fowler rises to his feet and reaches inside his robe. He reveals an antique revolver with a wooden handle and a spit-shined barrel. He walks to where Justin stands and says, "This is your opportunity for any final words."

The young man turns to his lover and gently says, "I don't regret it, Madison. I don't regret one single second I had with you. I know that to you it feels like it wasn't long enough, but it was perfect. When I believed beauty and love were forsaken in this world, you showed me just how alive and real they are. Know if heaven does exist, I'm begging the Almighty to allow my soul to stay with you. You are its home. So, think about me every day and know I'm doing the same. Live and fight, my sweet Maddie." Justin keeps his eyes trained on Madison as he's forced to his knees. "I love you, forever."

My hand reaches for my gun. I can't let them kill this boy; I must save him. Ryland pulls me into his chest as

Justice Fowler aims his gun at Justin's head. I half-heartedly try to pull away, knowing if I were successful, I'd be next to die and leave River alone. She would never forgive me, and I'd never forgive myself for abandoning her. Ryland wraps me in his arms, placing his palm to my ear and turning my face away from what's transpiring in the name of justice. He buries his face in my hair while my hands move from my gun to grip his belt loops. He holds on tight like he's willing a bubble to form and protect us from this inevitable travesty.

When the shot rings through the air, it's prolonged by the screeching cries of a woman whose beating heart has been ripped from her chest. It's the most haunting noise I've ever heard. The death of two people with a single bullet. I don't need to personally know Madison Lane to know her life just shattered into pieces. Every single day, she'll relive this moment and the pain accompanying it will cut just as deep as it does right now.

I feel a connection to her. It isn't just her life that has been altered— so has mine. For as long as I live, this will be a significant mile marker in my life. It will always be remembered as the day I knew, without an ounce of doubt, that the Affliction, which eats away at the minds of those craving human flesh, also diminishes the humanity of the healthy. This is the day that the tiny piece of me which still fights for all that is good in the world surrenders to the truth—goodness no longer exists beyond the walls of my home and the bunker buried beneath it. Those safely tucked away inside the house, hundreds of miles away, are my only motivation to carry on. They're the reason I'm going to finish this mission that brought me to this godforsaken place.

Chapter Twelve

I wish it were possible to scrub clean hideous memories the way one washes dirt from their hands. The lifeless body of Justin Reims, lying on the stone steps of the capitol building, in his own bright red blood, will fester inside of me until the day I'm dead. As Ryland, Wes, and I walk away, hidden in the dispersing crowd, I try my best not to look at his body one more time. But I fail. A morbid part of me takes a quick glance. I'll forever be haunted by this boy I never knew.

There's no attempt to stop us from leaving the capitol grounds. The guards must believe we've decided to ignore the justice's advice and are on our way to the Sanctuary.

I'd have the tiniest sense of peace if one other person was following our lead, but there's not. These people had an opportunity to save someone's life, and they stood silently by with no remorse as he was executed for falling in love. I'll never understand how any of them are complicit with living in a community like this.

An overwhelming sense of relief comes over me the moment we step off the property, and at the same time, emotional fatigue weighs me down. Trying to refocus on our objective is impossible. The rational part of my brain screams that I'm becoming a liability to my companions. If I don't get it together, and soon, I'll be the weak link that gets one of us killed.

We walk past a lamppost, and one of the bright orange flyers for the Sanctuary catches my eye. It's the piece of me that my aunt and uncle taught to question the establishment that has its curiosity piqued. I pull down the paper, fold it into a small square, and slide it into my back pocket. Is the Sanctuary purely a myth, or is there truth behind it? I'm not sure, but I won't be spoon fed my final verdict on the matter.

Once the capitol building is nothing but a tall tower in the distance, Ryland stops and slides into the shadows between two businesses. After quickly scanning the area, he turns to Wes and me. "The hospital is only two blocks away. The closer we get, the higher the probability of encountering something hostile. Take a minute to piss or stretch or whatever it is you both need to do. Going forward, we can't afford to be distracted."

No distractions? Ryland must be out of his mind. Peeing is going to do nothing for my inability to focus. Besides, if there were a shut-off switch to my emotions, I would've cut power to them a long time ago.

"Quinn." Ryland says.

"What?"

"Can you give us a second?" he asks Wes.

His friend's gaze jumps back and forth between us. "Yeah, I'll be over here keeping an eye on the street." Wes walks to the end of the alley, and with his back to us, leans one shoulder against a brick wall.

Ryland takes a step toward me, and instinctively, I take one back, colliding with a brick wall. With me trapped, he takes another step and closes the distance between us to mere inches. He drops his voice to a whisper and says, "Are you going to be all right to do this?"

I swallow a lump in my throat and lie. "Yes."

He places his hand on the wall next to my shoulder, his gaze burning into mine. "I know you're disturbed by what you saw, but for the sake of Wes and me, I need you to get past it for now."

"Okay, it's done," I say, trying to regain my much-needed personal space. Not many things on God's green earth muddle up my mind the way he does when he's close. My insides become a war zone of physical attraction versus common sense. Rational thinking must always win. I won't let myself fall victim to him.

He cocks an eyebrow. "You're sure?"

"Positive," I say in a firmer tone.

"Then you don't need me to kiss you to help you forget?"

"Are you... why would you—no!" I duck under his arm and rush past Wes, whose lips are pulled into a smirk.

Ryland catches up and strolls next to me on the sidewalk. He has me thoroughly flustered, and I wish he'd put a little space between us. There's a whole empty street with a sidewalk on the other side just for him. As my annoyance mounts, my temperature rises, and I'm compelled to address his poorly timed flirtation. "I can't believe you're even trying to cut jokes right now."

With his eyes on our surroundings and no attempt to hide his lopsided smile, he responds, "Who said I was joking?"

"God, you're obnoxious." I pick up my pace, and Wes

laughs from behind me as I take the lead.

The asshole, with his sexy accent, crooked grin, and offerings of a kiss is frustrating! I want to get this done with—kill what needs to be killed, find the steroids, and get home early tomorrow morning. Yet, he consumes more of my thoughts than any of that.

The clapping of running feet and grunting echoes through the quiet. A middle-aged man, with sickly gray skin, tattered clothing, and an open salivating mouth, charges across a parking lot. He's crazed with hunger and shows no signs of slowing down. I pull my gun from my pants, align my body with his, and open fire. My first shot grazes his jaw, dislodging it from his face. Dripping blood, it sways back and forth with each step he takes but does nothing to stop him. With a quick exhale, I pull the trigger again. This time his head rears back when the bullet meets his forehead, and he crumples to the ground.

"You're welcome," Ryland says as he walks up beside me.

"For what?"

"For infuriating you. You have a way of focusing all your anger on the task at hand."

I scoff. Of course, he had an ulterior motive when he offered to kiss me.

"For the record, I wouldn't have done it; not yet anyway," he says, raising an eyebrow and drawing his lips between his teeth to hide his smile.

I pull my gaze from his, grip my weapon tighter, and walk faster.

I'm on high alert again. It feels like Zs are lurking around corners, waiting for us to step closer. My peripheral vision plays tricks on me, and I swear the Afflicted are scurrying across the road in the distance and bounding from rooftops. The deafening sound of Wes's gun discharging behind me is a welcomed reminder that I'm not going insane.

He rotates around after shooting another Z. "Disgusting creatures," he mumbles, stepping over the dead body.

We reach the hospital's parking lot, and dread is like a sinking stone in my stomach. There is no telling what lurks inside the multilevel building. And whatever is inside will sense us way before we know they are there.

A metal door at the side of the hospital crashes open, and two Zs barrel out. Ryland quickly reacts and fires first, lodging a bullet into the head of the closest Z. At the same time, I step out from behind him and land a shot in the chest of the other. Both go tumbling to the ground. Keeping a safe distance, I look them over for any sign of what we're up against.

"What are you thinking, Mac?" Ryland asks.

Wes looks at the building, squinting his eyes. "It's a nest."

Ryland pinches the bridge of his nose. "That's what I thought, but I was hoping to be wrong."

I glance back and forth at them. "What's a nest?"

"Hospitals, prisons, or any place where there was once a ton of bodies. These locations have the potential of being a nest," Wes says, sweeping his arm in front of him. "Some of the Afflicted are hunters and seek their next meal, and others are driven by convenience. They'll remain where they are if the food source was once high, forming a nest."

I scrunch my nose and shake my head. "They build a little Z community, how cute. But what about nomadic Zs?"

"Hordes. I believe they consist of Zs who were

infected at the same time and ran out of fresh flesh. They stick together and hunt. You know they'll eat anything, even each other. It becomes survival of the fittest if there are no living beings around. Hordes provide them with a guaranteed food source. Someone is bound to catch something."

As gross as it all sounds, I'm impressed by Wes's knowledge. He's put a lot of thought into the habits of Zs. I'm sure it is partly what got him and his friends this far, knowing your enemy and all of that.

"There's absolutely no splitting up once inside. We stay within each other's line of sight at all times." Rylan looks directly at me. "No heroics."

"No worries, I left my cape in the truck."

His eyes light up for a brief second and his lips pucker as he fights a smile. "It's never stopped you before."

I can't help but give him a small smile of my own as I say, "Point taken."

"It's going to be foul inside," Wes says, pulling three handkerchiefs from his backpack and handing them to us. He wraps his around the lower half of his face, and Ryland and I follow suit.

Prepared for the stench, Ryland motions us to follow him. He holds a gun in one hand and a flashlight in the other, and when we reach the door, Wes eases it open. Ryland leans in, checking that it's clear before we enter the Z nest.

The corridor would be dark if it weren't for the two men multitasking. They hold a gun in one hand and a flashlight in the other. Unfortunately, I'm not feeling as skilled at the moment and need both hands steady on my weapon.

The hallway is thickly layered in dust and reminds me of the aftermath of an explosion. Tiny particles irritate my eyes as they float through the air, distorting my vision with tears. I'll never admit it out loud, but I'm a bit over my head right now. The unfamiliar layout of the hospital and its unkempt state has me at a disadvantage.

Reaching the doors at the end of the hallway, Ryland looks back at Wes and me. "Try to call it before you shoot it. We don't want to waste bullets or time by aiming for the same target. Also, we need to find a sign for the pharmacy, so keep your eyes open."

We slide into the corridor, and instantly, my palms sweat inside my gloves. In the distance, growls and moans have my heart racing like it is vying for a gold medal in a 40-yard dash. Wes was right—the muggy air is disgusting. Even through my scarf, I can smell the rot. Every type of decay festers around us—human waste, molding food, and decomposing bodies. It's the most repulsive thing I've ever encountered. I try to contain my disgust, but finally give in and dry heave.

"Hold it in, Ellery," Wes says from behind me. "If you start puking, it will cause a chain reaction."

I roll my eyes at the use of my last name; it's so militant. So not me.

In hopes of taking my mind off the stench, I respond, "You remember the most random things. I don't even remember your last name."

"I have semantic memory. I can remember a bunch of useless information. And it's MacVey, but Mac will work too."

Metal crashes to the floor, bringing our conversation to a stop. The noise ricochets through the empty walkway, followed by a raspy snarl. The Zs must sense our presence, but don't stampede to get to us. I hate when they're assholes who want to play with their food.

They've got me beat on speed and immunity to pain; I don't need them outwitting me as well.

"Fuck," Ryland hisses. His light shines on a revolting face, bolting down the corridor. "I got him. Mac, to the left," he instructs before firing.

Wes steps around me and releases two rapid shots into another Z running out of a room. I hardly have time to watch both creatures fall to the floor when my arm is yanked, pulling me back a step. I spin around to find the half-eaten face of a Z snapping its teeth at me. Its ear is severed from its head, and a strip of skin peeled away from its neck. I recover from the shock of its gruesome condition when we're almost nose to nose. I jam the barrel of my gun under its chin and pull the trigger. Its head explodes, sending brain matter and dark purple blood raining down on me. With my booted foot, I kick it, propelling its limp body into a wall before using the end of my scarf to wipe its guts from around my eyes.

Ryland stands several steps away, with his gaze boring straight into me. The bandana covering his lower face does little to hide the ticking of his jaw. I shift my weight and rest my hand on my hip, waiting for him to explode, but he turns to Wes. "I'm not saying this again, stay behind her." To me, he demands, "Get your flashlight out, Quinn."

"I handled it," I snap.

He closes his eyes and fills his chest with air. With a forced calm, he says, "Just get out your damn flashlight so you can see what's chasing after you."

Being the subject of Ryland's irritation is not something I'd wish upon anyone. It makes me want to lash out, and at the same time, it tears me up. It's fueled by his desire to protect. I understand that need and the guilt that drives it.

Without any further argument, I reach into the side pocket of my backpack and pull out my mini flashlight. I press the power and illuminate the wall across the hall. Like a much-needed ray of sunshine on a dreary day appears the sign meant to guide hospital visitors to their destinations.

"The pharmacy is this way," I say, walking in the direction of the arrow.

The further back we walk, the more intense the darkness. The odor is almost debilitating, and the occupants of the hospital sound crazed and restless. My heart bangs in my chest and my blood rushes to my head in dizzying pulses. This is feeling more and more like a death wish.

"Of course," Ryland yells and punches the wall.

I spin around to find a yellow sign taped to a locked door. *Due to renovations, the pharmacy is temporarily located on the second floor.*

"Looks like we're taking the stairs, boys," I say, pointing to the door leading to the stairwell.

Ryland shakes his head while I hold open the door for him. "I'm not fond of restricted spaces."

"Oh, really? I suppose we should just head on home then," I say, my voice dripping with sarcasm.

He grunts before walking inside.

The stairwell door slams closed, and we sweep our lights over the winding steps. The compact space gives us no room to maneuver. It's as if we are walking a tightrope with precise steps, and at the same time, there's an urgency to get to the other side. It's a deadly combination.

Halfway to the first landing, gunfire erupts in front of me. Without warning, Ryland's shoulder jerks back from the kick of his firearm. I grip the railing to keep from falling on Wes, and he places his hand on my lower back, helping me to stay on my feet.

I'm partially deafened by the ringing in my ears, but I still register Ryland yelling, "I could use some help, Quinn."

I drop to my knees and brace myself at his side. On the top landing stand several ex-humans who used to be doctors, caregivers, and patients. Many of the grotesque flesh-eaters have fed on each other; their exposed bones and shredded tendons hanging from their faces and limbs. Bloody hands reach out, and mouths salivate at the smell of our skin. Their numbers seem endless as they file in from the floors above. Not bothering with any order, they shove each other out of the way, trying to get to us.

Before I can release my first shot, the door we entered from swings open. We're trapped between the predators as they pour in from the top and ground floors. I'm torn, not knowing where to shoot first.

Like he's reading my thoughts, Wes yells, "Clear the landing."

Not needing to be told twice, I shoot alongside Ryland. During the seconds I was distracted, the Zs coming down made some headway. They trip over the bodies of their dead comrades, racing at us. Ryland aims for the back of the group, and I take the closer ones. High-pitched wails and low growls are amplified, reverberating off the concrete walls. The blasts and infinite screeching mingle together. The result is a maddening sound.

I glance back at Wes. With swift kicks, he throws our attackers back. They stumble over each other as he showers them with bullets. The Zs climb over the dead and press forward. "Start moving up, Shaw. I've got an idea," he orders.

While keeping his gun trained on those descending

the stairs, Ryland grabs a dead body by its hospital gown and throws it behind us. Wes moves over the corpse and kicks it the rest of the way down, piling his victims on the floor below. Following Ryland's lead, I pull on deformed legs covered in sticky, dark blood. I shove them out of our way and take the next step, making some headway. The attack from above tapers off, and my gun clicks empty. I cram it into my pocket and unsheathe my knife.

"Keep your aim high," I instruct Ryland, taking a couple of steps ahead of him.

Hand to hand combat is not my favorite method of slaughtering Zs. If I can reach them, they can reach me, but I have no choice. I dive for the nearest body, and it too moves to attack, grabbing my hair and pulling my head to its mouth. I use one hand to gouge my fingers in its unseeing eyes. When I have a slight advantage, I plunge my knife into its gut and yank up. I say a silent prayer that I'm strong enough to make it through its ribs and pierce its lungs. It hisses, throwing my head into the wall. My skull meets the brick with a crack. Running on pure adrenaline and anger, I disregard the pain and pull my knife from its body. Once free, I bury my blade to the hilt in its slim torso over and over again.

A hand reaches out and grips my upper arm, pulling me up. I spin to take out my next opponent, but Ryland stops me by holding my wrist.

Not the least bit fazed, he orders, "Run."

Together we rush up the stairs, stomping on the dead. Wes fires his gun a few steps below and hurries to follow us. There's a break in the horde raining down from the upper levels, but I'm not so naive to think we're out of danger. We've won a small battle in a war that has just begun.

As a unit, we climb the final set of stairs, heading for the wide-open door of the second level. I peer back at Wes. He pauses on the landing, surrounded by mutilated corpses. In his hand is something small, and he tosses it at the oncoming Zs.

"Go, go, go," he yells, bounding up the steps two at a time.

An earth-shattering explosion rattles the stairwell, followed by a scorching heat. Wes plows into my back, pushing Ryland and me into the second-floor hallway. We end up in a tangled pile of arms and legs on the linoleum tile. Wes scurries to kick the door shut as Ryland snatches the fire extinguisher from the emergency case on the wall. He wedges it in the door handle, locking the Zs inside. The men collapse to the floor beside me, and we all release a deep exhale.

I pull my scarf from my face—no longer caring if the hospital smells like rotting bodies soaking in a sewer—and use it to wipe away the sweat and blood from my forehead and cheeks. "Wes, tell me you didn't throw a grenade with all of us in there?" I ask through labored breaths.

"Yeah, I did." He smiles up at the ceiling.

I roll over to get Ryland's reaction. He's on his back, looking down the hall with his gun pointed at a Z running toward us. With little to no effort, he pulls the trigger, and the creature falls into a heap. Ryland rests his head on the ground, turns to me, and slides the bandana from his face. "Did I ever tell you that I absolutely hate confined spaces?"

I smirk and say, "I think you might have mentioned it."

Wes stands and shakes out his arms. "Let's get this over with before our sickly friend ends up dying."

I sit and bring my backpack around my body, taking out the extra clip from inside. With shaking hands, I reload my gun before refilling the used clip. I can't fight with a knife again; it's way too much work, and I'm on the verge of having a heart attack as is. I plan to keep my distance from Zs for the remainder of this run. The best way to do that is to riddle them with bullets.

Chapter Thirteen

"You're going to have to shoot the lock," Wes says to Ryland as we stand in a semi-circle around the door leading behind the pharmacy counter.

"It's going to attract attention as soon as I pull the trigger," Ryland says.

Both men are splattered with Z blood and a total mess. Ryland tore a hole in the knee of his jeans, and Wes has a dark purple bruise forming under his eye. I'm not any better off, my head aches from being slammed against the wall by the Z and then the floor when we dove through the stairwell door. It's surprising any of us are alert after the battle we fought.

"At least it's locked, so that has to be a good sign, right? I mean, if we can't just walk in, then neither can anyone else," I say.

Ryland keeps his focus on the door and shakes his head. "I'm not assuming anything."

I take a deep breath and turn to the pharmacy waiting room. It's in shambles with chairs turned over, magazines littering the floor, and blood smeared on everything. I can't help but think of all the people who were here waiting for their medication when brutally attacked. A single Z can overpower a handful of unarmed people, let alone those who are sick. This one room would have been a slaughterhouse.

"Just fucking shoot it, Shaw. I'll stay here and keep watch while you and Quinn grab what we need," Wes urges.

"I don't like that option either. We stick together, remember?"

Wes runs his hand over his face. "Well, something has to give if we want to get this done and make it back to Aiden."

"He's got a point, Ryland," I chime in.

In the short time that I've known him, one thing has become very evident—Ryland is the ultimate soldier who's not only fighting to win, but fighting for the well-being of those most important to him. The idea of leaving someone behind unsettles him, and he wants a workaround. It's all or nothing with him.

With a sigh, Ryland says, "Stay by the door and call if you need help."

"Of course." Wes assures him with a faint smile.

We take a step back, putting some distance between us and the door handle. In quick succession, Ryland lets loose two shots, and the lock falls to the floor. Using his booted foot to finish the job, he kicks the door open.

I sweep my flashlight over the contents inside, and my tense shoulders relax at the sight of the unscathed room and an array of medications. Ryland and I move forward, and without a word, we split up and hastily rummage through the shelves. We're not only searching for the steroids to save Aiden's life, but anything we deem useful. I remove my bag from my back, secure it to the front of my body, and fill it with medications.

My life no longer consists of simple tasks. Everything I do requires me to think outside of the box. There's a series of questions I always ask myself on a supply run. *Do I need this? Will I need this? Is this something I'll regret leaving behind come tomorrow?* I may never get another chance to raid an untouched pharmacy. Everything in here is something I want to take home.

"We've got visitors," Wes yells from the doorway and fires a shot.

I rush through the shelves. My body shakes and perspiration trails down the back of my neck. My movements become sloppy as I read the labels, frantically looking for any jargon indicating the contents of the bottles. Every time Wes shoots his gun, the blast stunts me. It is almost deafening as it echoes through the waiting room. My ears ring, wreaking havoc on me. It takes a second for me to gather my bearings, rendering me useless and wasting precious time.

In the next aisle, Ryland curses to himself. There's no doubt that the separation from his friend is making him anxious. If Wes isn't with him, then Ryland has relinquished the control he wants the most—the ability to protect.

I peer between the shelves to the front door. With his hands full, Wes no longer communicates with us. I count each shot, knowing he only has fifteen until he'll need to reload. Eight. I rummage through the next shelving unit. Nine. Tossing bottles of painkillers in my backpack. Ten. I check on Wes again to find two more Zs entering the waiting room. Eleven and twelve. I meet Ryland's panicked gaze. Thirteen. I zip my backpack and put it on. Fourteen.

Fuck it!

"Keep searching," I say, sprinting for the door and removing my gun from my pocket.

"Quinnten," Ryland yells.

Fifteen. Wes's gun renders useless as I enter the waiting room, geared up for a fight. He's on the ground with a large Z on top of him. The two desperately struggle for something they desire more than anything else—Wes for his life and the Z for flesh. Drool oozes down Wes's hand as he holds his attackers face away from his body. The Z scrambles to find the perfect angle to sink his sharp teeth in and rip the flesh from his bones. They're all over the place, and I can't get a clear shot without putting Wes in more danger. Before I can come up with a plan, a new batch of the Afflicted storm into the room. I take down the first two, but it's the third who has me tripped up.

At one time, he was a boy, no older than ten. His hair is missing, and bodily fluids stain his superhero pajamas. Not only was he a child when he was infected, but most likely a cancer patient. My heart shatters. Fate played a cruel joke on this kid, dealing him a horrendous hand.

My sympathy for the boy doesn't last long; he's a vicious little beast. The child Z leaps for me with his mouth wide open, and my pity for the life lost morphs into pure survival instincts. I take the butt of my gun, pistol-whipping him on the side of the head. The force of the blow throws him off for a second, but he rapidly recovers, charging at me again. Trying to avoid Wes, I align my gun with the Z's head and take a step back. One of the many overturned chairs catches my foot, and I tumble to the ground, landing on my back. I keep a firm grip on my weapon, but the flashlight dislodges from my hand, casting everything into shadows.

The boy springs over the chair between us, and the limited glow of the light catches the raging hunger in his white eyes. I extend my foot, forcing him to keep his distance while holding my firearm with both hands in front of me. His small body clears my outstretched leg, and he plummets toward me. I pull the trigger, a bullet ripping through his tiny head. Blood sprinkles down as his limp body falls on top of me.

I stifle the overwhelming need to cry. The young boy has nobody to mourn his death. It's cruel and unfair. Although I didn't take his life and set him free from an unnatural existence, it still brings me anguish to know it had to be done. I forgo my usual harshness for a dead Z. Instead of shoving him off me, I gently roll him to the side. This will have to suffice as paying my respects to his sad, short life.

I rush to help Wes who is quickly losing ground to his rival. The big Z presses in on him, its teeth an inch from his cheek. Wes tightly shuts his eyes, his face contorting like he's waiting for the second that his skin is ripped from his skull. Using my heavy boots, I kick the Z in the head every time it lowers to take a bite. When I've become an absolute nuisance, it bites down on the tip of my steel-toed-boot. I scream, trying to pull away. It shakes its head like a rabid dog, knocking me off my feet. I land with a thud vibrating up my spine. I don't let the shooting pain slow me down. I'm not sure if its teeth can chomp through metal, but if it does, it will reach one of my toes and break the skin. As soon as the saliva pooled around its mouth reaches my bloodstream, I'm a goner. I pray the steel is a strong enough barrier to withstand its sharp teeth.

The hulking Z traps Wes and me. Half of its body is on top of Wes, whose arms flail as he tries to get loose. I'm jostled around while it whips its head side to side. I can't line up a straight shot, so I give up on my gun, leaning back on my hands and kick. The sole of my shoe lands directly in the middle of its face. It's enough to break its grip on me. The Z screeches and turns back to Wes. I don't give the monster time to position itself for the kill, jumping onto its back and grabbing a fistful of its hair. The black strands are greasy, difficult to hold, and smell like the embodiment of death.

The Z thrashes with an unending supply of energy, but I'm determined to win. I press my gun to the Z's temple, waiting for the perfect moment. It pivots and snaps aimlessly at my arm as I squeeze the trigger. The Z topples over, pinning me to the ground underneath its dead weight. The air in my lungs drains out, and the pressure on top of me stops me from inhaling. It figures I kill the damn thing only for its corpse to suffocate me. I squirm around, trying to find a way out. My lungs burn, and my face heats from the lack of oxygen.

Muffled gunshots ring out, and the chaos dies thrusting everything into silence.

"Are you all right, Mac?"

"I'll be okay, but I need help getting this fucker off Quinn."

They roll the Z from me, and I gasp for air only to regret it right away. I brace my hands on the floor and dry heave. The adrenaline from the fight and shock from everything I endured is too much for my body to handle.

"Hurry and get it all out. We're not done yet," Wes says, resting his hand on my shoulder.

Fingers wrap around my arm, pulling me to my feet. "No time. Up you go."

It's not surprising that Ryland is entirely driven by the mission. Things like sympathy for almost being crushed to death are clearly beyond him.

My head spins, and I slump, gripping my knees to keep upright.

"Quinn, we don't have time for this. I'm going to need you to run," Ryland says.

I take two deep breaths and say, "Tell me you found it."

He knows right away what I'm asking. "I found it."

I couldn't do this again if we had to, at least not anytime soon. All I have left in me will be enough to escape this hell-hole alive.

"Let's get out of here," I say with a lazy smile.

It's what we all need to hear. We can return to the barn and wait out the night. It may not be as safe as the bunker, but at least it's a warm, safe place where we can rest our aching bodies. Of course, we first need to find our way out of this nest.

We exit the pharmacy and jog the opposite way we came, running through double doors and wide corridors, searching for anything that hints to a way out. The darkness makes it hard to see any distinguishing marks. It isn't long before we arrive at the pharmacy again and realize we ran in one gigantic circle.

"I think we need a plan B," Wes says, gasping for air.

"There were elevators located next to the stairs we came up," I suggest.

Ryland shakes his head. "That would be amazing if there were electricity."

"That's not what I mean. We can climb the elevator shaft."

He blows out a puff of air. "Confined spaces."

I toss up my hands. "You're going to have to suck it up, cupcake."

"I agree," Wes adds.

Ryland shoots his friend a warning glare and turns back to me. "Let's just get this over with."

There should be another stairwell located on this floor, but we don't have time. Our goal is to make it back to the barn before nightfall. For all we know, the sun set hours ago. When in a bind, it's best to use what you know, and in this case, we're sure there's an elevator shaft. The question is—where did the elevator car stop when the power went out? If it's between the first and second floors, we're screwed.

When we reach the elevator, the doors are closed. Wes and Ryland set to work using nothing but their hands to pry them apart. I stand watch, scanning in all directions for any unwanted followers. My nerves are worn thin, and I'm irritated listening to the two go on about how to open the doors. I clench my jaw and hold in the need to scream. Rubbing my fingers over my eyes, I try to ward off my headache and fatigue.

I drop my hands and shine my flashlight down the hall. It doesn't reach far, leaving most of the hallway in shadows and me squinting into the darkness. I blink once. Then twice. But the bodies at the end of the hall don't fade away. They're lined shoulder to shoulder with their hungry stares glued on us.

"Figure it the hell out boys because shit is about to get ugly really quick," I say, without taking my eyes off the Zs.

"Oh, fuck," Wes drawls.

"What are you waiting for, Quinn?" Ryland asks, scooting in beside me.

I take a moment to survey our surroundings. We could run left or right, but honestly, what's the use? They'll follow us and possibly attract more Zs. Standing here and shooting is not going to work either, we need an escape route, and fast.

The red cabinet mounted on the wall catches my attention.

"Wes, get the ax out of the emergency cabinet and pry those damn doors open," I command before firing my gun.

Wes runs to the wall and kicks in the glass while Ryland opens fire next to me. The Zs keep the steady pace, closing in on us, stepping over the dead as they fall to the ground. Shattering glass resounds throughout the corridor, and Wes yanks out the ax, swinging it at the stainless-steel elevator doors. The pounding of metal-on-metal mixes with the blasts of the guns, setting the approach of the Afflicted to a hectic beat. Ryland and I continue to decrease their numbers, but it's not enough.

"How's it coming, Mac?" Ryland's voice rises over the loud pop of my gun.

"Almost there," he responds with a grunt.

The ax skids across the floor in front of us and the leisurely pace of the Zs speeds up to a brisk walk. Ryland doesn't wait for confirmation. If Wes let go of the ax, it's because he has accomplished what he set out to do.

"Go, Quinn," Ryland demands.

I quickly turn to see Wes lower himself down the elevator shaft and hold his hand out to me. I hesitate. The Zs are halfway to us, and I can't leave Ryland to fight by himself.

He briefly meets my eyes. "I'm right behind you. Now, go!"

I back up and shoot one more Z before Wes's hand wraps around my ankle. He guides me to the first rung of a ladder along the front wall of the shaft. I divide my attention between the Afflicted and trying to descend to the next floor.

Hoping to clear the way for Ryland, I yell at Wes, "Move, move, move!" I hurry to get down, and before I can't see him anymore, I call to Ryland, "Come on."

I continue into the musty space, periodically glancing up. Each step I take causes a gut-wrenching fear inside of me. Ryland should be coming down by now. What if the Zs broke into a sprint once I couldn't see them? The Afflicted had already lost two perfectly good bodies, what if they were set on not letting the last one get away? My chest tightens, and I'm poised to dart back up when a body free-falls down the shaft. Its arms and legs flail and an unnatural screech echoes around us. The Z lands on the top of the elevator with a thud. I jump at the sound of a gun discharging and find Wes below me, releasing a fatal shot. I don't hear any gunfire from above, only the grunts of the Afflicted. Unadulterated dread takes over. I won't leave Ryland. Even if they have him, I won't let him suffer while they rip him to pieces. I'll do the most merciful thing I can—kill him myself. Tears sting my eyes as I grip the rung above my head and pull my body up. I shouldn't have abandoned him. We could have figured it out together, and both of us could have escaped. But I left him to fend for himself. How stupid! I set my resolve, dry my eyes with the back of my sleeve, and begin to rush upward.

"Wrong way, love."

My head whips back as the black soles of Ryland's boots move above me.

"Watch out," he calls down before letting go of the ax. It crashes onto the roof of the elevator next to Wes and the dead Z.

A frustrated scream calls to us, and Ryland stretches his arm and shoots the Z who appears in the opening above. It falls forward, landing next to its friend on the elevator.

Wes gets to work shoving the bodies to the side and splitting the metal roof of the elevator car open with the ax. It doesn't take him long to create a space big enough for us to slide through. The doors below are open, giving access to the first floor and freedom. Wes lowers himself inside and waits for me. With little grace, I wiggle past the jagged metal until his hands wrap around my waist, guiding me safely to the ground. I can't risk letting Ryland out of my sight again, so I stay put until he jumps down.

The minutes flash by in a blur. The three of us tune into our surroundings, making sure that nothing holds the element of surprise. We come head-to-head with a Z or two, but they don't stand a chance against our desperate need to get out of the hospital. We rush to the exit, bolt out the side door, and sprint away from the building.

I've never been so grateful for the setting sun painting the sky in pink, orange, and blue. Cold fresh air stings my face and fills my lungs, reminding me that I survived again. I want to drop to my knees and worship the concrete jungle around me. I swear I've been a prisoner in the depths of hell for decades and battled grotesque demons in a war for my flesh for a lifetime. Against all the odds, I prevailed with my friends and won another day on earth.

With the hospital well behind us, my body drains of adrenaline. The damage done to it in the last few hours is impossible to ignore. My arms and legs are heavy, and every movement I make feels overly complicated. Each breath is restricted by the buildup of thick mucus in my throat, and my head throbs from the multiple collisions it had with rock-hard walls and floors. But none of it is as painful as the burning in my foot. I fall behind the guys, my jogging hindered by my need to limp. Glancing at my shoe, I find the yellow fragment of a Z tooth embedded in the tip.

"Shit," I mutter, falling to the ground and frantically unlace my boot.

I toss my combat boot to the side and stare in horror at the blood staining my pink polka dot sock. The pulse in my neck pounds like a drum as my worst fear comes to fruition. The massive Z from the pharmacy gnawed through leather, steel, and cotton to reach my big toe. I don't bother with a brave face and holding back my emotions. I let the tears slide down my face and surrender to my fate.

Ryland stands over me, his eyes wide. "Quinn?"

They can't take me home. I might not be out of my mind yet, but come tomorrow, I'll start eating my own flesh. In the next two weeks, I'll lose my ability to verbally communicate, my sight will vanish, and I'll become immune to physical pain. By the end, I'll have a never-ending craving. There are no other options. This must end now, or in the middle of the night, I'll unknowingly attack the people I care about. I'd rather go on my own terms and still be me.

My voice is hoarse as I say, "Please take River with you when you leave. I know you guys will keep her safe. Tell her I love her, and I hope that in time she can forgive me."

Ryland shakes his head, his entire body rigid as he stares at me. He always possesses an awareness, like he is planning every step he takes, holding so tightly to the reins of what he can control. But now, it has slipped through his fingers, and the way his eyes dart around like he is searching for answers tells me he's at a loss.

I reach into the pocket of my jacket and hold out my

gun. "I don't think I can do it myself," I say, urging him to take it.

He swallows and looks blankly at my weapon. "I can't."

Tears and snot run down my face, but I don't bother to wipe them away. Unleashing my emotions doesn't make me weak. My strength is found in my willingness to accept my fate and forfeit my life for the safety of others. This is a dignified way to die.

"Please, Ryland. It's a mercy killing," I plead.

He clenches his jaw, and his eyes become glassy. "Please don't ask me to do this. I can't, Quinn."

As difficult as it is for me to accept, I understand why he says no. Although I was determined to crawl up the elevator shaft and do this very thing for him, I'm not sure I would've gone through with it. I may have just as soon chosen to go down with him rather than snuff out the light in his bright green eyes.

I won't risk the lives of those I care about for the selfish purpose of living one more day. The danger I swore to protect them from is now me. And I know what must be done.

I aim my weapon at my temple. Self-preservation screams at me and activates a rational fear. Will I die instantly, or will the kick of the gun throw off my aim, causing a long, drawn-out death? If my mark holds true, will it hurt, and for how long? I'm terrified of the suffering I might endure, but I can't let it rule me. It must be done.

Needing to control my fear, I turn my attention solely to Ryland. His handsome face with its minor imperfections is a flawless distraction. I wish he would smile so I could admire the deep dimples on his cheeks and the way it washes away the toughness of his demeanor. I'm saddened that I didn't get to witness the playful side of him more. He's more than handsome, he's beautiful, even in his state of disarray. The tips of my fingers tingle with the desire to touch him one more time and prove he's real. If things were different, I could have eventually fallen in love with him.

But things are what they are, and there's nothing I can do to change it.

I pull as much cold air as I can into my lungs and hold it. The gun at my head is heavy and my hand shakes under its weight. This is the right thing to do, I tell myself as my trigger finger tenses and prepares to discharge a bullet into my brain.

"Quinn, stop!" Wes yells. "It didn't break through. You're bleeding from the metal digging into your foot."

He steps into my view, holding the broken tooth in his gloved hand and my boot in the other. Ryland snatches my shoe from him and looks it over before tossing it to me. I lower my gun and examine the exposed steel at the toe. I blink a couple of times, making sure I see it correctly. The steel at the toe is bent but not broken. The indentation must have dug into my toe as I was running. I'm so thankful that I want to jump up and hug them, but I'm brought to a halt.

Next to me, Wes bends over with his hands on his thighs, catching his breath. His black hair sticks up on its ends around his head, and there is a greenish tone to his skin. Blood is smudged on his bruised face, and his jacket is shredded in several places. He looks terrible, and I've added to his stress.

Across from me, Ryland is in constant motion, with his eyes closed and both hands clench his hair. He's entirely drenched in the purple blood of Zs. He didn't look so filthy in the pharmacy and the only time I lost sight of him was when I descended the elevator shaft. There were no gunshots before he lowered himself, he must have used the ax. The carnage of hacked off body parts he left behind must have been substantial. As crazy as it sounds, I kind of envy him for having the opportunity to do it. I bet it was therapeutic to violently take out his aggression on the Afflicted. And yet, my blunder may have undone all of that.

I sigh as I watch the two. I've tried to keep space between us, but it's been impossible. The last thing I wanted was for the four men to wiggle their way into my life and hold some importance to me. Yet here I am risking my life for the spirited boy who lies dying in my bed. I've trusted Noah to take care of the person I love most, and when I saw Wes struggling with the Z, all I wanted to do was get to him and save him. I was totally set on not risking my life for anyone but River, and I crossed that boundary for him today.

And Ryland... For a moment, I believed he'd been taken by the Zs. My fear ignited an immense pain in the depths of my soul, which is crazy. He's a walking contradiction—an enigma I'm tirelessly trying to figure out. I can draw a definitive line with the other three men, but the same can't be said for him. There's so much to learn about Ryland Shaw and to think my chance may have been lost is unbearable.

Chapter Fourteen

My eyes spring open, and my heart races. Memories of the capitol building have plagued me all night. Every time I drift off, I see Justin lying on the ground, soaked in his blood while the girl he loves is pulled away in hysterics.

I've dozed off a handful of times only to be startled awake by the lucid dreams. No matter how comfortable I am, I can't find the much-needed respite from my overactive imagination. It's astonishing that my mind is even able to recall the day's events. I was beyond exhausted when we entered the barn well past dusk. I took one look at the ladder leading into the hayloft and wanted to cry. It was like looking up at the world's highest peak from the mountain's base. With my last ounce of energy, I climbed into the rafters where Wes and I scattered bundles of hay on the floor, making the surface softer to sleep on.

I turn to my side and discover I'm not the only one having trouble sleeping. Ryland sits at the edge of the loft with his back against the wall. One arm resting on his bent knees as his other hand fiddles with the pendant on his necklace.

He's a presence I don't think I'll ever become accustomed to. I'm used to making hard calls and taking significant risks, but he has changed that. He's demanded that I allow him to take some of my burdens, and the only reason I'm apprehensive to do it is because I can't rely on his help forever. If this mission is successful, Aiden will recover from his sickness, and the guys will move on. I can't overlook that reality and pretend this will last. He's also unbelievably attractive, which is unnerving. Too often, I find myself staring at him, memorizing every detail of his face. Even the filth from the day's battle doesn't take away from his captivating features—his strong jaw contrasting his perfectly shaped soft lips, or how the seriousness in his eyes vanishes when he smiles with a boyish charm. I might not get used to having him around, but after today, I want to take advantage of our time together and get to know more about him.

I crawl out of the bed of hay and brush off the straw clinging to my clothes. Ryland doesn't say a word as he watches me walk to him. I keep my distance, choosing to sit at the edge of the loft with my feet hanging over the side. I rest my arms on the bottom board of the railing and fidget with the mood ring on my finger.

"You should get some sleep. You have to drive in the morning and need to be alert," Ryland says in a hushed voice.

I rest my head on my arms. "I know, but I can't."

"Do you want to talk about it?"

There's nothing I can say to ease my mind. The things that happened at the capitol will most likely happen again. Those people were brainwashed into believing justice was served and nothing will change that. The only thing I can control in my life is me, and right now, anything is better than tossing, turning, and replaying the death of an innocent man. I don't want to talk about it, so I choose a random topic instead.

"What's your middle name?"

Ryland laughs. "You're losing sleep because you want to know my middle name?"

I roll my eyes and smile. "Don't flatter yourself. I'm desperate for a distraction, and this seems like a good start."

"If I answer, you have to as well." He leans forward, resting both arms on his knees.

"That's fair. My middle name is Hope."

"Kingston, my middle name is Kingston."

"Favorite color?"

He smirks and tugs on the front of his jacket. "Black, it hides the blood. You?"

"I like your answer, so I'm going with it."

He cocks an eyebrow. "You're a cheater."

I rush to defend myself and give another answer, but he moves on to the next question. "All right, since the Affliction, what do you miss the most? And you can't say your family, it's a given."

"That's easy, ice cream. And you?"

"Giran in the autumn. The leaves are the brightest red and yellow, and there is a hint of logs burning in the air."

I smile at his answer. It sounds like a romantic book or the name of a folk band. Besides layovers at the international airport in Giran, I've never been to the continent, I suddenly feel like I've missed out on what should be a mandatory life experience.

His long fingers move back to his necklace, twirling

the crescent moon pendant. Since meeting him, I've been fascinated by the symbol for Bogati hanging around his neck. I've spent many summers there with Josh, Amara, and River on humanitarian trips. It is the most underdeveloped of the four continents. While the rest of the world was on the verge of eradicating hunger and homelessness, Bogati still struggled to get their footing. Since the continent is Amara's childhood home, she made it a priority that we do what we could to help. It always held a special place within our family.

My curiosity gets the better of me. "If you are from Giran, why do you wear the symbol for Bogati?"

Ryland looks at his hand and flattens his palm, laying the symbol in the center, studying its metal shape. His silence lingers, and I become afraid that I've crossed a line, and our conversation is coming to an abrupt end, but thankfully, I'm wrong.

"If I tell you, then you must be prepared to share something deeply intimate with me."

My brow furrows. "It's only fair you tell me what you're going to ask since you know my question."

"I want to know about your mom and dad."

I look away and run my hand over my face. My biological parents are a private story that not only I but my family guard with care. I have my reservations, but I also want to hear what Ryland has to say. "I'll agree, but if you tell me your parents are from Bogati, I'm reneging. You know you're prying into something deep with me."

"That's fair."

For days, I've wanted some new insight into what makes him tick, and here's my chance.

"Do you remember Wes mentioning our friend Dylan?" Ryland asks.

I nod, recalling the exchange in the study about

linking the cell phone to the tower. It didn't take a genius to figure out Wes slipped when mentioning Dylan. Everyone hurried to move on from the topic.

"The crescent is his."

"Where is Dylan?" I quietly ask.

Ryland turns away and studies the barn below. Again, his hand moves to the pendant, rubbing it between his fingers, and his Adam's apple bobs up and down as he swallows. "The five of us had this brilliant plan. Each summer while we were at university, we would go on a vacation, just us guys. The goal was for each of us to visit places we always wanted to see. Aiden was the first to choose, so we spent six weeks in Oscuros. The next summer was Dylan, and he chose the islands off Bogati." Ryland chuckles. "We spent the entire summer fucked up. If we weren't high, we were drunk, and Dylan loved every minute of it. We sat on the beach, looking out at the vibrant blue water and passing around a joint. I've never been so relaxed in my entire life." He gives me a humorless smile. "It's hard for you to believe I could let go and enjoy myself, isn't it?"

The mourning in his eyes isn't just for the past but for a piece of him that is lost. It was free and careless—the very things that made him a young man in the prime of his life. I bet he didn't even know how important that side of him was until it was gone.

With my head resting on my arms, I smile. "Sometimes, you let your overbearing guard down, and I see little glimpses of it. So, no, it's not hard to believe. I actually like those moments with you."

His eyes meet mine, and the intensity of his gaze softens. He's not a hopeless case, just a broken soul in need of some mending like the rest of us.

"The trip to the Western Canyon of Stern was my holiday." He rolls his eyes as he speaks. "I had this notion that we should have a rugged experience, with hiking, camping, and canoeing. Dylan dreaded the entire thing. He was pissed we weren't going to party in the big cities on the western or eastern coastline. He was a bit repulsed by the idea of bathing in a river and cooking over a fire. But a pact is a pact, so he went."

A lump forms in my throat as understanding consumes me. There were initially five of them. I consider stopping him from going on, but there's this part of me wanting him to confirm my suspicions with details, so I wait for him to continue when he's ready.

"You know we missed the evacuation, but we still tried. We went to the Western Region capital in hopes of the authorities making an exception for us. We had spoken to our families and knew they were working to get the Giran government involved with our rescue, but they were met with countless roadblocks. Besides leaving our phones behind, the western capital was one of the worst decisions we made. Finding safe shelter became impossible over time. People weren't keen to help five young men. We were seen as a liability rather than a charity case. Eventually, we found an old, rundown house with boarded-up windows. It was disgusting, and I wouldn't wish it on my worst enemy. Sewage had backed into it and roaches and rats would scurry across the ground as we tried to sleep. Making matters worse, we were sloppy in the beginning, too trusting, inexperienced with self-defense, and too impulsive. The Afflicted were running rampant in the capital, and we were no match for them." He stops talking and blows out a massive breath of air.

My heart breaks for him, and he hasn't even told me how he lost one of his best friends. "Ry, you don't have to go on."

He bites his lips and continues. "The blackout changed everything. People were already panicked, but the loss of electricity unleashed chaos. We were struggling to find food and were surviving on candy bars split five ways or rationing out small bags of chips. It was late at night, and we were starving, so we ventured out, looking for something to eat. We were armed with one gun, a bunch of makeshift weapons, and a single, dying flashlight. We found a massive empty house with packed cupboards. The zombies came out of nowhere, and we didn't have a chance. We ran, but Dylan went back to grab his satchel. I went in after him, but..." He shakes his head and dries his eyes before the tears trail down his face. "The guys and I fought them off, and took with us anything we could give to Dylan's family. We've lost some of it along the way, but Noah still has his passport, and Wes has his phone."

"And you have the pendant," I finish, wiping at my eyes with the back of my hand.

"Yeah, I have the pendant."

There's no longer any question as to why I feel attracted to him. Ryland and I have an unspoken bond rooted in guilt. He blames himself for Dylan's death, and I blame myself for the separation of my family. There's nothing we can do or say to absolve us of our sins. They're our burdens to bear, and we're both more than willing to burn in hell for our transgressions, but in the meantime, we'll live out our penance doing our best to make sure those we love survive.

"You don't have to tell me about your parents."

I appreciate his change of heart, but I can't accept it. There's little I own which is worth anything in this godforsaken world, but my word is still precious to me. I won't minimize its value. "We have an agreement, and you most definitely upheld your end." Looking at my dangling feet, I gather my thoughts. No matter how I explain it, the story of my parents holds nothing but brutal truths. There's no way to ease into it. It is what it is.

"My mother and River's dad, Josh, are brother and sister. One day, out of the blue, she showed up on Josh's and Amara's doorstep. At first, they thought she had surprised them by coming to meet River, who was only two months old. My mom was twenty, on a full-ride scholarship to a university in the southern region, and she hadn't seen Josh in almost a year. It turns out that the reason for her visit was that she was seven months pregnant and terrified to tell my grandparents."

He runs his hand over the back of his neck and blows out a puff of air. "That's tough. Did no one know she was in a relationship?"

I shrug and say, "I don't know all the details. But I always found it strange that she had not been to a doctor while she was pregnant. That's kind of pregnancy basics there."

"Yeah."

"Anyway. Several days after her arrival, she went into labor with me. I was delivered early, but healthy. My mother, on the other hand, should have never had a natural childbirth. Her uterus ruptured, and they couldn't save her. The saddest part is her death was avoidable if she received prenatal care." My voice quivers with the last sentence, and I wipe at my eyes.

"I'm sorry, Quinn."

"Thank you." I take a moment to pull myself together. "According to my uncle, Amara fell in love with me the minute she saw me. He couldn't let his baby niece go, so they adopted me. Since there's no father on my birth certificate, nobody put up a fight over their decision." I grin, trying to make Ryland believe I'm okay, but the unanswered questions surrounding my conception haunt me. "They assured me that she loved me, and every day they spent with her, she grew more excited to meet me."

"Where's your father?"

I shrug. "I think Josh knows more than he's telling me. The best I can gather, he was older than my mom, and I think he already had a family. So, there you have it. I was one big oops and I don't know my mom or my dad. Josh and Amara have always been my parents."

"But you don't call them mom and dad?"

My heart sinks, and I quietly say, "I used to... before all of this. I called Amara Ma and Josh Papa."

He releases a deep breath. "We're quite the cluster-fuck, aren't we?"

"Yeah, we are."

It's nothing to be ashamed of. I doubt anyone surviving this apocalypse is totally sane. It takes a special kind of insanity to keep going despite flesh-eating ex-humans trying to devour you.

"Come here." Ryland gestures with a jerk of his head.

Without any argument, I slide down the wall next to him and unexpectedly find myself wrapped in his arms. I'm sure it's as much for his peace of mind as it is for mine. It's what we both need after scraping our emotions raw on the memories of our past. I cuddle next to him, with my head in the crook of his shoulder and the front of his blood-stained jacket clenched in my hand. I cringe as he nestles his face in my filthy hair and inhales the scent of death on me. Not that he smells any better, but he radiates warmth and strength. It more than makes up for the crusty, sticky feel of his clothes and the foul odor coming from them. It's nice to be in contact with another living being who wants nothing more than to hold me.

I release the tension weighing me down and sink further into his embrace. It's a welcome feeling to let go and allow someone to comfort me. I didn't realize how desperately I needed to unburden myself until I finally did it.

Chapter Fifteen

It is early morning when I park the truck in the garage. Ryland and Wes follow me to the bunker and patiently wait as I scan my finger into the security pad. The door clicks, and I slide it open, trying not to disturb everyone inside. The burning furnace in the far corner casts a warm orange glow that illuminates the mess of wires scattered on the kitchen table and Dylan's smartphone connected to River's old laptop. From the look of it, Noah kept on task while we were gone.

I turn my attention to the sleeper sofa and find my side occupied. Noah looks back over his shoulder at us with River encircled in his arms. I raise an eyebrow at the lack of clothing on his upper body and pray it doesn't extend to his lower extremities. I'm not ready to consider just how serious things are getting with him and my cousin.

"How did it go?" he asks with a gravelly voice.

"We got it," I say.

It's the most forthcoming statement I can make

about our mission. Saying it went great is not true. It sucked, it was hard, and I don't want to do it again. We accomplished what we set out to do, and that's all that matters.

I turn on the lantern by Aiden's bedside where he's been propped up to keep from choking on his blood. Unfortunately, it's done little to save his shirt from the red stains splattered on the front. His skin is a sickly pale, and his lips are chapped. Small beads of sweat line his brow, and he looks absolutely awful. Ryland steps beside me, handing me the bottle of steroids before I carefully shake Aiden.

"Hey, I need you to wake up and take these."

With heavy purple lids, he opens his washed-out blue eyes and weakly smiles. "How did it go, beautiful? Did you bring me back anything good?"

"Only the best stuff for you, stud. Open and take these; let's see if we can get you better again." I set a pill on his tongue and help him take a sip of water.

He swallows and falls back on the mountain of pillows. "Did you pick out a restaurant in the city for our date?"

I chuckle at his unyielding sense of humor. "I was thinking we should just order pizza and watch a movie. The nightlife in the city is overrated."

Aiden's head lolls to the side, and he looks past me to Ryland. "I feel like I have competition. I've never seen him so into a girl before."

My jaw drops, but I quickly recover. "All right, now I know you're delirious. Let's get you comfy and back to sleep so you can start healing." I rearrange his pillows before moving on and wring out the cloth soaking in clean water on the nightstand. As gently as possible, I wash away the blood around his mouth.

"Are you jealous?" Aiden asks, continuing to egg Ryland on.

"That you're choking on your own blood? I don't know, that's a tough one," Ryland quips with a cocky grin.

I run the cloth over Aiden's forehead and place a light kiss on his blond hair as he continues bantering with Ryland. "No, that the girl you like is tucking me in and kissing me goodnight?"

If he weren't sick, I'd flick him on the side of the head. He's trying to be funny, but I'm mortified.

"Are you jealous that I got to hold her in my arms last night and watch her sleep?" Ryland asks, lifting a questioning eyebrow.

With a wide-eyed shock, I look at him over my shoulder, but he isn't paying attention to me. The two men are in an intense battle of the wits and emanating too much testosterone. I need to get out of here, put some space between me and them. I go to my dresser and pull out a clean pair of leggings and a sweatshirt. Grabbing my toiletries and towel, I rush to leave the room. With a quick stop at one of the boxes in the basement, I gather my old comforter and pillow before heading for the top floor for a warm shower.

My mind is flooded with Ryland's taunting. There are a million other remarks he could have made to gain the upper hand over Aiden, but he chose to bring up our sleeping arrangement last night. Perhaps I'm reading too much into it, and the reality is that my home has been overrun by the sick and deliriously tired; both of whom are not in their right minds.

I lock myself in the bathroom and set all my necessities on the countertop. I stare at myself in the mirror like a curious bystander on the side of the road, gawking at an accident. I'm a total wreck—my hair is matted with clumps of blood and hay, and my face is coated in filth. The image looking back at me is haggard and beaten. She requires extensive work in order to get remotely back to her old self. My jacket is crusted in blood and uncomfortably stiff as I pry it from my body, followed by my less disgusting shirt. I unbuckle the knife holster from around my waist and check my pants for any weapons I may have overlooked. My hand reaches into my back pocket, and I pull out the flyer I took from the light post in Blythe. Moving to the closed toilet seat, I sit and unfold the paper.

I recall the judge at the capitol warning the people about the Sanctuary and what would happen if they were found with propaganda promoting it. He said people believed that by following the riddle they'd find safety or maybe a better life. It is hard to believe this paper holds such a great promise. There is nothing special about it except for its eye-catching orange color. In big block letters, it reads:

Dearest Explorer,
Follow the blue mist to the mountains aglow in the morning sun.
Trek the path that goes up, up, up to the dome in the sky.
Catch a glimpse of where the new founders dwell.
Safest of journeys,
The Sanctuary

I read the printed words over again, but they make no sense. What the hell does this all mean? Blue mist and domes in the sky—it's gibberish. What transpired at the capitol was utterly wrong, but the judge may have had a point when warning the people not to buy into this.

I fold the paper and place it in the front pouch of my

toiletry bag. I'll look at it again when I feel like I'm not on the brink of passing out, which won't be anytime soon. I sluggishly finish undressing and enter the warmth of the shower. It takes minutes to clean every disgusting thing imaginable off my body, but I don't mind. The heat relaxes my aching muscles. After brushing the knots out of my hair, I head to my old room. It's been ages since I've slept there. Having my own space is an ancient concept to me, and I miss it.

I put my loaded gun on my nightstand and open the curtains, letting the sunshine in. Taking my overstuffed comforter, I wrap it around my body and fall onto my bed. I study the area where I spent almost every night of my life. The pale gray walls with dusty white trim used to be decorated with clear twinkling lights and a collage of monochrome photos of my family and friends. The remnants of my past life no longer exist in this space. Its reflection of me has been wiped away, and now, it's a blank slate waiting to be designed into an expression of someone else's life.

Funnily enough, my room is an accurate metaphor for my uncertain future. Blank. The course my life has taken is new. Nobody has ever forged their way in a world like this. There's not a "How to Survive the Affliction Handbook," filled with helpful hints on how to better my life while trying not to be eaten alive. There's no list of high demand careers in a demolished continent or access to a post-apocalyptic dating site. I'm a pioneer, starting a new beginning and rewriting all the rules. And damn, it's a scary thought.

I pull the reins on my random thoughts and relax as my body sinks into the mattress. The past twenty-four hours haven't been gentle with me physically or mentally, and I need to unwind. It would be easy to lay here all day and ponder all of the what-ifs as I stare at the ceiling. It's a struggle at first, my inner dialogue keeps going off on tangents, but finally, the warmth of my bed lulls me to sleep.

My eyelids are extremely heavy, but my mind is aware of the sound of shuffling steps moving across the wooden floor. Something is sat on the nightstand next to the bed, and the mattress sinks under the weight of someone sitting next to me. Not only do my eyes not want to open, but my muscles are so relaxed I don't think I could move if I had to.

"Quinn."

A tiny cluster of butterflies takes flight inside of my stomach. The deep voice has become familiar to me in the last few days, but I can't say I'm entirely used to it. I'm still fascinated by each word, even when his tone is laced with frustration. It captures my attention and intrigues me. My body's reaction to Ryland merely speaking my name is proof of the effect he has on me.

"Quinn, are you hungry?"

I hum an indistinguishable answer, and at the same time, my stomach growls. The discomfort helps pull me away from the hold of my fatigue. I stretch my body and slowly open my eyes, bracing for the invasion of light. Instead, I find the room dimly illuminated by an oil lamp. Ryland is seated on the edge of the bed, looking down at me. The grime of our mission is washed away, leaving in its wake soft brown waves framing his cleanly-shaven face. He's dressed in a white t-shirt and gray sweatpants. The light colors against his skin making it look golden in the flickering flame of the lamp. His eyes seem to sparkle, and his lips form a lopsided grin as he looks down at me. He's quite the image to wake up to.

"Do you want me to let you go back to sleep?" he asks.

I move into a sitting position. "No. How long have I been asleep?"

"Almost twelve hours."

"Seriously, I've not slept that long in forever."

Guilt bubbles inside me. I was given the luxury of sleeping the day away and didn't contribute to our group. It could be argued that I spent the day before in harm's way, and I earned it, but I don't see it that way. It's what needed to be done, making it undeserving of a reward. Going to Blythe was my choice and not a reason for me to gain a reprieve from my responsibilities, not even a temporary one. Sleeping all day feels more like stolen time than a gift.

"How are you feeling?" Ryland asks.

I assess my body—wiggle my toes, roll my shoulders, and bend my neck side to side. "My head hurts a little from being knocked around too many times, but it could be worse."

He reaches into my hair, and his fingertips rub small circles at the back of my head. I'm torn between closing my eyes and staring at him as he massages my scalp. I want to give in to his touch, and lay my head in his lap, savoring the feeling for a while, but my bliss is short-lived when he grazes a tender bump, and I hiss in pain.

"Sorry," he says, withdrawing his hand.

I hide my disappointment that the head rub has ended behind a forced smile. "It's okay."

"Do you need me to grab you something for the pain?"

I shake my head and take a closer look at him. I've been witness to his worry for Aiden, but never has he directed it at me like this. Not that he *never* shows concern for me. Let's be honest, sometimes he can be a bit overbearing, but this degree of worry is unfamiliar. It's sweet, tentative, and a little strange, but it's something I could get used to.

"I'm just really hungry," I say as my stomach angrily gurgles again.

His gaze darts to the nightstand. "Everyone has already eaten, but I brought you some soup."

Ryland reaches for the two bowls, handing me one before taking the other for himself. I savor the taste of the warm liquid as it slides down my throat and hits my empty stomach. It's the same canned soup I've eaten more times than I can count, but tonight, it tastes a little better. It might be my extreme hunger, or a heightened sense of appreciation after making it through yesterday's ordeal. Or maybe it's my company that makes the flavor of the meal extraordinary. Either way, it's delicious.

"Why didn't you eat with everyone else?" I ask after I've inhaled half of my bowl.

"I just woke up a bit ago."

"You got a ton of sleep, too!"

"I had a difficult time falling asleep." Leaning forward, he sets his empty bowl on the nightstand and gets to his feet. He paces back and forth, running his index finger over his bottom lip and diverting his eyes from me. Every muscle in his body is tight, and his long strides appear to be a rigorous chore rather than a natural act.

"Ry?" I say, gently urging him on.

He doesn't answer as he moves to the window, leans his shoulder on the frame, and folds his arms over his chest. Looking over the property, he takes a deep breath and says, "I lied to you last night." He shakes his head, his hair gleaming in the moonlight. "Let me rephrase, I didn't lie, but I didn't tell the entire truth."

I sit up straight, my brow crinkled with concern. "What are you talking about?"

"Most nights, I can't sleep," he says. "Actually, I don't want to sleep, unless I absolutely have to. Every day, I try to push myself to my breaking point, hoping it's enough to make my body give out. I don't want to take the chance of being in an uncontrollable state of half-asleep and half-awake. Every moment of quiet I have is bombarded with images of him. Last night in the barn, I knew if I fell asleep you would join him." His words are said in a haunting voice while he stares at the yard. None of what he's telling me makes sense. But I remain silent and give him time to gather his thoughts.

"You claim it's mercy, Quinn, but where's the mercy for me? If it's the right thing to do, then why don't I have a moment of peace?"

I'm scrabbling for the right answer. He's in so much pain, and I'm unsure how to ease it. "I don't know."

"When you held out your gun to me, all I could see was him—his screams filling the house and the sounds they made as they ripped him apart. With every ounce of strength we had, we fought off the Afflicted as they attacked him. He was going into shock by the time I got to him, but he had enough energy to beg me to kill him. I was the one with the gun. I could end it quickly. I wanted there to be another way. I wanted to save him, but I couldn't. With my last bullet, I killed him and ended his suffering. It was the merciful thing to do, like euthanizing an animal. But he wasn't an animal. He was one of my best friends."

"Dylan," I whisper, covering my mouth with my hand to stifle a sob.

Most would believe he had done the right thing, but

he was left to carry the weight of his friend's death. He killed Dylan. And I'd asked him to do the same for me.

Without hesitation, I leap from the bed. I'm not sure if he wants my comfort, but it's all I have to give. I wrap my arms around him from behind and rest my cheek on his back. He tenses at the contact, but I don't let go, saying, "I wish I could take away your hurt."

He unfolds his arms, resting one hand on top of mine and propping the other on the side of the window to hold himself up. With his face buried in the crook of his elbow, his body shudders. There are no words coming from him, just an occasional rattled breath. I hold him tightly as he mourns all of his losses.

He didn't just lose a friend; his innocence was ripped from him as well. He was given no choice but to go against the very basics of human morals. Even small children know it is wrong to kill. When he fired the deathblow, it scarred him in a way that will never heal.

We've all lost tiny bits of who we are throughout the progression of the virus. Circumstances have forced us to abandon those things we don't consider essential to our survival. Certain emotions and consequences have no place in a society like ours. If the ultimate goal is to live, then we can't be bound to rules, not even those that are naturally designed to separate us from other animals. We've abandoned what defines us as human.

After several minutes, Ryland raises his head and turns to me with red-rimmed eyes and flushed cheeks. He leans back on the window, placing his long legs on either side of mine, and reaches out to me. I rest my hand inside of his, but don't move any closer. It would be so easy to fall into his arms and press my body against his. In fact, it's overly tempting.

Ryland plays with my fingers, comparing the size of

them to his own. "Yesterday, when you gave me your gun and begged me to kill you..." He shakes his head. "I can't go through that again, Quinn. I'm barely hanging on as is, but if I had to take your life, that would've been it. No matter how justified it is, I'm still plagued with crippling guilt. My soul can't withstand it again. I'd rather die."

I despise the very thought of damaging him beyond repair. He's the embodiment of strength and bravery, and now, he has revealed his weakness. His vulnerability is equally noble. It drives him to protect those around him. It's rare, even in a perfect world.

"I'm so sorry, Ryland. If I had known, I would have never asked you to do it. I wish I could take it back."

With my hand intertwined with his, he pulls me closer. His other hand slides across the side of my downturned face, using his thumb he guides it up. His facial features are set in severe lines saturated with compassion and vulnerability.

"You can't go rogue on me anymore. I know you're capable of taking care of yourself, but I can't risk losing another person I care about."

My chest tightens at the admission of his feelings for me. We were never supposed to get to this point. I've been relying on him to remain at bay, to keep the emotional gap between us while my defenses slowly crumble. The line separating our responsibilities is blurring. Whether I want it or not, he and the other three men have wiggled their way into my life and divided my focus from River.

I search his face for any sign that his feelings are clouded. Too many things can factor into an unnecessary meltdown—sleep deprivation, stress, and traumatic events—all of which he has experienced. As hard as I try, I can't find any fault in his resolve. It's terrifying.

I move to pull away, but he holds firmly to my hand. Desperation laces my words as I say, "Please don't do this. I'm failing to keep you out. I'm relying on you to stay strong and keep your distance. I can't afford even a second of letting my guard down."

"I can't take the words back, and if I could, it wouldn't change the truth." He smiles, but there's an air of sadness behind it.

Our boundaries have been compromised, and the odds of everyone we care about surviving have suddenly decreased substantially. Neither one of us wanted this, yet here we are.

He pulls me closer again, his hands sliding to my hips and under the hem of my shirt. His thumbs massage small circles at my waist, every little rotation sending a spark through my body. His touch comforts my aching soul while awakening a part of me I thought was dead.

"When we leave, I want you and River to come with us," he says.

I open my mouth and close it again as I search for the right words. We've fought side by side and looked out for each other. There's an unsaid agreement between us— we will not leave the other behind. It was a temporary promise that was never meant to extend beyond the time he is here.

"We can't, Ryland," I say.

"Why?"

"What if our family comes looking for us? This will be the first place they search."

He shakes his head and says, "And what are the chances of that happening? What if they can never come back? You've waited long enough."

He has a point, but I'm not convinced he's thought

this through. River and I are tightly shackled to this continent. There's no way out, and our future is paved for us in fear. Fear of Zs and fear of those who have not been infected by the virus. At least if we're locked away in our home, we can strive for some kind of normalcy. Ryland and his friends have an agenda. They plan to use their status as Giran citizens to cross into Oscuros. I just don't see how our situations can combine and have a positive result for us all. Whether it's the guys or us, someone is going to have to make a sacrifice. They will have to stay behind with us on this decaying continent, giving up their hopes of going home. Or River and I follow them to the border and are left to fend for ourselves with no constant food source, weapons, or shelter when they go. The gamble is too high, and I won't risk our lives without a solid plan.

"It's not like we can just pick up and go with you. How will you get the border guards to let River and me into Oscuros?"

"We'll tell them we're married, and you lost your passport. Noah will do the same for River."

I cock an eyebrow. The story has too many loose ends with no guarantee of working. And he knows it.

With a sigh, he says, "We have time to figure something out. Aiden's still sick, and I don't want to leave until he's at a hundred percent. River suggests we stay until spring, so we don't take the risk of him relapsing."

"Are you sure she's saying this for Aiden's sake, or is it for the sake of her and Noah?" I ask.

He tenderly brushes the backs of his fingers over my face and tucks a loose strand of hair behind my ear. Hundreds of thousands of bumps rise on my flesh, and I turn my face to the warmth of his palm. My lips sweep across the callused skin, taking a deep breath and filling my lungs with the scent of him. Damn my body for betraying me for his physical attention.

In a hushed voice, he says, "Does it matter?"

"No," I say, the confession easier to admit than I thought. There was a time when I counted down the minutes until he left with his friends. Now, all I want is for him to stay a little longer.

He pulls his lips between his teeth, wraps his arms around my waist, and pulls me so close my chest meets his.

All boundaries between us have vanished, along with some of my trepidation. I don't want to yield to my emotions. I need to keep battling. To give into whatever is occurring between Ryland and me is to relinquish my promise to right my wrongs. I'm selling my soul to the devil to momentarily abandon my responsibilities and indulge in something beautiful in a corroding world. Fuck, I don't even regret it.

I encircle his neck with my arms and tangle my fingers in his soft waves. With my face in the crook of his neck, I close my eyes and inhale. There's not a scent on earth I can compare him to. It's distinctly him—strength, passion, bravery, and dedication. He embodies everything I'm striving to be.

His hands press to my spine, and he buries his face into my disheveled hair. "I don't need an answer tonight. Just think about coming with us, all right?"

I can't fully surrender, so I say, "I promise I'll think about it."

Chapter Sixteen

"So, have you always been good with computers?"
From my place on the couch, I peer over the top of the book and watch River and Noah. She's seated on his lap with her arms around his shoulders while he works on her laptop to sync it to the cell phone. He wears a big, cheesy smile with his arms on either side of her. Even if he needed her to move, I don't think he would ask. He would just keep working around her if it made her happy.

It has been this way between them ever since we arrived back from Blythe two weeks ago. They were done downplaying their attraction to each other. River pulled me aside to ask if I would mind trading beds with Noah. I agreed and officially began my new rotation with Wes. We take turns sleeping on the top bunk and the couch in the study. The prime sleeping spot is away from the late-night giggles coming from the sofa bed.

I try to ignore River and Noah and focus on the paragraph I've read countless times in the last ten minutes, but it's impossible. My ears perk up, listening to Noah answer River's question.

"I've always liked electronics like video games and such. I didn't really get into computers until I was a bit older. My friends were talking about fake IDs and how expensive it was to buy them. I figured it couldn't be too difficult to replicate a piece of paper, so I researched it and gave it a shot. It turned out I was pretty good at it, so I started a little side business. The more I delved into computers and what they could do, the more I loved it."

River laughs and rubs the top of his buzzed head. "How cute. You were a little entrepreneur."

"Who knew criminal activity was adorable," I grumble, pulling my legs out from beneath me and stretching them across the couch.

"Someone sounds jealous," Aiden sings from the floor.

I glare down at him, but he can't see me. His back is to the sofa, leaning against it as he plays a game on my old tablet. His health is steadily improving. He no longer coughs up blood and sleeps most of the day, but it will take time before he's back to normal. He's overexerted by simple tasks like climbing the stairs or standing for an extended period. Each day, he pushes himself a little further, but his recovery is a slow process.

I scoff. "Jealous of them? Please."

Ryland sits on the opposite side of the couch from me, with one long leg crossed over the other and a book resting on his knee. He keeps his eyes glued to the pages and does a terrible job of hiding his smile.

"I'm not!" I say again.

"Of course not," Ryland says, placing his hand on top of my foot to stop it from anxiously bouncing next to his hip.

River's and Noah's relationship isn't the only one

progressing. Ryland and I have fallen into a comfortable groove of our own. Of course, the bond between us is different from theirs. Ours is a growing friendship. When I sleep in the study, our interactions are tame. He remains on the floor and I stay on the couch. From our designated sleeping places, we stay up talking until we're too tired to keep our eyes open. It reminds me of when River and I were kids, and we had friends spend the night—everyone laying on the floor and talking until the sun rose. It's pretty much the same thing, except Ryland is gorgeous, and I find my thoughts occasionally drifting in a way they shouldn't. I can positively say I've never felt the same inclinations for my childhood friends.

I sigh while dog-earing a page of my book and abandoning it to watch Noah and River dote over each other. The way they share secrets, sideways glances, and adoring smiles is impossible to ignore. Their relationship isn't what has me frazzled, per se. I like Noah a lot, and he's head over heels for my cousin. I don't doubt the sincerity of his affections or that he would never intentionally harm her. I'm simply envious that he has occupied her time for the past weeks. I miss it being the two of us.

Setting his book on the coffee table, Ryland lifts my feet over his legs and scoots closer to me. With his arm draped over the back of the couch, he leans in and quietly says, "You were going to work in the greenhouse today. Why don't you ask her to go with you? The two of you can get away from us for a bit."

"You want me to pull that apart?" I say, waving my hand in their direction.

"Yes!" Ryland and Aiden say as one.

Ryland smiles at his friend before continuing. "I think a little break from us will do both of you some good."

"All right," I say, playfully shoving Aiden's head to the side as I get up from the couch. "Riv, do you want to help me out in the greenhouse?"

"Yeah, I'll go with you," she says before pressing a kiss to Noah's cheek.

As we put on our jackets and strap on our weapons, I work to cast aside my jealousy. This is going to be the first time since the guys arrived that I'll get some quality time with her that doesn't consist of us locking ourselves in a bathroom. Between sharing chores with the guys and her taking care of Aiden, we haven't found time for just the two of us. I don't want to cloud this moment with resentment.

After taking a few calming breaths, I head out of the bunker with her. We walk side by side through the house until she stops shy of the front door and turns to me. Her gray eyes narrow, and her hands rest on her slim hips. "This little trip to the greenhouse isn't going to result in you lecturing me, is it?"

I raise my hands and take a step back. "Whoa, where is this coming from?"

"Don't think I didn't notice you watching us like a hawk with the annoyed eyerolls and snarky remarks. If you have a problem with Noah and me, just say it, but don't corner me so you can get all parental."

River has always been tough and never has she been one to mince words. She's unashamed when it comes to wearing her emotions for everyone to see. Her boldness is one of her many admirable traits.

"It's not my intention to lecture you, and I don't have an issue with you and Noah. I just wanted to spend some time alone. Even though I see you every day, I miss you," I admit.

"So, you have no ulterior motives in inviting me to come with you?"

I can't be mad at her for not trusting me. In the past, I've nagged at her about everything from going outside without me to splurging when we should be rationing food. Too many times, I've tried to rule over her instead of being her friend. My intentions are always pure, but they're not always right.

"No ulterior motives," I promise.

"Then what's up with all the snotty looks and comments?"

I shrug. "Jealousy, I guess. I'm not used to sharing your attention."

"You said before that you weren't jealous, but I knew you were." Her features soften, and she pulls me into a tight hug. "That's sweet. It's stupid you haven't said anything until now, but it's sweet."

I hug her back. "Sorry."

"I am, too. I'm not trying to ignore you."

"I know."

Our sentimental moment comes to an end with the beat of heavy boots walking up from the basement. I look over my shoulder as Ryland appears from the kitchen. He has on his jacket and is holding a gun. He comes to a standstill and casually slips his weapon into the waistband of his pants with a sheepish look on his face.

"What are you doing?" I ask, still hanging on to my cousin.

"I'm—I was going to..." He points up the stairs. "I was just headed upstairs."

There's nothing up there for him. The only time any of us use the upper level is if we're doing a security check on the property. Everything can be seen from there, the edge of the woods, Josh's workshop, and the greenhouse.

The greenhouse.

He's going to stand guard while we're outside.

"We'll wait for you to get in place before we walk out," I say.

With bright red cheeks, he gives a quick nod and hurries up the stairs.

River looks at me with raised brows.

"What? It calms him to know everyone's safe," I say, opening the door.

"Uh-huh." She steps past me with a smirk.

The inside of the greenhouse counters the sub-zero temperatures outside with its warmth and humidity. We discard our jackets and roll up our sleeves before taking the black aprons from the hooks by the door and slipping them on. A small workstation houses the tools we need to tend to the plants, and we each grab our favorites. Using the knowledge passed on to us by Amara, we jump into the task of caring for her beloved greenhouse.

As kids, we relished being in here, especially during the winter. We would make-believe it was a warm summer day, while inches of snow gathered on the ground outside. A small corner of the structure was given to us, and we grew our own tiny garden of flowers and vegetables. When we got tired of the tedious work of pruning and turning the soil, we chased each other up and down the aisles, laughing and screaming. Even with all of the fragile vegetation around, Amara never told us to settle down. Instead, she joined in on our fun, creating many unforgettable, happy memories with us.

After minutes of silence, River asks, "What exactly is the deal with you and Ry?"

I keep my eyes on the plant before me, clipping off its wilted leaves. "We're friends."

"You're friends who spend every other night sleeping in the same room?"

I glance at her and slowly reply, "Yes."

"You're friends who occasionally sit really close together on the couch and watch movies. The type who goes out of their way to make sure the other is safe crossing the yard?"

I stop and stare at her, but she pretends not to notice, continuing to tend to a tomato vine.

"Yes, we're that kind of friends," I say, not bothering to hide my annoyance.

The sibling rivalry that has always existed between us is ignited within me, and I seize the opportunity to return the favor. Just as a biological sister would do, I go for the kill, trying to embarrass her.

"So, did you and Noah do it on the sofa bed?"

The shears drop from her hand. She fumbles to pick them up, making a choking noise. When she finishes clearing her throat, she answers, "We haven't done that yet."

I'm a bit surprised since everything about their relationship has been fast paced. I wasn't sure if they had sex in the bunker, but I was confident that their relationship had reached that level. It goes to show how I don't know everything about the one person I'm the closest to. And maybe that's my fault. I haven't been the easiest to talk to when it comes to her and Noah.

River continues to explain. "We know you guys think we're crazy for jumping into a relationship. What you all don't know is that there are some things we want to build up to, and that's one of them."

I feel a little ashamed of my assumption. It seems she and Noah have put a lot of thought into how things should happen for them. It's clear it's not just lovesick stares and displays of affection. They're trying to build something lasting, and I have a new respect for them.

"Please don't take this the wrong way, but what happens to the two of you when they leave?" I ask.

"I've been meaning to talk to you about that, but I haven't found the right time," River says, setting down her gardening tool and removing her gloves. She walks over to the table behind me and clears a space before hoisting herself on top. Her long legs dangle from the edge, and she watches her feet while talking. "When were you going to tell me that Ry asked if we would leave with them?"

I pause and let her words sink in. I can't avoid this conversation or give her a half-ass answer. This is important, and we need to talk about it before she decides without me. I turn around and lean back on the table with my arms crossed. "Who told you?"

She cocks an eyebrow like I've asked the world's stupidest question. Of course, Noah told her because Ryland spoke to him.

"There's nothing to talk about. We can't leave." I try to be gentle, knowing the decision affects her relationship.

"You're going to make that call without first discussing it with me? I hardly think that's fair," she says, her voice rising with irritation.

I pull on each individual finger of my gloves until my hands are free. "Okay, discuss."

"I think we should go."

"Of course you do," I say with a sigh.

"Would you please just listen? I know you think I want to go because of Noah, but that's not the case. We've already spoken about it, and he said it's my decision. He's going to stay with me either way."

I lose control over the muscles in my jaw, and it drops open. "He will stay here if we don't go with them?"

Her eyes well up with tears, and her chin trembles.

"Yes. I told him that he needs to go home no matter what we choose to do, but he refuses. If I don't go, he's planning on staying with us."

"River, we can't go just because Noah won't leave without you."

She rolls her eyes, wiping away her tears. "I don't want Noah to stay for me and give up his life in Giran, but it's not why I want to go. I feel like we're sitting here rotting away in this house. I don't want to live the rest of my life like this, Quinn. I want a chance to live the kind of life I always pictured having."

"At least we're safe here," I say, sweeping my hand in the air. "There's no guarantee if we go that we'll get across the border. What if we get all the way there and are sent away? And then what if Noah changes his mind and wants to leave with his friends? Can you stand to watch him walk away from you? It'll be just you and me fending for ourselves while we try to get back here?"

She shakes her head. "I'm tired of playing it safe, and if Noah were to change his mind, then so be it. At least we tried and did something, other than sitting here in our safe little bubble."

I run my hands over my face, fighting back the fear building inside of me. "We can't take that risk. It's too big."

She jumps from the table and stands before me. Her shoulders square, eyes steadily holding mine, and her tone is firm with resolve. "You don't get to make that call for me. It's my life! I know you feel guilty about us being stuck here, but it's not your fault. I stayed behind because I wanted to. I wanted one last summer with you just as badly as you wanted it with me." She looks at the ceiling and humorlessly laughs. "I was as terrified as you were about leaving home and growing up, but staying here didn't change that, did it? Here we are, adults, and now it's time to go."

She's right. We've grown up and are stuck in the setting of our childhood as women. We have no choice in the matter, we're changing whether we want to or not. Perhaps her words about staying behind with me for the summer have alleviated a fraction of my guilt, but it doesn't mean that we should run into a situation that is almost sure to kill us.

"I just need some kind of guarantee that we'll be safe. When I think about leaving right now, all I can see is a hopeless situation. Maybe if the cell phone link works, we'll be able to get the word out to someone who will promise to notify the Giran government. Or even if we come up with a better plan than just telling the border guards you're married to Noah and lost your passport. We need something foolproof. If we have a solid plan, I'll seriously think about it. But until then, I just can't do it."

River is always the optimist, even now. "Then we'll have to find a way to get you what you need, because we're going to go, Quinn."

Her mind is made up, and I no longer have the desire to fight against what she wants. All I can do is pray that we find a way to make it happen.

Chapter Seventeen

"Quinn, do you have a red five?"

"Nope," I say to Wes.

He mumbles a string of curse words and pulls the top card off the deck.

Trying not to come down with a terrible bout of cabin fever, we've moved into the study for the day. The curtains are drawn back to allow in the natural light of the winter sun, and a fire rages in the fireplace. River, Wes, Aiden, and I sit in a circle on the massive woven rug in the middle of the room with a deck of cards. For hours, we've entertained ourselves by playing every card game we could think of, but we hit the bottom of the barrel about thirty minutes ago when we started this never-ending children's game.

It's been a month since these four men forced their way into this house and our lives. In the past, thirty days would seem minimal in our fast-paced world of school, study, and friends, but now, it feels like an eternity. We know who the morning people are and who are not, and the things to do to drive each other mad. Meal preparation and other chores have been equally divvied up, and our day-to-day now has a natural flow. I can't seem to recall what life was like before they arrived.

I look up from my cards and watch Ryland nervously pace back and forth, running his fingers through his hair. The dark circles under his eyes are evidence of another sleepless night, making me wish he could find a moment of peace. Holding his gun, he splits his attention between watching the property out the window and glancing at us. I gave up on trying to get him to relax and join us on the floor. He's on edge, and my best guess is it has to do with the cell phone up-link.

Noah has been perched behind my uncle's desk since sunrise and is not in any better shape. Brown strands of his hair stand straight up, and his dark eyes look weary from hours of staring at a computer screen. River's laptop sits open before him with the cell phone connected to it and a thick black cord running out the study window and across the lawn to the tower. This plan has taken a lot of time and effort on all of our parts, but Noah has been running the show. Under his direction, Wes and Ryland have wired the tower into the solar panels on top of the workshop. For weeks, Noah has been coding the program that will hopefully connect us to the other side of the world. He's confident that today everything will be up and running.

The call will be quick, no more than five minutes. After that, the phone will most likely malfunction if not explode due to all the power running directly to it. We have the chance for only one call, and then communication will be lost with the rest of the world again.

I'd be lying if I said I'm not a bit disappointed. I wish each of us could call our families and let them know we're alive. It must be awful for them to deal with the possibility of our deaths, but I especially feel for the boys' parents. They sent their sons off on a summer trip thinking it was temporary and they would return unharmed. Their children are lost, and they're left with the fading hope of one day being reunited.

My fingers are crossed that today will change everything for our families. I pray we reach the right person who can get the word out to our loved ones. Perhaps if a big enough fuss is made about the boys and how they have survived, their story will get to the right authorities, and we can be rescued. It's a long shot, but it's all we have. Just this one call.

With his hand back in his hair, Ryland steps away from the window. He stops in his tracks when he catches me staring at him. A forced smile pulls at the corners of his mouth, and I return it with a genuine one. It's the first real exchange we've had all day. It's not often I get to see this unnerved side of him, so I want to do what I can to help alleviate some of his stress.

"Hello, Quinn," Aiden says with a raised voice.

I pull my attention from Ryland. "Sorry, what?"

"Do you have a black nine?"

I try to focus on the values of the cards I'm holding. "A black nine?"

"I think we need to talk about our relationship," Aiden says, playfully throwing up his hands as if exasperated with me.

I raise an eyebrow and try to hide my smile. "All right, go for it."

River lets out a huff and Wes moans as our game times-out.

Aiden and I have continued with our harmless flirtation. I play along because it's amusing—an inside joke all our own. I thoroughly enjoy Aiden's company. He, on the other hand, does it because he believes our back and forth aggravates Ryland, but there's no sense of annoyance on his part. In fact, I think Ryland reacts more to make me squirm than to get the upper hand on his friend.

"You see, I'm starting to feel like someone else has caught your attention, and I get it. I'm just this sickly lad, and he's... tall. Perhaps he's also what others might find"— he raises both of his hands and makes quotation marks with his fingers— "pleasant to look at."

Ryland leans against the wall with his arms crossed over his chest and an eyebrow cocked. He doesn't look amused, and at the same time, the tilt of his lips says he is.

"I have a lot to offer," Aiden says. "I'm a sensitive man who enjoys long walks on the beach and candlelit dinners. I make up for my homely face with humor and my vulnerable side. I've heard I'm quite the catch."

I double over, my laughter filling the room.

Aiden is utterly ridiculous and far from being unattractive. Although, I do agree that his humor is the main contributor to his appeal. He has a way of drawing us all in. He may be a twenty-two-year-old man, but there's a youthful quality to him. The rigorous life he's led for almost two years hasn't left him looking as haggard as the rest of us. His eyes still sparkle with carelessness, and his smile isn't tainted with indifference. He embodies a typical young man just starting his life.

Ryland shakes his head. "There's no quality, no matter how amazing, that can make up for that face, Donnelly."

Aiden bows his head. "I'm destined to be alone."

I lean into his side, looping my arm in his and resting my head on his shoulder. "Don't listen to him." I stick my tongue out at Ryland. "I have to admit, the struggle to keep my hands off you grows harder each day." My words are meant for Aiden, but my eyes are glued to Ryland.

I'm only too aware of the indirect truth I've spoken. The nights when I sleep in the same room as him are a mixture of peaceful slumber knowing I'm safe and restlessness at having him so close. In the early morning, when he's consumed by sleep, my brain jars me awake with the need to look at him. From across the room, I watch the rise and fall of his chest as he lays on the floor in front of the fire. My body aches to slide next to him and mold to his back, wrapping him in my arms. I'm sure he doesn't need my comfort, but there are too many days where I feel I need his.

"Quinn, can I have a moment with you?" Ryland says, the playfulness vanishing from his face and replaced by a worry line between his eyebrows.

I give Aiden a quick kiss on the cheek. "By the way, you're absolutely handsome, not that you need me to tell you."

As I follow Ryland out of the room, Aiden brightly smiles. "I know, but I play it down for stolen sympathy kisses."

I roll my eyes. "Well played."

Ryland closes the study door once we are in the living room. The change of scenery has done nothing to calm his nerves, and again, he paces from one side of the room to the other.

I let him get a lap in before I ask, "What's going on?"

He stops and brushes his disheveled hair from his face. His chest expands with a deep breath, and he closes his eyes. "I can't properly express how grateful the four of us are that you let us stay. Both you and River made sacrifices for us even before we earned your trust."

His demeanor screams uncertainty, and it's the complete opposite of who I know him to be. We're still learning all the little things about each other, and I don't claim to understand him entirely, but something is off. To ease whatever is plaguing him, I move to close the distance between us. Keeping our bodies inches apart, I slide my hand inside of his.

"Thank you, and you're right, I was hesitant about helping you guys, but I don't regret it. I mean, Noah and River are happy, and I'm..." I reach up and move a rogue strand of hair that's fallen across his forehead.

He turns his lips to the inside of my palm and kisses it. My stomach flips at the touch of his warm lips lingering on my skin. My imagination runs wild. The thought that rules them all is if his lips would feel just as soft pressed to mine. I've never wanted to kiss someone as much as I do him.

"And you're...?" He urges me to finish my thought.

I'm always given the opportunity to be brave when I step outside of this house. However, when it comes to my emotional state, I cower. For once, I want to emulate the kind of courage Ryland portrays.

I glide my thumb across his jaw, willing his eyes to meet mine. Their green depths speak of his hurt and the tragedy he has endured. He's not always strong, just a master at masking those darker emotions. He has taught me that I can be afraid and brave at the same time. And this is one of those times.

My voice is coated in emotions, making my words break when I say, "I'm so glad you're here."

He cradles my face in both of his hands. His forehead meets mine, and his expression is full of pain. "I have something I need to tell you."

I swallow as my stomach sinks, but I fight to ward off any expectations whether good or bad. I just want this one pure and truthful moment with him.

"Ry, we're up," says a muffled voice from the study.

His eyes spring open, and we stay silent, waiting to see if we heard correctly.

"Shaw." Wes pulls the door open. "Noah says we only have a few minutes, and the phone is already heating up."

He lets go of me, and I swear I see a flash of regret in his eyes before he jogs back into the study. My head spins as every thought I held at bay comes rushing in. Questions about what he needed to say and if he planned on kissing me. But it doesn't matter. For now, I have no choice but to block everything out and follow Ryland and Wes back into the study.

Noah sits behind the desk with the phone in his hand and a blank computer screen before him. Everyone has gathered around him, waiting to see what will happen next. I stand off to the side and watch Ryland give a quick nod and step beside Noah. He maneuvers the laptop to face him as the phone rings. Within seconds, a grainy picture of a dark-haired woman appears on the computer screen.

I'm astonished. I had no idea Noah was working to make a video call.

"Dylan," the woman sobs over the sound of hysterical voices in the background. "It's his phone," she explains to those around her.

"Mrs. Kassis, it's Ryland." He leans down with both arms, supporting his weight on the desk.

She frantically nods. "I can see you, Ryland. Noah, Wes, Aiden." She greets them. "Where's Dylan?"

Noah turns his face into River's stomach, and his

shoulders shake while my cousin lovingly runs her fingers through his hair.

"I'm so very sorry." Ryland swallows a gulp of air, and his eyes shift like he is searching his memory for the carefully scripted speech he prepared for this moment, but it seems to elude him. "I couldn't save him."

"Ry." Aiden places a hand on his shoulder, but he shrugs it away. I know the guilt he carries feels like too gentle of a punishment for not returning a son to his mother. This is his one chance to lessen that guilt a fraction.

Dylan's mom is consumed by tears, and her makeup runs in black streaks down her beautiful oval face. "Did he— Is he one of them?"

"No," Aiden answers, giving Ryland a firm look that begs him to let it be.

The heartbroken woman's world has ripped wide open, and she doesn't need all the gory details of her son's death. Ryland cannot rely on her to absolve him of the sins he believes he committed. Not when her pain is just as deep, if not deeper than his.

"Where are you boys? Can you find a way home?" Mrs. Kassis sobs.

"We're working on it," Wes says, with a strained smile.

"Tell me where you are so I can send help. Your families—"

The screen blinks in and out, breaking up her words before smoke discharges from the phone. Noah quickly pulls the plug from the computer, saving it from malfunctioning just as a light flashes outside followed by a deafening crack coming from the tower.

I blink at the blank screen, processing what happened. This call was nothing like I expected. From the beginning, I assumed we'd contact the Giran authorities and plead our case to be rescued, but it was never their intention. Linking the cell phone to the tower was always meant to be an attempt to notify Dylan's family of his death.

The group next to me quietly exchanges brief sentences and comfort each other with promises of getting home. Even River is caught up in the moment, hugging each of them and whispering kind words while rubbing their backs.

Our chance of a more plausible escape plan has vanished.

Anger and frustration heat within me, and I want to scream. I was misled to believe they were trying to save us. Every time I spoke about this moment, I was never corrected by any of them. It was their intention to deceive me from the start. And it would appear everyone was in on it.

Without a word, I turn on my heels and rush from the room.

From behind me, River says, "No, let her go. She just needs some time."

I hurry out the front door, slamming it closed behind me. The ground is slick with ice from where the snow has melted during the day and refrozen at night. My feet slip as I sprint across the yard and into the woods. I leap over fallen trees and dodge large rocks. Low snow-covered branches cross my path, threatening to scratch my face, but I duck and shove them aside. It's not until I reach the edge of the lake, that has transformed into a massive block of ice, that my body gives out. I fall to the ground, pulling my legs to my chest and resting my head on my knees.

My unhinged emotions bombard me. One part of me is livid with myself for being upset. The death of Dylan has plagued his friends for far too long, especially Ryland. This was their chance to lessen their torment and honor their dead friend. In letting his mother know of his death, they were able to give her closure and gain some for themselves as well. I can't deny the call was the right thing to do, but at what cost? The tiny ounce of hope I had for River and me has been violently ripped away. For weeks, I've clung to the unlikely probability that this call would work in our favor. I'd built it up in my mind to this epic moment when someone would come to our rescue. In a matter of minutes, my dream was quashed, and reality put back into its place.

I can respect that the boys had a difficult choice to make. I honestly couldn't say what I'd have done in their shoes. I just wish it wasn't paid for with my trust.

I don't bother to hold back my tears. Their wetness and the unrelenting cold remind me that I'm still alive, and my fight is not over. But for this small moment, I give in to my hurt and sadness, letting them run their course until I'm unable to cry anymore.

Crunching snow under slow steps invades the quiet around me. I keep my head down, hiding the evidence of my weakness as something warm is placed around my shoulders. I wrap it around my body, realizing my limbs are shaking and teeth are chattering. I wasn't dressed for the freezing temperatures. I've sat here wallowing in my sorrow and welcoming hypothermia at the same time.

Extra heat radiates from the body that slides down beside me.

"I wanted to tell you about the call," Ryland says.

In the safety of the jacket, I keep my face hidden as I dry my eyes. "Why didn't you?"

"Not that it makes it any better, but I was trying before it connected."

I look at him over the fabric. "No, it doesn't make it any better. You let me believe you were calling for help."

"I know you, Quinn. There was no way you would've agreed to the call. You would have fought it."

"You're right. I would have pushed back. This was our one chance to find someone outside of this fucked up situation to help us. I'm stubborn, but not unreasonable. Maybe if you had given me a chance, I would have also come up with a compromise. We could have all gotten what we wanted."

"Do you honestly think you would have bent on this? You have a one-track mind when it comes to River," he says, keeping his eyes on the frozen lake before us.

"She's the only thing I have left in this goddamn world, but she isn't all I care about. Despite fighting it, I've grown to take the well-being of the four of you into account as well. Or is this all one-sided and I'm the only one considering you guys my friends?"

"No, Quinn. It isn't one-sided. You know that," he says, pure conviction lacing his tone.

His certainty jars a little of the fight out of me and my voice wavers as I say, "You could have at least put it up for a vote and given me a voice in the matter."

He turns to me, guilt etching deep lines into his forehead and around his mouth. "We did put it up for a vote, and you were outnumbered."

Through clenched teeth I say, "I guess we'll never know if I would have compromised."

I want to scream and unleash my fury upon him. From the moment I met him, I tried to hold him at a distance. I begged him not to let his guard down when I was miserably failing. He forced his way in, and I trusted him almost as much as my own family. He betrayed me, but he didn't act alone.

"River knew, didn't she?" I ask.

He nods. "Noah told her when we were in Blythe. Don't be upset with her, be upset with me. This was my fault. Hold me responsible and let me make it up to you."

"How? She's going with you no matter what. She thinks it is useless for us to say here any longer. The minute we leave, I have no safety net for her or myself. You can't guarantee we'll get across the border, and if we don't, it will be her and me fending for ourselves."

"I already told you we will work it out. I'll get you both across." He almost has me convinced, but the rational part of me knows it's empty promises. What we'll face at the border is unknown.

"How can I believe you when you've already deceived me?" I ask.

He flinches and says, "I'll make it up to you, I promise, whatever it takes."

There's only one thing worth a damn that he can give me right now. "If you want to make it up to me, then swear you'll protect River at all costs. I'm not delusional. I know you won't put her above your friends, but you sure as hell better put her above me. Swear to me, if a moment comes where you have to choose her or me, you'll choose her."

His eyes widen and he shakes his head. "That's not a promise I can make."

My heart shatters. He's my last hope of delivering River back to our family alive. "Then your promise of doing whatever it takes is just another lie."

He reaches out and wipes away a tear sliding down my face with his thumb. "Ask anything else."

I wouldn't go as far as to say his affections for me run as deep as love, but he does feel the need to protect me. I'm sure watching over River seems redundant to him. He has said that Noah will always look out for her, leaving him open to watch over me. But I need him to go against whatever drives him to protect me. If River and I can't both be reunited with our parents, then I'm going to make sure one of us does. It will be her, and I need his help to do it.

It pains me to hurt him, but I have no choice. "There's nothing else I want. Promise you'll put River's safety above my own."

His brows furrow and he frowns. I know he doesn't want to say the words; his integrity will not allow him to back away from an oath. Once he says he will put her first, he'll be held to it. That is exactly what I want.

Ryland takes a deep breath and quietly says, "I promise."

Chapter Eighteen

Ryland and I sit together in silence after he vows to make River's safety a priority over mine. It's not an immediate fix for my broken trust, but it's a soothing ointment that has us on the mend. I still feel conflicted about being left in the dark about the phone call and sympathizing with why everyone did it. Ryland was right when he said I would've put up a fight about the decision to call their friend's mother. I've been solely focused on the well-being of my cousin and me for so long that it's now integrated into every fiber of my being.

I've held tight to controlling what already feels like an unmanageable circumstance, and I'm not dealing well with being left in the dark. Even in the most dangerous of conflicts, I've not felt this hopeless since that day in the greenhouse when River told me she wanted us to leave with the guys. The phone call was our chance at simplifying an overly complicated plan to get to Oscuros and cross the intercontinental security checkpoint. Now, I'm left with nothing to help ensure we return to our family.

I may feel betrayed by Ryland, but I can never doubt

his ability to look after those he cares about. He's a loyal friend, and his dedication to them speaks volumes about his character. He doesn't say something unless he plans on delivering, and in this case, he's pledged to protect River. His oath has lessened my worry a fraction. It's the best I can ask for now.

Groaning followed by the swift movement of feet yanks me from my thoughts. I leap up, threading my arms through the jacket Ryland placed around me and freeing my gun from the back of my pants. Ryland steps in front of me, but I place my arm out, holding him at my side. There's no better time than now for him to start practicing self-restraint when it comes to defending me.

The movement comes from the pine trees lining the outer bank of the lake. The quiet surroundings make it difficult to figure whether we're facing one Z or a horde. Every step echoes like it is a thousand. I carefully listen while scanning the area. The rustling of leaves from above and the popping of the expanding ice on the water has me on edge. My heart hammers in my chest, and my skin raises in goosebumps.

"We don't know how many of them there are, so we can't risk running through the woods," I say. "If we stay here, we have a clear view of what is coming for us."

"No matter what, we stay together," Ryland replies.

I spare him a quick glance. "Keep the macho shit to a minimum, Ryland. You have a promise to fulfill."

He shoots me a glare—a mixture of amusement and annoyance. I meet it with a cocked eyebrow.

Three Zs break through the line of trees and barrel at us. Their bodies are worn down from going without fresh food and feasting on each other. Tattered clothes hang from their deformed frames, and chunks of flesh have been ripped from their bodies, healing into angry red and purple scars. One's arm swings wildly at its side as it sprints, but it does little to hinder the Z's pursuit.

Standing side by side, we open fire. It's not easy hitting three moving targets zigzagging down the rocky shore. They stumble, but quickly recover, bobbing up and down as they go. When I get one in my line of sight, it manages to duck out of the way, wailing as a poorly aimed bullet collides with a nonlethal part of its body. The closer they get, the tighter my grip becomes on my gun. My palms sweat, making the metal slippery in my hold.

Ryland is the first to make a kill, blowing a hole into a Z's heart. It tumbles to the ground and the others only seem to cast it a quick look like they are logging it to memory as an easy meal after they're done with us.

I take the stance my uncle taught me and concentrate on hitting a precise mark. Looking down the barrel of my gun, I aim at a Z's head. The first bullet grazes the side of its face, ripping away the pasty flesh on its cheek. I quickly recover and release another shot this time to its forehead. It falls to the ground, nothing more than a lifeless sack of skin and bones. I turn my attention to the remaining Z and shower it with bullets along with Ryland. It's within arm's reach when the death blow is given, and it crashes at our feet.

With the last Z dead, I slide behind Ryland, pressing my back against his and survey the bank of the lake. I work to steady my breathing, each large gulp of chilled air burning my lungs. Using the seconds of silence to let the pain subside, I listen for any sign that we're still being hunted.

"It's now or never, love," he says, and I nod.

We're going to have to run through the thick forest which will provide us with little to no visibility. The Zs will hold the advantage with their pinpoint hearing and impeccable sense of smell. Thankfully, I've always been on the winning side, and today will be no different.

"Are you going to actually let me lead the way?" I ask.

Ryland smiles over his shoulder. "I'm working on suppressing my chauvinistic habits, aren't I?"

Rolling my eyes, I say, "Stay close and watch your footing."

I run into the snow-covered foliage with Ryland on my heels, mimicking each of my movements. I bound over obstacles and keep focused on my surroundings, anticipating an attack before it happens. As I bolt through the woods, my neck whips back and forth, scanning for movement in the shrubs. Every muscle in my body is tightly wound and ready to change course at a second's notice.

The immediate loss of warmth at my back is followed by the horrifying sound of animalistic grunts and the wrestling of bodies. I turn to check on Ryland and find he's no longer behind me but lying on the ground with a Z on top of him. A female sits straddling his hips. Her brunette hair is matted with pine needles, and the checkered blouse she wears is missing buttons, exposing her bra. Ryland presses his gloved hand to her face, fighting to keep her unnaturally long, sharp teeth away from his flesh. She's like a rabid animal, but instead of foaming at the mouth, long strings of green mucus-filled saliva stream from her lips. She calls out in a shriek, struggling to get her teeth into him while her long claw-like nails hold him in place.

Ryland's loaded gun lays in the snow outside of his reach, so he throws sharp punches to the side of her head.

Each hit does little to discourage her. There's no fear in his eyes, just pure determination to win even if the odds are highly stacked against him.

I leap into the scuffle and grab a fistful of her hair, yanking her face away from him. She turns to the side and snaps her teeth centimeters from my hand. I curl my fingers into a fist and drive it into her temple.

"I'm. Not. Your. Snack," I emphasize each word with a punch to the head.

She shoves me to the ground, and her disgustingly long fingernails pierce my shoulders, holding me under her. I buck up and down to shake her off, but she won't budge. She closes in with her teeth poised to sink into the middle of my face. Rancid smelling saliva strings across my cheek and her hot breath saturates my airway. I'm on the verge of vomiting as I await the sting of her bite.

A shadow moves over us, and I raise my eyes to meet Ryland's cold stare. He aims his gun at the side of her head and fires. The sound of the single gunshot ricochets through the trees, and the decaying body on top of me is kicked away before it can pin me down.

Between heavy breaths, Ryland says, "I hate Zs."

With the back of my sleeve, I wipe the spit and blood from my face and look up at him with a smirk. "So much for not pulling any macho bullshit."

"I think it is more like survival bullshit," he says, holding his hand out to me and pulling me to my feet.

A bit wobbly on my legs, I brace myself against his chest as I regain my wits. His arm wraps around my waist, holding me to him as he says, "Also, saving you is what I do best."

The lopsided grin that his lips form is amazingly sexy. If it was any other day, I would have caved. There's no argument that we're good together, not only as a Z-fighting team, but as *more*. But it's not any other day, and we can't be *more*. No amount of racing heartbeats and butterflies in my stomach will change that. It doesn't matter how my lips ache to feel his or that my entire body tingles pressed against his chest. I can't be any more important to him than I already am.

I'll save his life a hundred times over and never think twice about it. My world would become an unbearable place without him in it. No Z, no human, not one damn thing will keep me from fighting for him, but I'll never be able to admit it out loud until my first mission to my family is complete. I can't afford to cloud our emotions further. We must stay focused on saving the others.

Letting go of him, I step out of his embrace. "We need to get out of here."

A flash of hurt darkens his eyes as he recognizes my dismissal for what it is—a resounding call for distance.

Without another word, he follows me out of the trees.

We approach the house where Aiden, Noah, and River are lined up on the patio while Wes has taken guard on the second-floor balcony.

"How many were there?" Aiden asks.

"Four. Did you see any?" Ryland replies.

Noah searches the landscape. "No, we heard your gunshots."

"We'll have to patrol tonight. It's too dangerous to pick up the dead and burn them," Ryland says.

"Don't worry, I've got the first shift. I'm ready to kick some Z ass," Aiden says, clapping his hands together.

Ryland sighs and we share a glance. At least one of us is looking forward to guard duty.

Later that night, I sit in the high-back chair in my

aunt and uncle's room. With my gun at my side, I keep guard over the land around my home. The house is pitch-black and hauntingly quiet except for the steps Noah takes as he wanders through on foot-patrol. So far, we've had an uneventful evening. The four Zs are turning out to be nothing more than a fluke. But we're better off safe than sorry.

I take advantage of the time alone to calm my mind. For hours, I've been immersed in thoughts of River and the guys' betrayal. I don't want to waste my time being upset with River, and the friendships I've built with the four men meant something to me when I woke up this morning. I can't just throw it away. These five people have been the reason for every burst of laughter and happy moment I've had since the Affliction. They can't be discarded, and I can't pretend they no longer hold value.

I shift in my chair and sigh, running my hands over my face. I'm in major need of a mental reprieve. I wish the logical part of my brain would malfunction and flip to white noise. I could go for a peaceful hum while I stare blankly at a wall.

"Can I talk to you for a second?"

I turn to the doorway to find Noah waiting for permission to enter the room. His clothes and hair are rumpled, and he appears uncertain of himself. Like everyone else, his interactions with me this evening have been numbered. I've not exactly held out an olive branch with an offering to make amends. I need tonight to come to terms with things, to sleep on it and start anew in the morning. Noah apparently has other plans.

"What's up?" I ask, returning to looking out the windows.

He walks into the room and stops by my side. There's worry written on his face; the likes of which I've not seen since I first found him and Wes huddled around Aiden in the study. He takes a couple of deep breaths and says, "I want to apologize for today. It was wrong of us not to let you know what was going on."

I cross my arms and ankles, leaning back in the chair. "You guys did what you had to do." I'm not going to let myself get worked up about this again. What's done is done.

"It doesn't make it right."

"No, it doesn't," I agree.

He slides his gun into the back of his pants and stuffs his hands into his pockets. "I know you felt like the call was your only chance of getting you and River to safety, but it's not. I won't leave her, Quinn."

I'm sure he believes what he's telling me with every fiber of his being, but the realist in me rears its ugly head. "You say that now, but what happens when we get to Oscuros, and you get to pass, and she doesn't? Are you really going to sacrifice a chance to go home to your family for her?"

He squares his shoulders and closes his eyes for a moment. "I understand everyone is skeptical of my affections for her. One month doesn't seem long, but it has been enough time for me to know I love her. I resent every second I'm asleep; they're priceless intervals of time I could spend learning more about who she is. Every word she says I cling to, and each of her touches are filed away as cherished memories." He drops his head and looks at his shoes. "It sounds wild and obsessive, and maybe it is, but I want her to devour every single nanosecond of my time."

He glances up at me, and I find myself smiling back. This is the type of man who deserves the love of my cousin. It's not about his beautifully spoken words. His whole being radiates with his adoration for her. There's nothing for me to question. He wears his love for River like a second skin.

His posture straightens as he says, "It's not just her, I care about you too, Quinn. You're her family and best friend. I won't leave you alone to watch after her."

I shake my head. "I'm freaking out about leaving. I wish there was a sure way to get at least her across the border. If I had that, then I could handle the rest."

"Hopefully, telling the border guard we're married will work."

I lean forward in my chair and rest my chin on my hands. "I think we need something more substantial. If it were as easy as saying you're married, more people would've made it out of here."

He looks at the ceiling like it holds the answer. "We could break into a government building before we leave and forge marriage licenses."

His last statement resonates with me and sparks an idea. I fan it and allow it to grow and gain momentum. I test it against one opposition after another until I'm sure it's almost foolproof. With the details worked out, I ask, "How sorry are you for what went down today?"

He slowly says, "I'm really sorry."

I grin knowing I've roped Noah into helping me execute the next best thing to a guarantee. "Well, if you really want to make it up to me, I have an idea."

Chapter Nineteen

I pull my legs to my chest, wrapping my arms around them and resting my chin on top. Looking out at Devil's Lake, I try engraving into my mind every single detail. Ever since the decision was made to leave, I've spent at least an hour a day watching as the ice melts away from the water's surface. Now that winter has finally given away to spring, the lake is filled with fresh, cold water. The breeze makes tiny waves that catch the sun's rays, reflecting them off the surface like millions of sparkling diamonds. I curl my bare toes in the heated sand and savor the grittiness against my skin. This little piece of heaven in the midst of hell has been my refuge for my entire life, and tomorrow morning, I'll wish it farewell.

"I know you're worried," says a gentle voice from beside me.

The sound of it is as familiar as this shoreline. In fact, I've known both for as long as I can remember. I take in the sight of my cousin sitting next to me. Her posture matches mine with her long tawny legs pulled to her chest.

Tight, spiral curls have escaped the bun on the top of her head and frame her heart-shaped face. A mirror image of my light gray eyes stares back at me as we give each other half-hearted smiles.

With a lazy shrug, I say, "A little worried, but we always manage."

It's a lie. I'm more than a little concerned but confessing to it will do nothing to alleviate the feeling. We're going to leave behind the safety and certainty that our home offers in exchange for a shot in the dark chance to cross the border. Every careful choice we've made, every battle we've survived has led us to the ultimate suicide mission.

She scoots closer to me. "If it's any consolation, it's good we aren't going to be alone."

"I know," I say, as I rest my head on her shoulder. "If I keep telling myself it's okay, I might start to believe it."

She places her head on top of mine. "I'm sorry for the way I went about things. I never should have kept the purpose of the call from you. It was selfish to let my fear of hearing *no* get the better of me."

River has apologized countless times since the day of the call, and I've forgiven her every time. I understand that she felt it was the right thing to do... and that love sometimes makes people do stupid things.

"I forgive you," I say.

"We're going to be all right, Quinn. We're going to do this together."

Not wanting to argue, I let my disagreement flow out of me with a sigh. We've agreed on the decision to leave, and the only thing left to do is be prepared for what lies ahead.

Footsteps approach and we reach for our guns, scrambling to our feet.

"It's only me," Noah says, walking out of the woods.

The tension eases, and River and I sink back to the sand. Noah sits on the other side of her, sandwiching her between us. From the corner of my eye, I watch as her hand intertwines with his like magnets drawn together.

I feel a tinge of jealousy at their connection. They're so in tune with one another that they move like a finely choreographed dance. Their parts have been practiced over and over again until it has become as natural as breathing. River knows all his little idiosyncrasies, and Noah has learned the telltale signs of her body language. They have only known each other for a little less than three months, but it could easily be mistaken for a lifetime.

Breaking the silence, River asks, "Were you able to use my dad's old map program to print some more detailed city maps?"

I briefly lock eyes with Noah as he says, "Everything is ready to go."

"Are the others done bringing the supplies from the bunker?" I ask.

"Yeah, they're ready to load the truck whenever you are."

I stand, brush the sand off my clothes. For a final time, I look out over the lake which has been a staple place in my life. Maybe someday I will find myself on its shores again. But for now, it's time to say goodbye.

The normally empty living room has a pile of boxes stacked in the center. They contain everything needed for our trek from Devil's Lake to Caprielle—the city just beyond the Oscuros border. We expect the fifteen-hundred-mile journey to be grueling, but we're working to minimize as many foreseeable problems as we can. I sidestep the supplies and enter the study to join Aiden,

Wes, and Ryland. The three men stand around the desk shuffling through printed maps. They raise their heads, and each gives me a quick greeting as I squeeze into the circle.

"I wish there was another way to do this. Passing through four major cities doesn't sit well with me," Wes says. His black hair has grown shaggy over the last couple of months, and his bangs hang over his blue eyes as he looks down at a map. He traces our route with his fingertip while I study the tattoos on his arms.

It wasn't long ago that I realized he was hiding the ink under the sleeves of his always-present hoodie. Most of the markings are a collection of random drawings that work together to suit him perfectly. But one tattoo on his outer forearm stands out from the rest—the compass that looks just like the one on Ryland's arm. Each of the boys have the symbol somewhere on their body as a representation of the adventures they shared.

With a grunt, Aiden stands straight and crosses his arms over his chest. All of the boys have gained some weight and muscle since they first arrived, but it's the most noticeable on him. His light skin no longer holds a gray undertone and the blue of his eyes sparkle. He pulls on the short strands of blond hair next to his ear while he thinks out loud. "If we try to bypass the bigger cities, we'll just be adding time. At this point, the best we can hope for is to make it through Hudson with the SUV and walk two hundred miles on foot. If we're lucky, we can make it to Caprielle in a week and a half."

Ryland rubs his jaw. "Aiden's right, hopefully, we can make it through the major cities with a vehicle." He looks at me and asks, "Do you have any thoughts on this?"

"I don't like the idea of traveling through so many big cities either, but the longer we're on foot, the more likely we are to encounter Zs. We really don't have a better option."

Ten weeks and two days—that's how long it's been since the night I first laid eyes on Ryland Shaw, and everything has changed. Well, almost everything. Two have remained the same. He's still painfully handsome. So much so, that on a daily basis, I catch myself staring at him. The second thing that hasn't changed is that I'm always working to fortify the wall I've built between us. It's nearly impossible. I literally have to lecture myself on all the reasons to rein in my hormones when I'm around him. I counter the heart-melting effect of his lopsided smile with thoughts of his pigheadedness and rationalize our rare intimate discussions with the memory of how he misled me. I remind myself that his overall goal has little to do with me and everything to do with him and his friends. Daydreams about being wrapped in his arms are canceled out with nightmares about the moment he walks across the borderline and doesn't look back. Every second in his presence is a struggle to maintain my distance.

Ryland closes the atlas and stacks the printed maps on top. "We can stand here and stare at these all night, but it's not going to change what the best route is."

Aiden and Wes both agree.

"Are you guys ready to swap out the vehicles?" I ask.

Wes jingles the keys to the truck. "Yeah. I'm going to miss cramming into the back seat of the old girl."

I smile at his fondness for the vehicle that has served us well. "I'll let you drive it back to the workshop, and we'll meet you there."

Wes practically skips out of the room and to the side door leading out to the garage. The rest of us head to the far back corner of the property where Josh's workshop sits. Like the bunker, it's protected by a security scanner, and I use my fingerprint to unlock the door. Thankfully, all of its solar panels didn't short circuit when the phone call went dead. I flip the switch on the wall and light up the inside of the metal structure. A newer model SUV sits in its massive glory in the middle of the room. This was Josh's baby. He had already equipped it with a state-of-the-art electrical system able to power the engine using electricity and minimal gasoline as the backup energy source. Noah worked day and night attempting to create a mobile charging station, and it's almost perfect... almost. The SUV will be fully charged when we leave in the morning. The electrical charge will last for the first four hundred miles of our journey. After that, the fuel system will kick in for the next six hundred. During this time, the solar panels Noah rigged to the top of the vehicle will recharge the battery and hopefully supply us with another couple hundred miles. After the final cycle, the SUV will no longer function, leaving us to walk the rest of the way.

Once we return to the house, the boys load the SUV. I go to the bunker to secure other priceless items like photo albums and jewelry that have been passed down through generations. Hopefully, at the very worst, the shelter will one day be reopened in a more peaceful time, and viewed as a time capsule of the typical family pre-Affliction instead of a haven.

To commemorate our final night in the house, River insists we have an over-the-top dinner. She has thawed out what may be the last remaining roast on the continent. The greenhouse is stripped of all its ripe fruits and vegetables, and the dining room table and chairs are dusted off. We find Amara's antique plates and silverware and set it before each of the six seats. Dozens of candles light the table and surrounding area, setting everything in a buttery glow.

River insists that everyone dresses up for the feast. So, while the roast is cooking, she rummages through several of the boxes in the basement until she finds the one containing a few of our old semi-formal dresses. She kicks the boys out of the bunker and the two of us spend the time getting ready for the evening.

To appease her unrelenting need for a formal dining experience, I sit at the kitchenette table with an array of bobby pins and hair accessories sprawled out before me. She twists and turns my thick hair into an elaborate updo before moving on to my makeup. I try to bat her away several times, but her persistence pays off. She even convinces me to wear a cream-colored dress she says is suitable for the occasion. When I exit the shoe-box-sized bathroom yanking on the hem of it, I come to a stop.

"Is that the dress you bought online and your mom wouldn't let you wear to the end of the year dance?" I ask.

She twirls around, and the puffy, short skirt floats up, showing a hint of the tight lace shorts she's wearing underneath. "It sure is. This dress deserves a night out. Just look at it."

It isn't exactly a dress. The upper portion of the voluminous mini skirt is lined with black lace details and paired with a matching crop top. It leaves a good two inches of the brown skin on her abdomen exposed. Amara usually didn't judge us for our clothing, but this "dress" had crossed the line. The second River modeled it, Amara put her foot down about wearing it in public.

River slips her feet into a pair of black stilettos before directing me to turn around. I spin in a full circle and find her scowling when we're face to face again.

"I look stupid." I march back to the bathroom.

"Stop!"

I peer at her over my shoulder.

"You do realize the back of the dress is see-through? I can see your bra."

I crane my neck to look behind me. "You want me to not wear a bra?"

"You look smoking hot, but your bra is out of place."

"Oh, for Christ's sake." I stomp back into the bathroom to remove the garment in question.

I come back out to find her holding a pair of strappy, silver heels in one hand and a matching bracelet in the other. I take the items from her and put them on.

"Pick up a dish to carry upstairs, but don't grab anything that will spill on the dress. We'll send the boys to get the rest," she says, placing a lid on the bowl of mashed potatoes.

River's desire to orchestrate the perfect dinner is out of control, but I get it. When we leave the house, our lives will become completely practical. All the tiny luxuries we still have will be a thing of the past. But we still have tonight, and we are going to make the most of it.

As I walk through the ground level of the house, hushed male voices drift through the air. The soft glow of candlelight dances at the entryway of the dining room to the gentle sound of acoustic music. Baritone laughter rings out in the mellow atmosphere and greets me as I enter, but it quickly comes to a standstill. I place the dish in my hands down and slowly lift my gaze to find four sets of eyes focusing on me.

With a playful grin, Aiden says, "I should've pushed harder for a date. You look absolutely incredible."

My face heats up, and I duck my head while situating the dish in the middle of the table. When the wave of embarrassment fades, I slide into my chair and casually take in each of the boys. River offered them the pick of Josh's dress-shirts and suits, and they used the pieces to create their semi-formal ensembles.

Aiden and Noah both chose white button-up shirts, but Noah opted to pair his with a black tie, perfectly knotted at the base of his neck. Aiden wears a dark-blue blazer. The most casual of the four men is Wes. He couldn't give up his black jeans with a hole in the knee, and he accessorized the dress shirt with his black hoodie. Finally, I take in the sight of Ryland. He is in all black. The sleeves of his button-up shirt are rolled below his elbows, leaving his tattooed forearms exposed. His soft chestnut waves frame his face, and his green eyes look two shades lighter than usual. As always, the man is breathtaking.

"Gentlemen," River says in a singsong voice entering the room.

All attention shifts from me to her. I smile to myself, watching their jaws hit the floor. I'm pretty sure this is the reaction she was hoping for. Noah scrambles from his chair and takes the dish she brought from her. He places it on the table before holding her hand and guiding her in a spin. With a devouring look in his eyes, he pulls her into his arms and tips her back for a dramatic kiss.

I look away from their public display of affection to find that I'm wrong. She hasn't captured the attention of everyone in the room. Ryland leans back in his chair with his hands in his pockets, and his eyes glued onto me. Never have I been the girl who has gone out of her way to draw a guy's attention, but he makes me want to test those uncharted waters. I lick my lips and fuss with my table setting, trying to pretend I don't notice him. He shifts in his seat and runs his fingers through his hair. With a bit of courage, I look at him through my eyelashes and bat them.

In reply, his jaw clenches and one side of his mouth lifts into a smirk.

"Ry." River's raised voice breaks the spell between us. "If you want to eat, you better go help your friends bring up the rest of the food."

With a sweeping look, I discover we're the only three remaining in the room.

Ryland stands and answers, "Of course."

When he's gone, River turns to me with huge curious eyes. "What was that?"

"What?"

"You were flirting with him, batting your eyes, and licking your lips. Oh my god, Quinn, I've never seen you do that!"

"He was staring," I say, like it explains it all.

"Damn right he was staring. You look amazing," she says, just as the boys return.

The food is delicious, and the red wine helps to aid the lively conversation. Everyone takes turns telling stories about our lives before the Affliction. It becomes a game where we try to embarrass each other with recounts of our most unbecoming moments. We laugh, enthralled by the stories, and giving little mind to the war raging on around us.

I have to hand it to River; the dinner party was a great idea. For a fraction of time, we're six normal young adults sipping on wine and dropping sexual innuendos. We're self-absorbed and careless. It's a refreshing feeling. I get to experience what it could have been like if the Z virus never existed. I would've gone to college and spent weekend nights with a group of newly made friends. We'd get drunk and not give a damn about anything but the moment. My life would have solely revolved around me.

After dinner, we work in a tipsy haze to clean up the

mess in the dining room. When the dishes are packed away, everyone retreats to the study with the last bottle of wine to take advantage of our final night of freedom. I sneak away to the bunker to grab some clothes to sleep in. There's a good chance that with low inhibitions, this could be the night Noah and River try to take their relationship to the next level. I really don't want to be in the bunker when it happens. Besides, nothing in the world sounds as good as sleeping in my own room one last time.

As I head up the stairs, the bathroom door opens. I stop dead in my tracks as Ryland walks out. He has on nothing but a light gray pair of sweatpants sitting low on his hips and a towel to dry his soaked hair. Seeing him like this brings back memories of the first time I witnessed him shirtless in the bunker. I couldn't keep my eyes off of him then either.

He pauses as he catches sight of me. The short dress with its sheer back feels like it's leaving me completely exposed. The skin of my bare legs rises into thousands of tiny goosebumps, and I silently curse myself for not changing into my pajamas before leaving the bunker.

"I—I didn't know you were up here," I say.

"I needed a shower," he replies, balling the towel in his hands.

I wonder if his shower was cold and if I had anything to do with it. I pucker my lips to the side and scold myself for having such a thought. Ever since the call to Dylan's mother, I've been able to hold on to my feelings of mistrust, allowing them to be the foundation of the wall I've created to keep him out. We're more than civil to one another, but our budding friendship was stunted that day. The only bond we seem to share anymore is forged by our desire to save our friends and hatred for Zs. We're still an unstoppable duo when kicking Z ass, but as soon as the battle is over, the wall is erected again. I've been content to stand on opposite sides of an emotional void.

"What are you doing?" he asks, pointing at the clothes in my hands.

"I'm going to sleep up here. Something tells me Noah and River will need privacy tonight."

He raises an eyebrow. "You might be right about that."

"Yeah," I say, turning to my room.

"Quinn," he calls before I shut my door. "Can I talk to you for a moment... in private?"

I take in his state of undress and swallow the lump in my throat. My thighs clench as forbidden thoughts dance through my head. I don't think I can concentrate with the hourglass inked on his sternum on full display or the sight of his naked arms or his wet hair. Fuck, I'm in so much trouble.

I open my door for him. "Sure, come in."

He hangs his wet towel on the stair's banister and enters my room. I shut the door and move past him to the window. I need something to keep me distracted from looking at him. My traitorous brain is already imagining the way the shadows will highlight the lean muscles of his chest and arms. His skin will be welcoming, looking so smooth that the tips of my fingers will tingle with the need to touch him. I force the thoughts from my head and focus on the treetops off in the distance.

"Are we ever going to move on from what happened, or are you going to keep pushing me away?" The graininess of his voice is proof of his hurt and regret.

I shake my head. "We are moving on, and why should I let you get close when we're on borrowed time? In a week and a half, we'll part ways. I want to make it an easy separation."

I close my eyes and will myself to stand firmly in place as the soft steps of his bare feet move toward me. If I back down, he'll sense my weakness, and I won't have the chance to keep my upper hand on him. He stops short of touching me, but the heat radiating from his skin sends a shiver down my spine, and the fresh scent of soap from his clean body invades my senses, fracturing my resolve.

"I've done everything you've asked me to do. I've made the promises you asked me to make, and I've respected the boundaries between us, but for what?" he quietly asks.

"So we can both walk away from this whole."

"What if the only time I feel whole is when you're with me?" I gasp as the tip of his finger glides over the row of buttons on the back of my dress. Between each clasp, the fabric parts, allowing him to touch the skin down my spine. His voice is a soft hum as he says, "What if the moment you leave is the second I fall apart?"

My head spins, and I tell myself it's from the wine and not his touch and words. "You won't."

"Tell me you believe you won't fall apart without me," he whispers, his lips brushing the shell of my ear.

I vigorously shake my head. "I won't."

"You're lying." He presses his lips to the curve of my shoulder, making my skin prickle with goosebumps. My breath leaves me when his fingers move into my hair. The tiny ping of my hairpins hitting the floor resound throughout the room as he continues to speak. "Throughout the day, you try to casually glance my way in hopes it will be enough to curb your curiosity. You pray it will hold you over until tomorrow when it's safe to steal another look. When we're alone in a room, you say a quiet prayer that I'll be the first to break and to pull you into my arms. And for the first time in God knows how long, you brave the nightmares that sleep brings for the off chance that you'll dream about me."

His words have me at a loss. I never expected him to have the slightest inkling about my feelings for him. He has me totally pegged from my unspoken wish for him to hold me to the dreams of a safe alternate universe where we can be together. He brushes my hair from the nape of my neck and replaces it with his lips.

I struggle to keep my bearings and ask, "How do you know that?"

His smiles against my skin before he lifts his head, and I immediately miss the warmth of his breath. Thankfully, the feeling is short-lived. He turns me to face him, laces his fingers through my hair, and moves so close our mouths are separated by a mere sliver of space. "Because it's how I feel about you."

His lips are soft as they move against mine, and I close my eyes and savor our first kiss. For months, I've wanted to have my body pressed into his and his arms holding me close. I've wondered if his kisses are as perfect as the shape of his pink lips. Now I have my answer.

His kiss is deliciously slow, lingering like he's cherishing the feeling. I'm lost in the heady taste of him, mixed with a hint of red wine. Combing my fingers through his hair, I pull him closer, silently begging him to deepen the sweet kiss as electricity charges every cell of my body with euphoric bliss. I don't know how I'm supposed to go the rest of my life without ever feeling this again, but that's what is destined to happen.

I'm cruelly brought back to reality, and slowly separate my mouth from his. Resting my forehead on his chest, I catch my breath. I'll live the rest of my life without his kisses. No matter how this all plays out, his future is inevitable. He will return to Giran. The chances of those holding another continent's passport crossing the border are a hundred times better than those who do not. The truth is that we'll go our separate ways, and I'll know what it's like to fall apart without him.

"Quinn?" The worry in his voice rips me apart. Ever since I saw him sitting defeated under the tree in the forest surrounded by Zs, I've wanted to protect him, even though I feared to care for another person. I've fought to stay my course, but he has conquered my defenses and claimed his stake. He's stolen a piece of my heart.

"Please don't make this harder than it already is," I beg.

He brushes down my hair and kisses the top of my head. "I'm trying to save us, love."

Us, but there is no us. At least, there's no us beyond the here and now.

He pulls away and guides me to sit on the edge of the bed. Kneeling before me, he removes my shoes as I quietly watch. He wraps the blanket from my bed around his shoulders before climbing onto the mattress and holding his arms open. I can't stop myself. I curl up next to him, resting my head on his chest. I swear, only this once will I forfeit my resolve and allow him to win.

With hooded eyes, I listen to his deep voice vibrating through his chest as he says, "At least for tonight, let me hold you. You are the only thing that can save me from my nightmares, Quinn."

Chapter Twenty

Six hours in a vehicle with five other people feels like being trapped in a small moving crate with windows after a while. The air is thick and humid, and every tiny brush made against my skin is irritating. No matter how quiet people try to keep their conversations, they're amplified in the confined space. Thank goodness we're in an SUV and not a compact car, or I would have murdered someone by now.

My lack of sleep is likely the main contributor to my irritability. Sleeping while Ryland was wrapped around me proved to be difficult. I was fascinated with everything about him, the deep exhale and inhale of his breathing, and how he mumbled incoherent words that I tried to decode. As the sun rose, I took advantage of the first rays of light to study his face. Damp curls clung to his neck, and his lips parted slightly, releasing soft breaths. I couldn't pass up the opportunity to marvel at him.

Aiden's head falls on my shoulder for the umpteenth time. Unlike me, he has no problem falling asleep. Twenty Zs could be chasing us down the road, and he'd be out until someone shook him awake. I place my hand on the top of his head ready to push him away but change my mind. It's useless. I slouch down on the bench seat we share and sigh in frustration.

Ryland looks through the rearview mirror, his eyes crinkle on the sides as he gives a lopsided grin. "Push him onto his side."

"I have," I reply flatly.

"Kick him onto the floor. That's what I would do." Wes chimes in from the passenger seat.

"Don't do that. I'm comfortable," Aiden mumbles, wrapping his arm around my waist.

"Seriously, your body is like a heating pad. You need to move to your side."

He lifts his bright eyes to me and smiles. "Let's just cuddle this out for a bit."

I shake my head at his ridiculousness, but don't bother pushing him away. The man doesn't seem to compute personal space. To be honest, I don't really mind. It's good to know that at least my friend is getting some much-needed sleep.

The sound of shuffling comes from behind me, and I look over my shoulder to see what's going on in the backseat. River is lying on top of Noah with their legs tangled together. Both are out cold.

I haven't gotten all the details from her, but according to Wes and Aiden, the bunker was locked last night, and neither of them could get in. I'm assuming River and Noah took their relationship to the next level. I'm happy for them. They have found each other and show no fear for what their future will bring.

The most obnoxious siren blares in the distance. I ignore it and find comfort in my awkward position. My face is pressed against the window, and Aiden is pinning down the lower half of my body. Both of his arms circle my waist while his hot sweaty head rests on my hip. I'm not sure how long it's been since I dozed off, but I'm not ready to wake up yet. I clench my eyes shut, but it doesn't block out the wailing coming from outside.

A female voice echoes through a loudspeaker saying, "Pull over and put your hands up, or we'll open fire."

"Shit!" Ryland punches the steering wheel, and the SUV comes to a slow stop on the side of the road.

With his hands held high, Wes gazes out the window. He shakes his head, and I swivel around to get a look at what he sees. A police cruiser has pulled up behind us with blue lights flashing on its roof. Three uniformed women exit the vehicle with weapons drawn. They're decked out in all black with combat boots and aviator sunglasses. A woman with a silky onyx ponytail and an exceptionally tall blonde with spiky hair walk toward us. The third member of their group, a petite woman with cropped dark hair, kneels by their car with a terrifying weapon.

"Does she have a rocket launcher pointed at us?" I ask.

"What do you think the penalty is for speeding during a zombie apocalypse?" Wes says with a chuckle.

"Shut up," Ryland snaps.

Wes doesn't let Ryland get to him and continues joking. "Flash them those dimples and pour the charm on thick. Hopefully, you can wiggle your way out of this without getting us blown up."

Ryland grunts in reply.

A tapping comes from the window right behind me, followed by the woman with a ponytail barking, "Everyone sit up."

I glance at the back seat to find Noah and River rubbing their eyes and looking around in confusion.

"Where are you boys headed?" the blonde asks Ryland.

"Just passing through."

She slams her hand against our vehicle. "Don't play cute with me. Are you with the Raid?" She doesn't even give Ryland a chance to answer the question before she pulls the door open. "I need you to step out of the vehicle and keep your hands where I can see them." She turns to her partner and instructs, "Get the rest of the men out and have them line up against the car."

The woman with black hair opens Wes's door and pulls him out, demanding Aiden and Noah do the same. The boys stumble over each other, rushing to exit, and I watch through the side view mirror as Ryland is led back to the police car. The blonde forces him to lean over the hood and frisks him.

"Where did you find the girls?" she asks.

Ryland shoots her a glare over his shoulder. "What do you mean where did we find them?"

River leans forward in her seat. "I don't think these cops like the boys very much."

I press my finger to my mouth. "*Shh.*"

The blonde looks at Ryland with disgust. "Did Blaze send you out to find them? Is the Raid becoming so desperate that your leader has you plucking helpless girls from their homes?"

"They're hardly helpless," Ryland counters.

She grabs the back of his neck and presses his face to the hood of the car. "Don't fuck with me. They're women, human beings, who deserve your respect. They're not your toys to do with as you want. They're not slaves to bow to your every disgusting desire. You pigs make me sick."

The SUV shakes as the other woman throws Noah against the side. He looks at River through the window with excruciating pain written on his face.

"You Raider boys like to pin women down and take what you want from them. Let's see how you like it," the officer spits as she presses her gun to Noah's head.

River climbs over the seat to get out. "I think she's planning to murder my boyfriend."

I check that my gun is secured to my lower back and tug my shirt over it. "I got this," I say, throwing open the door and getting out on the opposite side from where Noah, Aiden, and Wes are detained. I don't need to look back to know River has followed me. She's a pissed off girlfriend, and hell hath no fury like a woman whose man is being held at gunpoint.

"Let him go," I order the blonde who is handcuffing Ryland.

"You don't have to be scared. We're here to help you," the woman crouched next to the cruiser with the military-grade weapon says.

I pull the gun from my back and point it at the blonde. "I said, let him go."

She tilts her head but makes no move to release Ryland.

I could try to advocate on the boys' behalf and tell her she has them pegged all wrong, but I fear she might think I'm a victim who has become dependent on my captors. She needs to view me as confident and in control of things like her.

"I won't ask you again to unhand my man." I fight to keep a straight face and not cringe, but Ryland looks up with a smirk on his face.

"They didn't kidnap you to take you back to the Raiders?" the blonde asks.

"The who?"

"A gang of disgusting chauvinistic pigs who pillage nearby neighborhoods. They take young girls and force them into sexual slavery," the black-haired woman explains.

"No pillaging and all sex is consensual," Ryland states with a wink at me.

I roll my eyes and amend his statement. "Some of them are still working on the chauvinistic pig part though."

All aggression fades from the blonde's demeanor, and she smiles. "At least he's working on it." She unlocks the handcuffs and releases Ryland before extending her hand to me. "I'm Dex, that's Reese, and Ty with the rocket launcher."

"Quinn." I put away my gun and shake her hand.

"Sorry about that." Reese shrugs with a coy grin. "We're not used to seeing a vehicle full of men who aren't trying to round up women in these parts."

Wes rotates his shoulder. "The Raiders should avoid you at all costs. Your arm-lock is brutal."

Reese beams at his unintentional compliment.

Ty lets the weapon half her size hang from her body as she stands. "Where are y'all heading to?"

"Caprielle," Ryland answers, rubbing the feeling back into his wrists.

"It's going to be dark in fifteen minutes, and you don't want to drive through the east side of Loury once night falls. The Raiders will be out in full force. They'll hijack your truck and..." Dex looks at River and me with deep sadness. "It won't be pretty."

Ty crosses her arms over her chest. "Not to mention

the Afflicted around here are prone to be more active at night. They're like roaches."

Aiden steps forward and says, "We were planning on stopping for the night anyway. Do you have any suggestions?"

Dex hooks her finger over her chin, and her eyes travel across each of us. "You can stay with us, but we do require payment."

"What kind of payment?" Ryland asks.

"We barter," Ty says. "Food, supplies, services—everything holds a value."

We don't have much, but I'm sure we can forgo a couple of items for a safe place to sleep. It beats sleeping in the backseat while a gang of women-stealing men roam the streets. "We have some prescription medications that may help with some common sicknesses," I say.

Dex nods. "We can work with that. Stay close and follow us."

As we turn to file back into the SUV, I notice a bright yellow flyer attached to a light post. I don't have time to read it, but the last couple of words stand out: *The Sanctuary*.

"Quinn," Ryland calls.

"Coming," I say over my shoulder, snatching the paper off the metal pole, sliding it into my pocket, and jogging back to the vehicle.

"You're not going to need that," he says, holding the back door open for me.

I shrug and climb in. "I know, it's just interesting."

We carefully follow the police car, winding through the streets of Loury. As the sun sets, the city looks like a ghost town. The iconic tourist traps I'd seen on television are skeletons of their former glory, with signs hanging haphazardly from the building fronts, and the high-end shops and eateries looted. Two years ago, people would have lined the sidewalks carrying shopping bags, and we would have been bumper-to-bumper in rush hour traffic. What was one of the most populous cities in Stern now appears vacant.

We briefly come to a stop at the entrance of an underground parking garage where a man and woman stand guard. Dex leans out the driver's side window of her car, pointing at us as she talks to them. When she moves again, the man waves us through as well. The structure is mostly empty, and the only light inside comes from the headlights of our vehicles gliding along the walls. Once parked, I reach under my seat and pull out a small flashlight. The six of us collect our backpacks and climb out to meet the women at the back of our vehicle. Shining my light on the side of their police cruiser, the emblem on the door catches my attention. It's not a cop car like I first thought.

"Palace Mall Security," I read out loud.

Reese giggles. "Yeah."

Ty joins in saying, "Everything a girl could ever want or need in one convenient place." She does her best impression of a commercial announcer's voice, "Palace Mall: your shopping destination."

I smile at how ironic it is that these badass girls, fighting for the freedom of other women, are driving a car belonging to a mall—a place where the stereotypical woman is supposed to spend all of her free time and money.

I open the back of the SUV, careful not to hint at the food or weapons we have stored in the boxes. These women have been exceptionally kind to us, but I can't bring myself to fully trust them. I hand River the first aid supplies and leave it to her to choose the medications we can stand to part with.

"I apologize if this sounds rude," Ryland says to Dex, "but will our vehicle be safe here?"

Ty answers, "Our security detail is the best. You have nothing to fear. I give my word that your belongings will be here in the morning."

Reese smiles and wraps her arms around Ty's shoulders. "Ty is our head of security, and her team is unbeatable."

They meet eyes, grin, and Reese winks at Ty. Their faith in one another is all it takes and a sliver of my reservations fade away.

"Follow me," Dex says.

With our weapons drawn, we exit the parking garage and stroll the empty sidewalk to the front of the mall. The building is at least seven stories high, and the exterior of the upper levels is made up of glass walls. The ground level is also constructed of display windows, but they're covered from the inside by sheets of metal. We reach the main entrance—a set of double steel doors—and Dex knocks. A small section slides open and a man on the other side says, "State your name and provide your identification."

"Captain Dex Wells," she says, placing an ID card into the slot.

A fully armed man opens the doors and promptly closes them as soon as we're all inside. The lobby of the mall is dimly lit by candles placed on the top of a round concierge desk, and an elderly man wearing a vintage band t-shirt sits at the counter. His bald head is framed by wispy, white hair, and his eyes are magnified by the thick lenses of his glasses.

"Welcome home, Captain Wells," he says.

Dex's expression softens as she replies, "Thank you, Cal. These are our guests for the evening. Can you please supply them with candles?"

"Of course." He reaches under the desk, pulls out votive candles inside of glass holders, and lights them.

"Please make sure you let them burn in the glass and return it to me, so I can use the melted wax to make more," he instructs.

Now that each of us has a light source, Dex guides us on a tour of her home. "To the right is the hotel which serves as sleeping quarters for our permanent residences. We've been lucky with our resources and have found ways to rig the toilets, but we're still working on the pump for fresh water," she says with pride.

Fear and regret course through me, and my stomach ties into a knot. We had access to all the simple necessities these people are trying to obtain, and we sacrificed them for the unknown. I pray it's worth it in the end.

We continue to the escalators—now regular stairs—and climb to the second level of the mall. My neck cranes back as we step foot onto the next floor. A massive structure made of hundreds of glass plates stands in the middle of the common area. It extends from the center of the floor all the way up to the top of the building. Every level is built around the colossal chandelier while still allowing those on the upper floors to look down.

I pull my attention from the mall's focal point and take in the sound of conversation and laughter. Families are scattered throughout the common area in the middle of the mall. Children run after each other in a fierce game of tag as the adults engage in discussions.

"Children," River says in awe.

Reese smiles. "Yes, children. They too need a place to live."

"It's just that I almost forgot kids could still exist," River says, watching the children race around.

The old storefronts are still just that. The signs above their entrances are creatively put together using the lettering from the old mall signage. It's not as well thought out as a pre-quarantine mall, but charming in its own way.

Continuing up the escalator, Dex explains how each of the seven levels is designed to meet the needs of a particular demographic—families with children, teenagers, intellectuals, artists, social butterflies, and so on. The layout of each level is the same, but the atmosphere is different. When we reach the fifth floor, designed for the arts, there are people gathered around a man singing and playing the guitar. The stores are geared at selling paintbrushes and musical instruments. There's even a marijuana store with an assortment of baked goods and homemade bongs. Even during an apocalypse, there seems to be a market for everything.

The final stop on our tour is the seventh floor, focusing on social activities. Couples walk hand in hand around the common area or sit with their arms around each other on cushioned chairs. A restaurant has been converted into a nightclub equipped with a live band and dancing. As we pass through, a group of college-aged girls giggles, looking over their shoulders at Ryland. I struggle with the need to move closer to him and possessively lock my fingers with his, but I manage to keep my distance.

Of all the stupid feelings I can have, I can't believe I'm jealous. This crazy notion of *if I can't have him, neither can they* has awakened in me. He's not mine, and I can't hardly blame them for staring at him, yet I wish they wouldn't.

"Keep glaring like that, and you might be able to set them on fire," Aiden says in my ear.

I close my eyes and fight against my humiliation. It's not the first time Aiden has guessed my feelings for Ryland. He has a gift for reading people that often has me wanting to smack him for being so damn observant. He places his arm around my shoulder and pulls me to his side. I shove a hand into my pocket and concentrate on my feet as we continue to walk. The folded-up flyer I tore from the light pole tickles my palm, and I shift my jealousy and embarrassment to curiosity.

"Dex, did you say the old bookstore is now your library?" I call to the front of our group.

She slows her pace and waits for Aiden and me to catch up to her. "I did."

"Is it a common area I'm allowed to use?"

"Of course."

"Do you want me to go with you?" Aiden asks. The look on his face says he's trying to be polite but would rather remain in the social atmosphere.

I shake my head. "I'm good. Stay and have fun."

I don't need to tell him twice before he fades into the crowd, leaving me to research the Sanctuary on my own.

Chapter Twenty-One

Other than a couple of small groups deep in discussion, the third floor of the mall is relatively quiet. I walk into the bookstore and am greeted by a middle-aged woman at the counter. Her curly brown hair veils most of her face as she returns her attention to the book in front of her. Not a single soul lingers in the aisles as I study the books on the shelves. Not one of them is a duplicate. My guess is that Dex and her people have salvaged as much as they can from local libraries. With the world in shambles outside of these walls, it's comforting to know they're trying to preserve parts of our old way of life.

I find a quiet corner in a back aisle, remove my backpack, and place the candle I was given onto the floor beside me. Taking the new Sanctuary flyer from my pocket, I unfold it and read:

Future Settler,
The war raged when the waters turned red.
Untouched land was paid for in crimson currency.
Follow the path of the green general.
He knew the quickest way.

The Sanctuary

The riddles the Sanctuary leaves behind are utterly bizarre, and I'm thoroughly intrigued by the challenge. I dig out of my backpack the flyer I found in Blythe and lay it beside the other on the floor. Nothing is named, but there are little clues that can lead to something bigger— mountains surrounded by blue mist and water that turned red. It's not clear but it is a start.

I pick up my candle and head to the aisle labeled *History* and scan the shelves for books on past wars. Perhaps the water turned red after a particularly bloody battle, or maybe I can find something about a general. With several selections in tow, I wander back to my corner and set to work searching for answers. I carefully read through the text about the most brutal war that took place in Stern, taking care to note battle sites and any reference to water contamination. Scouring endless pages when I have such little direction is a daunting task. It's very possible that I'm going to leave here with no clues to help solve the riddles.

I crack open the next book and pause when a soft glow comes from the end of the aisle. Ryland. The flickering flame of his candle dances over his handsome face and reflects in his eyes as he moves closer. With each long stride, his hair sways in amber waves around his neck. I wouldn't be surprised if he sprouted wings and took on a heavenly glow.

He sits beside me and places his light next to mine, looking at the papers on the floor. For a moment, he studies the bright pages and then leans back on the shelf behind us.

"I don't know how I feel about your new hobby," he says, with a cocked eyebrow.

"It's something to do, and a little mental challenge never hurt anyone." I pick up the Sanctuary's riddles and use them as a bookmark. "Why aren't you with the others? You could be living it up right now. There was a group of girls eyeing you like you were the last drop of water in a barren desert."

Ryland bows his head and runs his hand through his hair, hiding his reddening cheeks. It's interesting that Mr. Tall-Dark-and-Handsome doesn't do well with being admired. I wonder if it has always been like this, or if there was a time when he used his looks to his advantage. There's still so much to learn about him, and the thought makes my stomach drop as I accept that I'll never fully get the chance.

"I'm not the least bit interested in any of them," he says, darting me a sideways glance.

I know exactly what he wants. He's hoping I ask why not, so he can say something about me being the only girl he's interested in. He made his feelings for me very well-known last night. I get that he's attracted to me, and I also know his options have been scarcely limited. I'm still young and prone to mistakes, but I'm not naive enough to let him bait and hook me.

"That's too bad. I thought a couple of them were cute," I say, with a shrug and slide a history book in his direction. "Well, if you're going to hang out with me, then you might as well help."

He glares at the thick textbook and back at me. I return his look with raised eyebrows and a hand gesture that urges him to get to work. With a groan, he lays on his stomach and asks, "What am I looking for?"

I follow his lead so we are side by side. "The flyer mentions a green general. I'm thinking maybe this person made history by going to war as a new general."

He nods in understanding, and we both dive into our books. The library is peaceful and empty, with only the occasional turning of a page. The lack of light is hard on my eyes, but it also adds to the ambiance of a boy and a girl hidden in the back corner of a quiet bookstore. I must admit, I'm struggling to concentrate on the words before me. My mind drifts into daydreams about a parallel dimension where Zs don't exist. I imagine Ryland and I cramming for our college history exam. We're just two normal students enjoying the comfortable silence. As we read our feet would *accidentally* touch or we would brush shoulders and lock eyes. Eventually, it would be too hard to not steal a touch and then a kiss. I close my eyes and force my wild imagination to come back to reality.

Not even before the Affliction did I find myself indulging in daydreams the way I do now. Simply being near this man has me always acting out of sorts.

"What are you thinking about?" Ryland asks.

I jerk my head up and struggle to get my mouth to work. "I was—I was just thinking about how normal things now seem fictional and what used to be make-believe is now real. Things like, I don't know, studying together. Did you ever study with a girl for a test before?" I want to slap my head with my palm as soon as the words leave my mouth. Clearly, I have little tact when dealing with a guy I'm attracted to.

Ryland clears his throat and says, "I had a girlfriend when I was in grade school. Her name was Kate, and I'd walk her home every afternoon. We weren't allowed to be alone in her room, so we would sit on the couch and do our homework together."

I cross my arms over my book and rest my chin on top. "Did you ever try to take advantage of your study dates?"

He laughs while turning to his side and propping his head up with his palm. "I was a teenage boy with raging hormones. What do you think?"

I'm torn by his confession. A part of me hates to think about him being intimate with another girl, but then again, I love hearing about what his life used to be like. I find myself wishing I would have known him before the world around us went to shit.

"I think you would intentionally come up with ways to touch her, but you tried to make it look like an accident. I can picture you sitting way too close when she was showing you something in a textbook or playing footsie with her while you pretended to read on the other side of the couch," I say.

His eyes brighten with amusement. "You make my intentions sound more innocent than they were. What about you?"

"Remember, I'm a small-town girl with limited experiences. I've known most of the boys in Devil's Lake since we were kids. I've fooled around a bit, but nothing serious. I never had a study date, or a real date for that matter, but I was okay with that. I was going off to college and would finally experience all the firsts I missed out on."

He scoots closer to me. "Is that what you were actually thinking about, all of the things you never got a chance to do?"

I concentrate on the far end of the aisle, not wanting to see the pity in his eyes when I truthfully answer him. "Yes."

"You know, if I were on a study date with you, it would be different from when I was with Kate."

I give little regard to the warning sirens going off inside my head as a single question breathlessly leaves my lips. "How?"

Mission accomplished, he's baited me—hook, line, and sinker.

He tucks a strand of hair behind my ear, and says, "If I didn't kiss her, it was all right, because there was always tomorrow. I let my uncertainty hold me back from pursuing what I wanted. I no longer have time to waste, and I've learned not to let my insecurities rule me. I'm older and much bolder in pursuing the things I want, Quinn."

Living for the moment is a concept I've not been able to dabble in as an adult. Whether I like it or not, I've been tethered to my guilt and an all-consuming desire to right my wrongs. Every single day, I curse myself for the things I should have done differently. My choices have become heavy burdens that make my heart ache. And I'm slowly adding to my regrets, waiting for when they eventually break me.

I want nothing more than to abandon my cautious mindset. When all is said and done between Ryland and me, I don't want to look back and second-guess a single second. For a moment, I want to play with fire and do the things I know I shouldn't. I want to be a typical nineteen-year-old girl trapped in a bookstore with a hot guy and open to possibilities. I want to relinquish my self-control and be reckless. For a tiny span of time, I want to be like Ryland said—*bold*.

I lift my head from my arms, leveling my eyes with his and close the short distance between us. He stays perfectly still as my lips brush against his. They're warm, soft, and giving as I press into them. If it weren't for the moan he makes, I'd have thought he was turned off by my advance, but he's toying with me. He remains unresponsive, letting me take control and do all the work. I'm dying to feel him kiss me back. Frustration has me pulling his bottom lip between my teeth and gently biting down. He smiles before giving in and deepening our kiss.

This is the kiss I yearned for last night before my nagging conscience brought it all to a crashing halt. His tongue brushes over my lips, sending shivers through my body. Every movement we make is slow and methodical, with an endless exchange of emotion—desire, reverence, contentment, and fear. Yes, there's fear hidden in our kiss. Fear that it will end, fear there won't be a chance to experience it again, and fear we'll have to let each other go. I never thought I could be so terrified by one kiss.

Ryland is the first to pull away. He closes his eyes and places his forehead against mine as we catch our breath.

Since the quarantine, I haven't had many moments I can store away as happy memories, but this kiss, this one perfect kiss, will never be forgotten. I'll come back to it again and again when I need to remember that not everything in this world is horrific. It will be my mental refuge when I feel like reality is caving in on me. It will be the beauty that makes me keep fighting when River is safely returned to our family.

With my heart rate back to normal, I move away from Ryland. "All right, back to the green general," I say, pointing to his book.

With a lopsided grin, he agrees and sets back to reading. I sit beside him and cross my legs, placing my book on top. We work quietly for some time, keeping on task for the most part. Every so often our gazes will meet, and we exchange smiles before turning back to the page in front of us.

Ryland is the first to finish skimming through his

book. He closes it before telling me about a battle in the mountain range along the east coast. A unit of indigenous soldiers was led by a man who was promoted to general only a week before the battle.

I feverishly flip through my book, trying to tie the events with anything to do with red water. My finger slides over the words as I go, but comes to a stop when Ryland's legs appear on either side of mine. His warm body presses against my back, and he sweeps my hair away from my neck, placing it over one shoulder. His arms circle around my waist, and his soft lips travel from the curve of my neck to my ear, sending a tingling sensation creeping up my spine.

With a shaky laugh, I ask, "What are you doing?"

"Reading over your shoulder," he says, pressing his lips to the sensitive area behind my ear.

I purse my lips, hiding a smile. Damn him for being so attentive and attempting to give me a small piece of the life I never had.

Playing along, I go back to reading. He behaves for only a few seconds before his fingertips inch up the hem of my shirt. When he reaches my skin, he makes the smallest back and forth motion with his thumbs over my waist. The butterflies taking flight in my stomach make it impossible to comprehend any of the words on the page.

"Explain how you're researching with your eyes closed," he says, and his palm slides across my abdomen.

I bite my lip and force my eyes open. "I'm trying, but you're making it hard."

"You want me to go away?" He ends his question by kissing the side of my neck.

"No."

I unfold my legs and stretch them in front of me,

placing the book on my thighs and lean back against him. I literally stare at one word, no longer caring about what I should be reading. He works up the side of my neck again and nibbles on my ear as his hands ease their way up my torso.

"I feel bad for distracting you. This might be the only chance you get to figure out the clues," he whispers before he strokes the sensitive area beneath my ear with this tongue.

"Why do you sound anything but apologetic?"

"You're right. I'm not," he says with a low growl.

He nips at my neck, and my hands clamp down on my mouth to muffle a high-pitched squeal. Without warning, he shoves the book off my lap and crawls around my body. He kneels before me and grabs the backs of my knees, knocking me off balance. I fall back on my hands. Bracing himself above me, he leans in and presses his lips into mine. He wastes no time coaxing me into deepening the kiss. His tongue slides past my lips, and I tangle my fingers in his hair. Gripping his neck, I let him guide me back until I'm lying on the floor with his leg between mine.

Our little game of make-believe has been abandoned for something real and passionate. Every logical thought I have is pushed to the back of my mind. I want his body pressed into mine and my hands on him. For one night, I need to forget everything but him.

I gather his shirt and pull it up his torso.

"We're not alone," he reminds me, looking toward the front of the store.

"Just your shirt. I want to feel your skin against mine," I say, kissing his jaw.

Ryland pulls his t-shirt off, exposing the dark tattoos on his chest and arms. I want to take my time and trace each one with the tips of my fingers. I'd give anything to watch his eyes darken as I follow the roses on his hips with my mouth. Instead, I substitute the flowers for the spiraling designs on his collarbones. His head falls back, giving me access to his neck. I work my way down, sucking and biting. Pulling away, he lifts his body from mine, and I instantly miss the weight and warmth of him. But my disappointment has no time to set in as a new sensation takes over.

With his eyes glued to me, he dips his tongue below my navel and nips at the sensitive skin before licking a straight line up. He gathers my shirt until it's bunched above my black bra and kisses the valley between my breasts. My hips lift from the ground, and I muffle a moan into his soft hair. The feel of his hands and mouth on me is unreal, making me hate the restraints of my clothes. I tug my shirt off and practically melt when his skin presses to mine.

"Fuck," he groans, his palms sliding over every naked part of me. When his thumb brushes the underside of my breast, his gaze locks with mine. "Can I touch you here?" he asks.

I swallow past the anticipation and nerves building inside of me and nod.

"I need your words, Quinn. Do I have permission to put my hands and mouth on these hard, pretty nipples?"

Oh. My. God. Ryland has never been one to sugar coat his words. He says exactly what he is thinking with no remorse. It appears that he doesn't hold back when it comes to sex either. His voice alone has my body responding but add the dirty words and I'm a goner.

"Yes, Ryland. Please."

"That's my girl."

He holds my stare with his as he lowers the cup of

my bra. The chilled air of the library brushes over me, and I ache for him to warm my skin. He doesn't disappoint, gliding his fingers over the hard peak of my nipple. It is only a whisper of a touch, but it sends a hot wave of desire through me. My back arches from the ground, making my throbbing center grind against his thigh.

"You like that?" he asks, his warm breath brushing over my skin.

"Yes," I hiss as his tongue follows the same path as his fingers.

He draws my nipple into his mouth and my eyes roll into the back of my head. It should be a sin for someone to ignite so much pleasure with just their mouth. He sucks and nips at my breasts, and I can't get enough. I lace my fingers in his hair as my body moves of its own accord, searching for the right amount of pressure between my legs.

He grips the back of my thigh and lifts my leg. "That feels good, doesn't it?"

I whimper in response and Ryland reacts by pressing his hard cock against my thigh. He sucks hard on my nipple while twisting and pinching the other.

"Ryland?"

"Tell me what you need, love. I want to give it to you."

I bite down on my lip and squeeze my eyes shut. I don't know if I can voice what I want, the boundaries I want to cross. No one has ever wanted me to do that before. But isn't that what this moment is all about, getting what I want? If I hold back, I'm not being true to what I hoped this would be.

I take his hand from my thigh and slide it between us. "Touch me. I want you to make me come."

"God, you don't know how many times I've

imagined you saying that to me."

He unbuttons my pants and slowly lowers my zipper. His hand slides down my panties, giving me the chance to back out if this isn't what I truly want, but I do. I want this memory too. I want any and all that have to do with him touching me.

"You're so soft and wet for me, Quinnten," he says, sliding his fingertip over my clit. He draws steady and firm circles against me. Each rotation brings me closer and closer to the release I need. When mewling sounds escape me, he places his other hand to my mouth.

"Open," he commands and slips his fingers over my tongue when I do. I suck on him as he continues to play my body like it was designed just for him. "Save all those sweet sounds for when we're alone and I'm the only one who gets to hear them."

I roll my hips against his hand, his fingers stroking me closer and closer to my release. I'm almost to the edge but I feel too empty. I want him to consume me, to take and take.

"Do you want more?" he asks, tugging on my nipple with his teeth.

I nod and he slides another finger into my mouth. I suck harder as his thumb moves to my clit, and he eases a finger inside of me. When he presses against just the right spot, I clench around him. Every muscle in my body winds tight as I give into the blissed-out feeling of him inside of me.

"Come for me, love."

My growing pleasure snaps, sending me soaring. No longer bound to this continent and my troubles. All I feel is Ryland and me, and I never want to return. But I can't fly forever and with each slowing rotation of his fingers, I ease back to reality.

Ryland kisses me one more time before holding himself above me on his elbows. He brushes the hair away from my cheeks while his eyes catch the dancing flame of the candles and roam over me. I admire every detail of his face—the slope of his nose, his pink lips that are swollen from my kisses, and the sharp curve of his jaw, which is lightly covered in a five o'clock shadow. I don't think I've ever seen someone as gorgeous as him.

"You're absolutely beautiful, but you are stunning when you come," he says, bringing his glistening fingers that were inside of me to his mouth.

I press my face to his arm, hiding my burning cheeks but peeking at him from the corner of my eyes. He sucks them clean and the lopsided grin that I adore graces his face. If only this moment didn't have to come to an end.

Ryland fixes the cups of my bra as I fasten my pants. When I'm semi-presentable again, he pulls his backpack over to him and folds his discarded shirt into a pillow. Resting his head on top, he reaches for me and says, "Come here."

Of course, I do as he asks. I can't resist.

He wraps me in his arms, and I place my head on his chest, mindlessly tracing the outline of the hourglass inked into the middle of his torso. I promise myself I'm only going to indulge in him for a few more minutes. Afterward, it will be time to erect my protective walls and guard my heart again.

"Quinn."

My shoulders are gently shaken, and I begrudgingly open my eyes. I'm on my side, and my head is on top of a familiar tattooed arm, warm breath brushes against my ear, and four sets of eyes look down at me.

"Good morning, sunshine." Wes smiles. "It looks like

you had a good night. Did you sleep well?"

"Yes," I groan, rolling onto my back and looking at Ryland beside me. He meets my stare with a smile and a groggy "Good morning."

"Where exactly is your shirt, Ry?" River asks, with a slight grin.

Ryland and I both look at his bare chest. *Holy shit!*

"I used it as a pillow," he lazily replies, giving no hint as to what transpired between us last night.

I take in the entertained looks on the faces above me. Thousands of assumptions running through their heads as they itch to bombard us with sexual innuendos and questions. Our friends are going to make it impossible to forget what happened between us during the next leg of our journey.

Chapter Twenty-Two

The sun is high in the sky above the Rove River. The massive steel bridge over the body of water allows for a perfect view of the cluster of high-rise buildings making up the Hudson skyline. The city used to be sophisticated and hold the promise of excitement and opportunity, but now, it's utterly terrifying. The dense landscape of steel and cement is the ideal hiding spot for Zs.

The six of us sip at our water bottles in total silence, keeping an eye on the city. We abandoned our final safety net over an hour ago and continued our journey on foot. We knew the SUV wouldn't take us all the way to Caprielle, but we had hoped it would make it past this last major city. We're now at the mercy of the elements, people with devious intentions, and Zs.

Whatever happens from here on out will require fast thinking, and in many ways, be left up to chance. We're relying on our limited resources and ingenuity. Our lives are so intertwined that one false move is the difference between life and death.

River is the first to come to terms with our fate. She doesn't falter while securing her quiver onto her back and taking a step forward. I admire how brave she is. Not once has she given any sign that she regrets our decision. She never looks back or drops a remark about our situation. Even if it is all for show, I wish I could find an ounce of the bravery she exudes right now.

It's not only the change from vehicle to foot that has me frazzled, but the events from the night before. Ryland and I are finding it difficult to fall back into the swing of things. I've spent the day searching for the right words to say to set us back to how we were before, but it's to no avail. We've crossed a line, and now, my emotions and body are waging a war against me. I can't forget the feeling of his fingers inside me or quit replaying how it felt to kiss him. I want more, to kiss him harder, to touch him the way he did me.

God, I hate myself for being so pathetically enamored with him.

"Don't go drifting off now. Stay focused," Ryland says from beside me, gazing at my fidgeting hands.

I release my mood ring and cross my arms. "I'm focused."

"Good. Keep it that way, Ellery."

"Will do, *Shaw*," I say, rolling my eyes.

Our group holds a tight formation as we enter the city square, weaving around the tall buildings and using them to hide us. My palms sweat and my heart beats out of control as the skyrises close in around us. Our movements are precise, and the weapons in our hands are lifted and ready to fire at any sign of trouble.

After what feels like hours, the scenery shifts from elaborate skyscrapers to storefronts. Striped awnings shade the open doors of local markets and clothing boutiques. Graffiti covers the sides of red brick buildings and trash litters the sidewalks. It's clear that these streets were desolate and forsaken long before the quarantine.

The sound of hollow clanking stops us in our tracks. Four sets of hands reach out to River and me, holding us in place. No matter how hard I try, I'll never talk our companions out of their need to protect women. I step to the side, looking in the direction of the noise. A green bottle rolls out from one of the alleyways and crosses the street several yards ahead of us. It hits the curb with a clink, and we jerk in unison. River moves next to me, positioning her bow and arrow between the shoulders of Noah and Wes, aiming for the alley. We hold our breaths and stand completely still, waiting for something or someone to reveal themselves.

When nothing happens, the tension subsides, but we all still hold firmly to our weapons. I don't even complete a step when a gravelly screech pierces through the quiet followed by a sprinting Z. Dressed in rags with long brown hair trailing behind him, the Z races for us. The sound of cutting wind and a snap join the ruckus he makes. As fast as he appeared, the Z drops to the ground with an arrow protruding from the middle of his chest.

River rolls her shoulders and glares at the dead body with a satisfied grin.

Our relief is short-lived. As if he had rung the dinner bell, the wailing cries of Zs saturate the dead city. We're officially under attack.

Ryland glances at me from over his shoulder. "Are you ready?"

"Don't worry about me. I can handle myself."

"I know you can."

As a small horde comes around the corner, I widen

my stance, take aim, and fire along with the others. Two of the Afflicted stop dead in their tracks and hit the ground upon arrival. The others give little consideration to the deceased and push forward. They have their sights set on us as we scurry to land fatal blows to stop them.

"Behind us, Quinn," River says.

At least a dozen Zs come up on us at our rear.

I press my back to Aiden's for cover and pull the trigger of my gun. Fear courses through me and my arms shake, making it difficult to steady my aim. Every shot must count, there's no time for miscalculations. We're outnumbered, in an unfamiliar city, and the odds are quickly stacking against us.

"Now would be the perfect time for a great idea," River states, releasing an arrow into the horde and landing it into a decaying chest.

I don't have a single clue how to get out of this. The shops lining the street pose as much of a threat as our attackers do. There's no way to tell if a building is a trap or offering asylum, but staying on the street is turning dangerous. As soon as we pick off a few Zs, more come to take their place. Every second, they grow closer, and we have mere minutes before we are surrounded with no way out.

Over the blasts of rapid gunfire, Wes yells, "See that restaurant to the left? We need to move to the alley beside it and get the horde to follow us."

The weight of my panic lifts from my shoulders. Thank God at least one of us devised a plan.

"Do you mind elaborating, Mac?" Noah asks, continuing to fire his weapon.

"Yes, I do mind, Noah. I'm gutted that after all this time you don't trust me."

Ryland looks in the direction of the alley. "Why do I have the feeling your plan entails an explosion?"

"Because you and I both know blowing shit up is the best way to gain the upper hand," Wes snaps.

I flashback to the last time Wes blew something up. He could have killed us, but it worked.

With nobody else offering a better alternative, we inch our way across the street. We can't afford to aggravate them, so we refrain from any sudden movements. And with each passing second, the continuous stream of ravenous bodies closes in on us.

We slide along the outside wall of a red brick building and pass a huge, white propane tank that gives us a little cover. The trek to the rear corner is nerve racking. A thoroughfare with several dilapidated dumpsters runs along the back of the building. They are the only obstacles between us and a major street.

Wes moves to the back of our group and patiently waits for the Zs to file into the alley. He pushes us around the corner and says, "Get ready to run and don't stop."

As we move out of sight, the Zs go mad, quickening their efforts to reach us. Using the corner of the building to shield himself, Wes opens fire on the propane tanker. The first shot is a direct hit, but nothing happens. Panic rages inside of me, and I bounce on the balls of my feet. There may be nothing in the tank, in which case, we're screwed, but it's our best bet. Wes releases another shot, but this one isn't meant to create an explosion. It stops a Z who has broken free from the horde and is within reaching distance of us.

Unable to step out of the safety that the wall provides, I squat behind Wes and slide my arm around the corner. I clip off the Afflicted as he focuses on the primary target. Again, he shoots, and nothing happens besides the sound of the bullet hitting metal.

"Come on, Wes," I plead.

He fires again and heat flashes across my face. I'm dragged along the ground by the collar of my shirt while I scurry to my feet. A ball of fire is hot on our backs as we sprint through the alley. Zs cry out, but not because they're being burned alive; their long-awaited fresh dinner is on the run.

My lungs burn and legs ache, and I silently urge them to continue to move. I'm at the back of the group, fighting to close the gap between my friends and me. I push forward, upping my pace, but my feet slip out from beneath me. I land hard on my back, knocking the air from my lungs. My head rolls to the side as I struggle to pull in a breath, but my efforts are cut short.

Barreling toward me is a crazed Z, shaking its head side to side with thick saliva stringing from its mouth. Wanting to close the distance between us, it leaps into the air. I raise my gun and shoot it in the middle of the face. Purple blood showers down on me, and its body skids to the ground.

Someone grips me under my arms and yanks me onto my feet.

"Nice shot, but watch where you're going, all right?" Ryland says, playfully scolding me.

He doesn't give me time to reply. Taking my hand, he pulls me behind him. When we emerge from the cover of the brick buildings, we're not greeted with the sight I was hoping for. Although Wes's plan immensely decreased the number of Zs pursuing us, many made it out. Burnt flesh hangs from their exposed bones and angry lesions ooze with blood. They're utterly grotesque times a thousand.

Our group disperses into pairs, Aiden and Wes, Noah and River, and me with Ryland. The Zs also break off into clusters, each zoning in on particular pairings. Yet again, we are outnumbered.

It's unnerving the way the Afflicted snap their teeth and flail their arms. They desperately want to grip anything—hair, clothing, or a limb—and pull us to their mouths. They reply with grunts and aggravated screams when we avoid their advances, and they're sloppy and unorganized in their quest to subside the unquenchable hunger driving them.

Ryland and I stay close with our backs pressed together. As quickly as possible, we pick them off one at a time, but they're unrelenting, giving little mind to being the next to die by our bullets.

A lithe male pulls ahead of the group, racing for me. I prepared to meet him head on when a terrifying wail resonates through the chaos. River. My head snaps in her direction as a Z drags her to the ground. His hands wrapped around the braid at the back of her skull, and her bow and arrow lie beside her just outside of her reach. Noah curses trying to get to her, but he can't break away. The Z barreling toward me rams its body into mine, pushing me back into Ryland. He stumbles forward but keeps his footing. I tumble to the ground with the Afflicted landing on top of me. My gun is jolted out of my grip, and I thrash my arms and legs, making it difficult for the Z to pin me down.

With no other choice but to fight hand to hand, I swing my fist as hard as I can at the monster. My blow whips his face to the side for an instant. It's long enough for me to grasp the greasy, black hair lying across his forehead and hold him at arm's length. I use my leverage to look in River's direction and find her in a similar predicament, only her efforts to hold off her attacker are failing. The Z pins her to the ground, and her arms are wedged between their bodies with both her hands on its chest. She vigorously pushes it away, but it is massive compared to her.

"Ryland!" I scream over the chaos. "River needs your help."

With a significant part of my focus on my cousin, I begin to lose my own battle. I give a swift tug on the strands of hair and regain an inch or two of space. With my other hand, I reach frantically for my gun. My fingertips brush the warm metal barrel, but I'm too far away to get a firm grip. Again, I glance at River. Strings of the Z's saliva drape across her neck as she turns her face to the side, putting as much distance as she can between her and it.

"Please, Ry, she needs you!" I beg.

The Z on top of me uses my moment of panic to his advantage. Without warning, he jerks his head to the side, loosening my grip on him. On pure instinct, he dives his teeth to my cheek. I don't want the last thing I see to be his face charging at me for the kill, so I close my eyes. I don't give up on reaching for my gun and stretch my arm one more centimeter. All the while, I brace myself for the pain of my flesh being ripped from my bones.

Bang. Bang. Bang.

With a jolt, the weight on top of me is gone.

I open my eyes to find Ryland standing above me with his gun aimed at the Afflicted who was attacking me. I don't bother to thank him or avoid the purple, gooey blood seeping into my clothes, but instead, I look for my cousin.

The Z lies draped over her body, it's face pressed against hers. I rip the Afflicted off her, expecting a fight, but its mangled head falls limp to the side with a bullet hole blown through its temple. I shove it to the side, and my hands move of their own accord, brushing the blood from her face and neck. I feverishly search her skin for any signs of a bite. It's not until she blinks that I feel a wave of relief wash over me.

"I'm fine," she says, struggling to sit up.

I pull her into my arms and hug her so tightly she's unable to breathe. I have no clue how she is still alive, but the *how* doesn't matter right now. She is still with me and that is all I care about.

Shots continue to blast around us, and a hand encircles my bicep, pulling me to my feet. "This is our chance to get away. We have to go now," Ryland says.

Noah pulls River into his arms and brushes back the curly wisps of her hair to examine her face before he presses his lips to her forehead.

Our group is a bit worse for wear, but we're all alive. We stay bunched together and alert while jogging down the road. Every so often, the blast from one of our guns echoes in the deserted city, ridding the world of one more of the Afflicted.

In the distance sits an endless body of water. We continue to trudge on until we're standing on its boardwalk. The men take a moment to survey the area, looking for a safe place to recoup for the night. I can't even think that far ahead. Something in my gut tells me all is not well. I think we've been lured into some type of trap, so I scan the area for anything out of sorts. For the first time in hours, we're alone. I check myself. Maybe I missed something, and the Z who attacked me did more harm than I thought.

I do a quick self-assessment and find nothing. Bewildered by the feeling I scan the faces around me until

I land on River. She stands against one of the metal posts, holding the thick rope that acts as a barrier to the lake. All the color has drained from her face, and her gaze moves to her hand clenching her side. Red liquid soaks into the material of her shirt and seeps out from in between her fingers.

"Riv," I say, my voice not sounding like my own.

She lifts her hand to stare at the blood staining it. Terror washes over her features before her eyes meet mine.

Chapter Twenty-Three

Noah falls in step with me, and together we rush toward River. He lifts the hem of her shirt, revealing the rip in her smooth skin. The entire world goes silent as we stare at the blood flowing from a jagged semi-circle. My eyes widen, and my heart sinks to the pit of my stomach. She stumbles back, her legs give out, and Noah catches her before she crashes to the ground.

"Quinn?" he says, my name a plea for help.

No other words need to be spoken. His mind is surely flooding with the same thought as mine—she's been bitten.

I've failed her, and now she'll turn into the one thing we despise the most in this godforsaken world. River will become one of the Afflicted.

Noah effortlessly lifts her into his arms. Her head rests on his shoulder and relief washes over her face. I rip the bottom of my shirt off and do the same to the back of Noah's. Balling up the fabrics, I place them to her side.

Noah's face pales at the sight of the material already turning crimson and tears pool at the corners of his eyes.

He steps back with River held tightly to him and repeatedly mumbles how sorry he is. She wipes the tears from his face and assures him everything will be all right, and he has nothing to be sorry for.

"Quinn, come and wrap the shirt into place. Tie it tight to slow the bleeding," River says as the others gather around us. I do as she asks while she talks to the guys. "I'm going to need stitches, so we need to find somewhere that's somewhat clean for the night."

She's in denial, shocked that this is her fate. We've talked about what we wanted to happen if we were ever bitten. At the time, we agreed to kill the other to prevent the Z virus from consuming us. Of course, it was the thought process of two young women who believed it would never come to that.

No.

No!

I refuse to believe this is it.

"Riv, what do you want us to do? Tell me how to fix this."

"You are going to have to sew me up, and let's get to Caprielle," she weakly says.

I nod and dry my eyes with the back of my hand. "Okay."

Noah's head jerks up, his gaze locking with mine. "She can't—they won't let her pass once they see the signs," he says.

I open my mouth to tell him to shut up, that she will be fine when River's laughter catches on the wind. "Oh, my God, Noah! You're planning my funeral. It didn't bite me. Its fingernails were super long, and it stabbed all four into me." She looks at me and nods. "I'll be okay, Quinn."

My legs give out and I fall to the ground. With my

face buried against my knees, I cry like a baby. Rage, relief, fear, and unconditional love course through me all at once. I physically can't handle the magnitude of my emotions. I thought I fucking lost her.

Noah lets out a string of words that is a combination of a prayer and curses, before pressing his lips to River's.

Ryland clears his throat and brings us back to the task at hand. "I have a plan that will give River a chance to recover and give everyone a break from the Zs." He looks out at the endless lake before us. "We just need a working boat."

He leads the way to a marina where dozens of abandoned boats are tethered to the dock. We choose a yacht that looks to be in sailing condition and has a roomy cabin. It's not the most extravagant craft in the harbor, but it's just what we need.

It turns out that we have made it to Ryker Lake— an enormous body of water that borders Oscuros as well. It's a major risk to use the waterway to cross into Oscuros. But we should be able to sail to Coft—the city on the Stern side of the border. From there, we'll have to continue the ten-mile journey by foot to the border crossing. It sounds promising in theory, but nothing about this journey has gone to plan.

Once the boys do a quick security check of the yacht, they leave Noah and me to help River into the hull while they raid the other docked vessels for supplies. She directs us to place her on the long built-in couch across from the kitchenette. Noah sets to work gathering clean towels, and I divide my attention between her and digging through our medical supplies for the items needed to suture River's wound. She walks me through the process of preparing the needle and my stomach roils at the thought of what comes next. River and I love helping people, but there's a reason I wanted to study psychology and not general medicine. I'm not one to deal well with those in physical pain, so being designated as her surgeon is terrifying.

"Is there something I can give you for the pain or to at least numb the area?" I ask.

Taking a deep breath, she shakes her head. "Just do the best you can and don't go too deep with the needle."

With one last look at the needle I've strung with medical thread, I set to work with shaky hands. River bites a wooden pencil that Noah found in one of the drawers and holds his hand in a death grip. Beads of sweat form on her brow, and she struggles to keep conscious. I do my best to work quickly, but it's hard. I hate the feel of her skin resisting the sharp end of the needle and the little droplets of blood forming around each stitch. It takes everything I have to push myself to stay on task.

After wrapping her injury and giving her painkillers, Noah carries her to the primary bedroom, and they settle in for the evening.

I finish cleaning before heading up to the deck. Other than the stars and moon in the clear night sky, I'm in total darkness. The yacht gently rocks with the movement of the lake and has a calming effect on my rattled nerves. I take a seat on one of the several padded benches and try to relax.

Ryland, Wes, and Aiden load an array of necessities onto the boat. Containers of gasoline, small tanks of propane, the standard non-perishable food items, and fishing gear are among their finds. I've never been on a boat like this before, but from what I can tell, the weather seems perfect for sailing. If it weren't for the concerning state of River's health, I might look forward to the journey.

It's not long before Aiden releases the yacht from its tether to the dock, and the boys work together to hot-wire the ignition. As we pull away from the land, I reflect on how I'm not going to have to worry about Zs for the first time in two years. Since they need their lungs and they lack common sense, water and the Afflicted aren't a good combination. I'll be able to concentrate on mending River, instead of protecting her. It's a comfort I was starting to believe I'd never have again.

Once we can no longer make out the outline of the Hudson skyline, Aiden drops the anchor. It turns out he competitively sailed while he attended university. He doesn't claim to be an expert, but he says he has the necessary knowledge to navigate us to Coft and keep the boat afloat. This is his first time taking the lead since I've met him, and I've never seen him so elated.

Wes and Aiden go down to the hull to start dinner, leaving me alone with Ryland. With his arms crossed over his chest, he moves to the edge of the deck and looks out over the water. His hair catches on the night breeze and dances around his head, and his tense shoulders relax. Keeping his back to me, he asks, "How's River?"

The anger I've been trying to shove down for the past few hours bubbles up within me at his question. He promised me he'd take care of her over me. We had a deal, and he broke it. River paid the price for his broken promise. She lost blood. She endured stitches without anything to dull her pain.

"Fine," I snap, not bothering to hide my irritation.

He turns to look at me, with his eyebrows raised. "How are *you*?"

"I'm pissed," I say.

"At me?"

I jump to my feet, square my shoulders, and close

the distance between us. Looking him straight in the eyes, I press my finger into his chest. "You swore to me that you'd put her first; that you would protect her instead of me!"

"You couldn't reach your gun, Quinn."

"I don't give a fuck!"

His jaw flexes and a vein on the side of his neck pulsates. "I do! I give a fuck! I care if something happens to you!"

I stumble back a step, his words like a blow to the gut. It steals a little of the fight from me, and it takes me a moment to remember why I'm so angry. "You made me a promise. And because of your blatant disregard of it, I had to sew my cousin back together. I had to watch as she writhed in pain, and it didn't have to happen."

"I'm sorry she got hurt, but Noah was making his way to her. They got it under control. There was no reason for me to leave you to fight on your own."

Noah was there? I was so grateful to find her alive under the Z that I didn't even consider how it died. As always, I was focused on River, and Ryland was monitoring everything around us. Always the planner. Always the protector.

Ryland speaks again, pulling my thoughts out of the battle and back to the heated conversation at hand. "I'm not sorry for saving your life, even if it means I broke my word to you. I warned you the day you made me promise that I couldn't keep it. I won't take back what I did, and I can't say it won't happen again." Sorrow consumes his jade eyes. "Please don't be upset with me."

I slide my hand down my face and release a long sigh. "I'm sorry for coming at you like that. I didn't see Noah. And I'm not mad. I'm just scared that we all won't make it to the border crossing."

It's the truth, my darkest confession. I'm terrified I will fail. And it's not just River I want to see to safety. Ryland, Aiden, Noah, and Wes need to go home. I'm determined to see that happen.

He cups my cheek in his palm, and I close my eyes, savoring the nearness of him. I love the way his rough, callused hands feel against my skin. It's a reminder of the trials he's undergone and his ability to prevail. Ryland's the strongest person I know, and that's why I'm so desperate for his help. He can give me the peace I crave.

"If it comes down to you or her, for me, it will always be you, Quinn. But what I can promise you is this: I will protect her just as I would any of my friends. I'll treat her equal to them."

Every last drop of the anger I had in me is gone. He has reduced me to the equivalent of a melted puddle at his feet. He never let me down, and I wholeheartedly believe he never will.

"Thank you," I say, my words hitching on the emotion building in my throat.

It's more than I expected from him. The guys mean the world to him, and there's nothing he wouldn't do to keep them alive. His life's mission is to return them home to their families. I know he'll do the same for River.

He gives me a weak lopsided smile. It's painful to know I'm the cause of the sadness behind it, but there is some solace in knowing this feeling won't last forever. He'll be free from my hold in less than a week and can carry on with his life the way it should have always been. He'll not only be able to leave behind the Affliction, but me as well.

Chapter Twenty-Four

I'm not a natural sailor. I had two episodes of seasickness which came with an audience witnessing me puking over the side of the yacht. On the bright side, I've always wanted to go on a cruise. Of course, I pictured somewhere tropical and not Ryker Lake. I suppose you accept what you can get when a deadly virus is ravaging the land.

We've remained in Stern waters for fear of not being able to protect ourselves if we ventured too close to the Oscuros shore. The last we heard, boats were being forced to turn back or sunk if they refused. It would be impossible for us to make our intentions known from the water, so we're sticking with the original plan of crossing by land.

Honestly, the lake isn't so bad. The freshwater is tranquil and clear. I occasionally catch sight of land in the distance—a gentle reminder we're not lost at sea. In some ways, it's like Devil's Lake, which only adds to its serenity, and at the same time, makes me homesick.

Since being on the boat, I've spent much of my time taking care of River while the boys handle the sailing. She's been in a ton of pain and has mostly slept, leaving me to entertain myself. I've rummaged through the closet and drawers in her room and found swimwear and t-shirts. It beats the blood-stained clothes I had on before.

The moments I'm not tending to my cousin I spend sprawled across one of the outdoor benches. From here, the late afternoon sun shines down on me, warming and tanning my pale skin that's slathered in expired sunscreen. I sit contentedly with a history book I commandeered from the Hudson bookstore and absorb as much information as I can. I'm determined to solve the Sanctuary's riddles, although it's not top of the line entertainment, it's something relaxing to do to bide the time.

Today is a double bonus, not only do I get to relax in the sun, but everyone is below deck. Aiden dropped the anchor about an hour ago. Him and Ryland believe we're a few miles from reaching the docks in Coft. With the sun's impending descent, we don't have enough time to make it to the border before nightfall. Everyone agreed that with River's injury it was best we have one last worry-free night. Come tomorrow afternoon, we'll again face all the dangers found on Stern soil.

Tomorrow holds no guarantees for any of us. The hours we put into planning a flawless departure from this continent may end up being for nothing. We could reach the border only to be turned away, and then what will happen to us? We've tossed around ideas, but never settled on a firm contingency plan. There were brief talks about continuing down the East coast and hope another opportunity comes our way, but they're nothing more than passing thoughts. We're banking everything on this one shot.

I look up from my stolen book as shuffling footsteps approach and am happy to see River slowly walking to me. Her hand is pressed to her side to help alleviate the pain, and the coloring in her face has returned to normal. It's a welcome sight after her poor condition for the past couple of days.

"I'm surprised Noah let you walk out here on your own," I say, scooting over on the bench.

She curls into a ball beside me and pulls her shirt over her knees before resting her head on my shoulder. "He dozed off, and I made a break for it."

"The hard life of having a loving and overprotective boyfriend. But seriously, how are you feeling?"

"Tired, but better. I just need some fresh air and sun."

This short journey has taken its toll on her. Dark bags underline her eyes, and the lightheartedness she generally exhibits has diminished. It kills me to think she's being changed in a way that will permanently alter the traits I love most about her. I wish this weren't the route we had to take, and I had an easy, sure-fire solution for reuniting her with her parents.

I wrap my arms around her and hug her close. To lessen my torment, I remind myself she wanted to leave with the boys. Being with Noah makes her happy, and I'm more than dedicated to helping her maintain this joy she's found in the worst of circumstances. The love I have for my cousin rivals full-blooded siblings, and it knows no boundaries. If things don't go fully to plan, letting her go will be the hardest thing I'll ever do, guaranteed.

"Riv?"

"Yeah."

I clear my throat, holding my mounting emotions at

bay. "I'm sorry we didn't go to Bogati. I'm sorry I asked you to stay behind."

Wisps of hair have broken free of her messy bun and brush my cheek as she shakes her head. "Don't be, I'm not. There's not another human being I'd want to survive the Affliction with. If it weren't for *our* decision to stay behind, I would have never met Noah, and I might not still be with you."

There is that positive and confident girl I've always known. She hasn't lost that part of her yet.

"I just want you to be safe, and know that no matter what happens tomorrow, it will be all right. I promise you don't have to worry."

She tilts her head. "I know, Quinn."

"I love you."

"I love you, too," she says, cuddling next to me again. Taking my hand in hers, she examines the mood ring. "The color of your ring was always black or red in the beginning. You were always stressed and anxious. Now, more days than not, you're amber, meaning you're confused, but there have been rare days when you're pink or even blue."

"Remind me what those colors mean again," I say.

"Pink is happy, and blue is love and romance."

I stare at the stone and wonder if it really does work. Have there been moments in the last few months where I've felt happiness or even love? When the boys became an extension of my family, they made our house feel like a home again. And Ryland... My chest tightens as the answer becomes clear, but I don't dwell on it. I can't. Come tomorrow, the shade of my ring will permanently return to a gloomy hue.

Wes and Aiden come running out of the hull. They hysterically laugh as they charge toward the back of the boat. The two pull their shirts over their heads and toss them to the ground before cannonballing into the water. They resume their rowdy behavior as soon as they break the surface, wrestling with one another. River and I have become immune to their hijinks, knowing that our floating refuge has allowed all of us a chance to be carefree for a short while.

Noah scoots in next to River on the bench seat. He pulls her legs into his lap and runs long calming strokes along her calves. "You should have woken me. I would have helped you up the stairs," he says in a gentle but reprimanding tone.

Accustomed to his doting, River effortlessly brushes him off. "I'm feeling better, and I can handle walking up a few steps."

His brown eyes look her up and down as he presses his lips firmly together. Being an attentive boyfriend, he knows arguing will be a losing battle. Poor Noah now joins me in the rankings of people who will do anything to keep River happy.

Ryland eventually emerges wearing nothing but a worn pair of jeans that cling tightly to his long legs. He casts the three of us a quick nod and strolls to the boat's stern. He leaps over the steps leading to a platform with a ladder into the water. With his arms crossed over his chest, he looks out at the lake. The setting sun is the perfect backdrop for his lean figure. The collection of black tattoos on his arms and torso are highlighted by the golden light, and his hair flutters around his face, catching the warm spring breeze. He's godlike.

His hands reach for the front of his jeans and the fabric slides down, revealing a toned, pale ass.

"What are you doing?" I yell.

Holding his jeans below his ass, he looks over his

shoulder at me. Without missing a beat, he says, "Swimming."

"But—"

"It's called skinny dipping, Quinnten. It's perfectly natural." He laughs as he continues to disrobe.

I gape at the sight of his naked form from the back. Never would I have imagined Ryland skinny dipping for fun. It seems immature and beneath him; not something a man on a mission would do. Yet, I forget he's barely twenty-two. He should be out at all-night parties, playing beer pong, and streaking down a neighborhood street to fulfill a silly dare. Instead, he's wielding a gun and fighting hand over fist to lead us to safety. The free-spirited young man before me is who he should always be.

He looks back at me again and motions his head to the side. "Come join me," he says before diving into the water.

"You're drooling." River says, wiping her finger across my chin.

"Shut up," I mutter, shaking my head and moving her hand away.

Did I seriously turn into one humongous raging hormone at the sight of Ryland? Was I gawking at his bare ass? Did all normal brain function seize up on me when I saw his perfectly rounded, muscular butt? Yes, yes, and *yes*. I press my palms to my eyes. The worst part is that I'd been caught. There's nothing I can do to talk my way out of it.

A splash of water rains down on me, and I quickly turn in my seat to look over the side of the boat.

"Come swim with me," Ryland demands again as he treads water.

"Tomorrow isn't guaranteed, but this moment of happiness is. Don't let it pass you by," River says so only I can hear her.

She's right. This might be my last chance to give in to something I want, just one more stolen moment with Ryland.

I pull off my shirt, revealing the yellow bikini beneath. My first reaction is to cover my exposed stomach, but I force my hands to remain at my side as I walk to the ladder. Set on making the most of right now, I jump away from the boat, hoping to make a big enough splash to get Ryland. The water engulfs me, accepting me into its depths. Although on the verge of freezing, it's refreshing. I relax, reveling in the weightless feeling as my body sinks. When my lungs beg for a breath, I kick my way back to the surface. Pushing my hair from my face, I uncover the huge smile that has my cheeks burning.

Ryland swims up next to me, and I kick away from him. "You're naked!"

He cocks an eyebrow. "And you already got an eyeful."

I vigorously shake my head. "I didn't see everything. I just saw you from behind."

His fingers intertwine with mine, and he moves behind me, leaving just enough space so our bodies don't touch. "Do you like what you saw?"

A shiver races down my spine and my next words slip out of my mouth. "Do you think I liked it?"

"It doesn't matter what I think. I want to hear you say it."

He moves closer, his body barely grazing mine. My brain stops working again, caught on the way his wet skin feels. Every warning alarm should be going off inside my head. What we are playing with is dangerous and bound to leave us in pain. But I don't push away, instead I lean into his chest, marveling at his warmth against my back.

"I liked what I saw, Ry," I whisper.

Everything around us goes silent—the lapping water, the wind—everything but my pounding heart. I question if he even heard me until his arms wrap around my waist. My eyes flutter closed, and my head rests on his shoulder.

"Was that so hard to admit?" he asks, kicking his legs to move us farther away from the boat.

I slide through his arms and turn to face him. "Is that what you want; me to tell you that you're hot? Come on, Ryland. I thought you had more confidence than that."

"Maybe I've spent the last few days replaying what happened in that library, and I can't forget how I felt when you told me what you wanted."

His words trigger that need inside of me that I've been suppressing for days. I knew it was a risk to give into it, that I would want more. He is freely offering me that again. It's tempting. *He* is so fucking tempting.

I cock my eyebrow and force my lips into a smirk. "So you want me to tell you how much I desire you. Is that what you were hoping to accomplish when you stripped in front of me?"

He meets my playfulness with his own. "Did it work?"

"No." I swim out of his reach, splashing water at him. "You'll have to try harder."

He dives under and grabs my ankle, pulling me back to him.

I laugh and scream, kicking out of his grip. "You plan on chasing me until I give in."

"If that's what it takes. I heard women like the chase."

I begin to swim toward the front of the boat with him trying to catch me. He's a fast swimmer, and several times, he pulls at my leg, but he never gets a firm grip. We round the corner, and he closes the distance between us. My breath hitches as his arms wrap around my waist and pull me toward him. We hold each other's gazes as my hands come to rest on his shoulders. All the air releases from my lungs as I take in the sight of him.

"I want to kiss you," he says.

"I thought you wanted me to tell you what *I* want."

"I'll beg for you if that's what you want, Quinn." He brushes his lips over mine.

Every cell in my body sparks to life. I wrap my legs around his hips and grasp the hair at his nape, pulling him closer. He opens to me and I sweep my tongue over his. The taste of him spurs me on. He tastes like a warm summer morning and sweet mint. His kisses are addicting, and I need just one more. One last kiss to appease the nagging ache inside of me. It throbs at my very core, reminding me how empty I am without his fingers inside of me. I curse the little yellow bikini that keeps me from fully feeling his body pressed into mine. I want it all with him, to surrender the last bit of restraint that keeps me from giving in. But I can't do it.

Sliding my hands to the top of his head, I release my legs from around him and push him under the water, breaking our kiss. Freed from his hold, I bolt toward the back of the boat. I pray my immature actions come off as playful, but they were nothing but weak. Perhaps my weakest moment since the Affliction. But every second I spend with him is dangerous. He's becoming pivotal to both my physical and emotional survival. I want to hold on to him and never let him go, but I can't. I won't destroy a chance for him and the others to return to their families.

I must stay focused on the task ahead of us.

I pull myself onto the boat's platform and hurry to replace Ryland's warmth with a dry towel. Hiding my face inside the terry cloth, I calm my frayed nerves.

Ryland reaches the yacht and struggles to slide on his jeans over his wet skin. As he passes me, I contort my lips into a sassy smile, like I've won our water fight. Unlike me, he wears no guise to hide his emotions. He appears totally dejected. My stomach turns as I take in the look of hurt on his face before he disappears into the hull.

I can't bring myself to look at him for the rest of the night. With a fake smile, I work my way through a couple of rounds of poker with some cards we found. The entire time, I think about returning to dry land, gaining some personal space, and for those I care about to cross over into safety.

After River and Noah retire to the primary suite for the night, I excuse myself. I literally feel a thousand times lighter when I shut the door to my small room and fall into the bed. It was a struggle not to react to the sound of Ryland's voice throughout the evening and to break down into an apology for hurting him. Stopping the kiss was the right thing to do, but a better option would've been never to kiss him in the first place. I've let my guard down around him too many times, and now, we're both bound to get hurt.

I toss and turn in bed as my brain races all over the place. It replays the look in Ryland's eyes as he passed me on the deck. I'd rather give into nightmares about Zs then relive that moment. Gripping my hair at the roots, I stare at the dark ceiling. I can't go into tomorrow with this lingering between us. It will eat at us and put everyone at risk. I have to make this right somehow.

The sound of my door slowly sliding open pulls me from the newest round of guilt. I hold my breath as the tall, shadowed form walks in and quietly closes us inside. He doesn't say a word as he slips into the bed behind me, pulling my back to his front. He nuzzles his face into my hair, breathing me in.

I go rigid at his touch, unsure of what to expect.

"It's all right, relax. I've got you," he says.

Never have I thought of myself as above or under anybody. Like everyone else on this planet, I'm doing the best I can with what I have and who I am. I'm not any better or worse... until now. I don't deserve Ryland's quick unspoken forgiveness. My actions are unworthy of his affection, yet here he is.

Before I can contain it, a sob escapes me, and I silently curse myself. My silly weakness will do nothing to correct the situation. If anything, I'm adding to all the stupid things I've ever done in his presence.

He pulls me tightly to him and says, "*Shh.* Let me hold you, Quinn."

I nod. He could ask a whole slew of things from me right now, and I'd do any of them to make up for my behavior. It seems unfair that what he asks is also what I want.

"I'm sorry, Ry. I didn't mean to hurt you," I say.

"You did nothing wrong. I know you're wary of giving in to your feelings, and I shouldn't have been so damn charming," he says, smiling into my hair.

I giggle. Actually, giggle. Ryland continually surprises me with his ability to make me react in ways I thought I was no longer capable of.

"It was your ass. You have a really nice ass."

"I know. It's one of my finer assets," he says and kisses the side of my head.

There was a time not long ago when I felt I couldn't

care for anyone beyond my cousin. Yet, I've not only sacrificed my life for Ryland, but for his friends. I was sure I'd never feel nervous flutters or kiss a boy again. He's found a way to make me feel alive, and at times, normal. I'm not sure what force placed him in my life, but I'll be eternally grateful for my time with him.

I've said it before, and it still stands true, if our lives were different, I could've easily fallen in love with Ryland.

Chapter Twenty-Five

en miles, ten miles, I repeat to myself as I step off the boat. My backpack is heavy with everything useful that I could cram into it. The gun in the waistband of my jeans is loaded, and my knife is strapped in its holster on my hip. I've taken every precaution I can to make it to the end.

The six of us have filled our stomachs and went over all possible scenarios before pulling the boat into a harbor. It's bittersweet saying goodbye to the one place that has provided us with a shred of normalcy since we left Devil's Lake.

River hasn't fully recovered and needs Noah's help climbing down the ramp to the ground. Her movements are slow, and if we're placed in a situation that requires us to run, it may be next to impossible for her. We plan on protecting her by keeping her in the center of our group at all times.

I say a silent prayer while we walk to the land crossing. I hope it's quiet and uneventful, but the chances are good that won't happen. Coft is not only most likely swarming with Zs, but the military presence it had makes the people a threat as well. We need to get to the main highway as quickly as possible, so we'll have a wide-open space in front of us with minimal obstructions blocking our view.

"You look nervous," Ryland says, walking beside me.

"I'm just anxious to see how this all turns out."

He places his hands in his pockets, surveying the area around us. "Do you think you'll leave for Bogati as soon as you get out of here?"

I've honestly not thought past this part of our mission. Making it across the border has been such a long shot, and I haven't bothered to entertain it. The best I've done is come to terms with saying goodbye.

I shrug. "I guess it's up to River. She's the one who has ties to both Giran and Bogati. I'll go where she goes, for now. What about you? Do you think you'll go back to school?"

"I don't know. I kind of want to go home and live on my mom's couch for a bit."

"That sounds nice," I say, keeping my focus straight ahead.

"You can come with me."

"Yeah, and we can sit together on your mom's couch, and she can cook for us while we catch up on all the television shows we missed."

"Why not?"

I smile and roll my eyes. "We'll see."

We follow the highway into the heart of the city. When tall buildings close in on us, we defensively hold our weapons at the ready. Grunts and footsteps penetrate our tranquil surroundings, drawing our attention in every which way. Our circle closes in around River, and we place our backs to her, moving down the road. Sweat slides down my face, and my heartbeats are so fast that I can count them by the pulsing in my ear. Like a slow crescendo, a chorus of earth-shattering screams calls out, sending a chill down my spine.

The crumbling buildings around us come to life with flashes of dark silhouettes moving inside. The Afflicted pour out the doorways and windows, trickling into the street. Dozens of them, in various stages of the Affliction, move toward us. I've never seen anything like it in the past two years.

I glance at the steel frame hovering over the water in the distance—the land crossing. We're so close to it. Unfortunately, we're also faced with the impossible odds of making it there alive.

"Whatever you do, stay together," Ryland barks.

"Hang on to my shirt," Noah says to River, pressing her to his back to shield her from the Zs.

Aiden moves to Noah's side while Ryland, Wes, and I guard the rear, ready to open fire. The first Z races forward, eager to devour us and not share with the rest of the horde. I steadily walk backward, my jaw painfully clenched as I focus on my target. Holding my gun with both hands, I fire and hit it in the head.

All hell breaks loose—bullets colliding with Zs.

The Zs surround us with their arms outstretched, grasping at thin air as they try to reach us. Unseeing white eyes skip back and forth and their nostrils flare, breathing in our scent. They growl with hunger, their mouths hanging open with long, thick wisps of slobber dangling from their chins. They're starving animals who've come to claim their feast.

My gun clicks twice before I realize I'm out of bullets and I frantically release the empty chamber, dropping it to the ground. "Shit," I hiss, reaching into my backpack and fumbling for a new clip.

Ryland's voice resonates through the chaos saying, "Communicate with me, Quinn."

"I'm good, I'm good," I say, pulling out the new magazine and slamming into the bottom of my gun.

I bite my lip until I draw blood as I open fire again. I need a reminder that although I've outsmarted these creatures hundreds of times, I still bleed. All it takes is one wrong move for them to gain the upper hand. No sooner does the thought cross my mind, and Aiden is torn away from our group.

He screams, punches, and kicks as he struggles against the Z. It climbs onto his back, holding him in a headlock while trying to bite his neck. Aiden repeatedly delivers violent blows to its face, his fist coming dangerously close to its mouth. All it takes is one misaimed punch, and he will join the rankings of our enemy.

Ryland breaks from our group, charging into the scuttle. Fury radiates from his eyes and each of his swift movements is filled with determination. He won't watch as another friend is torn apart right in front of him.

Another Z leaps out of nowhere, slamming its body into Ryland. They crash to the ground, and he swiftly throws back his elbow, colliding with the Z's nose. He seizes the break in their scuffle to line his gun with its mouth and pulls the trigger. The Z's head bursts open from the back, ejecting brain matter and blood.

Not bothering to get to his feet, Ryland crawls to Aiden. Grabbing the Z's leg, Ryland yanks and throws it off balance. The Z tries to maintain its hold but is unsuccessful when Aiden administers a punch to the center of its neck.

It falls backward with a fleshy thud, and Ryland unloads three bullets into its chest.

Aiden offers Ryland his hand and pulls him to his feet. "Thanks."

"Hold off on the thank you until we're across the border," Ryland says, wiping the sweat from his brow.

The two men fall back into the folds of our group, picking up where they left off.

I scan the area, devising a plan. Aiden's attack was too close for comfort, and the Zs are growing tired of the chase. We won't be able to hold them off much longer. The only chance we have to make it will be a distraction.

"Quinnten, I know that look. No heroics, love."

I shoot Ryland a side-glance. "I can lure some of them away and give you more time."

"No!"

"Let me do this."

"Absolutely not. We stick together."

I shake off Ryland's refusal to let me go and continue to fire at the Afflicted, knowing that breaking from the group is the only option we have left. I step forward, poising myself to sprint as soon as I see an opening.

Boom!

The Zs at the front of the horde crash to the ground in a ball of flames.

I stumble back, shielding my face from the heat of the blast with my arm. A firm hand grabs mine, and Ryland pulls me in front of him and pushes me forward. Together, we run to the center of the bridge. Out of breath, I hunch forward with my hands on my knees. Movement in the corner of my eye catches my attention.

Wes stands on the bridge's railing with a huge smile

on his face and his blue eyes shining with pride. He salutes the burning horde and says, "What a way to use the last grenade."

I laugh with a mixture of relief and amusement. "You're out of your mind."

"But in a good way, right?"

I don't get a chance to answer. A dozen Zs break through the flames. Through the tears welling in my eyes, I watch as the charge toward us. It's useless to fight back. They'll continue to come, and we'll never be able to kill them all. All that is left to do is brace for their impact.

Pop. Pop. Pop.

Rapid-fire blasts through the air, instantly followed by the whizzing of bullets over our heads. I spin around and find several figures in concrete towers, firing upon the Afflicted from the other side of the border crossing.

"This way," I yell to the others.

We rush to the checkpoint, and I take one final glance over my shoulder. Many of the Zs lifelessly tumble to the ground, but most disperse in several directions. I'm astonished. They're actually surrendering.

"Weapons on the ground and hands where we can see them," says a commanding voice over a loudspeaker.

We exchange alarmed glances, and Ryland gives a quick nod. Together, we gently place our guns on the pavement and raise our hands over our heads. No more than fifty yards away is the border guard station and beyond it a massive concrete wall. Armed guards line the top of the monstrosity with their weapons trained on us.

"This is a closed continental crossing. Stern citizens are not permitted to enter the continent of Oscuros," the disembodied voice says.

"We're not Stern citizens," Ryland replies, holding up his passport. "We're Giran citizens requesting asylum with the Giran embassy."

The authoritative voice falls silent, and everything comes to a standstill. We nervously shift from side to side, knowing this is the moment of truth.

Two men wearing black uniforms with bulletproof vests exit the station. Their hands hover over the guns in their holsters as they approach us.

"Do all of you have passports?" asks a guard with sandy-blond hair and a mustache.

"We have our marriage licenses," River unzips her backpack, searching for the two documents we took months ago from the regional court office and Noah forged.

The guard with jet-black hair and dark umber skin scowls and says, "That's not what he asked. Do you have pass—"

"Yes," I interject, holding up two Giran passport booklets in my shaking hands.

He glares at the engraving on the covers before turning on his heels and heading to the wall. "Follow us."

The other guard falls behind our group, urging us forward at gunpoint.

Everyone remains silent as we follow the guards to the checkpoint, the taping of our steps creating a steady beat. My nerves are frayed, our first plan to cross into Oscuros has been uprooted with no hope of being salvaged. I'm not surprised, the marriage licenses were a flimsy attempt at best. I just pray that by some miracle my plan B works the way it should.

Pulling the reins on my growing anxiety, I allow my curiosity to take over. "Why did the Afflicted run once you opened fire on them?"

The guard's dark eyes examine me up and down before he answers with indifference, "They've learned we'll kill them if they set foot on our territory. Like an animal, they can be trained to a certain extent, but never tamed. Occasionally, one will try to reach the wall, but we're here to quickly put them back into their place."

I'm dumbfounded by this information. I never considered Zs to be intelligent beyond their preferred hunting methods. The terror they can cause has been elevated to a new height, making this the perfect time to leave them and this continent far behind.

We reach a booth sitting before a concrete barrier, blocking the road into Oscuros. The two guards who gathered us stand watch as a third takes Aiden's passport and enters his information into a computer system. I lean forward, tapping River on the shoulder with one of the passports in my shaking hand. Her eyes widen as she takes the book, and I return to my place at the end of the line next to Ryland.

"Where did you get those?" he asks under his breath.

"I know a guy who's really good at creating fake IDs," I reply.

His brows rise with surprise and a grin splits his face. "Noah. His criminal activity worked in your favor."

"It would appear so."

Every muscle in Ryland's body relaxes. He clearly has faith in his friend's ability to forge government documentation, which is a good sign. We can't risk the guards second-guessing the legitimacy of what Noah created.

Before Aiden's passport is returned to him, the guard says, "I'll need you to wait for your friends on the other side of the barrier. Once everyone has been verified through the database, all of you will be escorted to a quarantine area to be examined and tested for the Z virus.

If everything comes back clean, you'll be handed over to the Giran authorities."

Everyone nods, and the guard blocking the small entryway steps aside. I can't believe it; they're going to let the boys go home.

River steps forward, handing over the passport, and every normal function of my body stops. I don't know how extensive the database is, but if there are pictures to accompany the information, she'll be screwed. Noah replaced Dylan's image with hers, but it won't match what the government has on file. There's no way she'll be able to pass as him.

I stop breathing as the guard eyes her. "Dylan Kassis?"

Without missing a beat, she says, "That's me."

The guard examines the passport again, comparing it to his computer screen.

"Please, my wife has been injured, and I just want to get her home," Noah begs.

The guard scratches the back of his neck, dividing his attention between the information in his hand and the girl before him. He isn't falling for it. She doesn't match the information before him. River isn't going to make it across.

The resolute glare he gave us when we first approached softens. "The quality of the pictures in this system sucks. But you have a non-Stern passport and that is all that's required to cross, Ms. Kassis," he says, giving the booklet back to her.

The breath I've been holding leaves me in a *whoosh* as I watch River walk across the border.

Noah looks back at me as he hands over his documentation that is missing its cover. Worry is written all over his face even though he knows he made the right choice to change Dylan's passport to look like it belongs to River. Wanting to ease his concern, I mouth the words *thank you*, and he responds with a timid nod.

Ryland places his hand on my lower back, moving me in front of him.

"No. You go ahead, I need to find something really quick," I say, kneeling on the ground and unzipping my backpack. I mindlessly rummage through the contents as Ryland hands the guard his passport. I can feel his gaze shifting between the guard and me as he waits for his approval to pass.

My stomach turns and the lump in my throat makes it difficult to swallow. When Ryland is given the okay, I grab his hand. "Get her to her family," I say, letting go of his fingers.

Confusion washes over his face as I slide my arms through my backpack. The guard tries pushing him through, but he drags his feet. "Wait. Hold on. Quinn."

"Your passport, miss," the other guard says to me.

I pull Noah's cover off my Stern passport and smile. "I'm not a Giran citizen." I show him my booklet which Noah was unable to alter with our limited resources.

Ryland stops struggling and stares at me in wide-eyed shock.

The guard's explanation of why I can't cross is nothing more than white noise as I take one last look at the people I love. They're finally somewhere safe where they can forget about the nightmares of the Affliction. I've completed my only goal for the past two years the best way I could.

"I'm just here to wish them farewell," I finally say to the guard.

"Quinn?" River says, and Noah wraps her in his arms, holding her in place as she pushes against him. "No, let me go. Quinn!"

"I love you, Riv," I say, choking on the words as I step away.

"I love you, too. Please don't do this, don't leave me," she wails, going slack in Noah's arms. He holds on to her while tightly squeezing his eyes shut and biting on his lips.

I brush the tears from my eyes, turning my back on her and the boys for fear of breaking down.

Needing her to believe I can be strong on my own, I trudge up the strength that River helped to ignite in me. She has been my life support when I felt like the whole world was going to swallow me whole. She gave me a reason to keep on going when I wanted nothing more than to give up. She's my best friend, and there's nothing I wouldn't do for her, including walking away.

"Quinn!" she screams again.

My body feels like lead, but I force myself to keep moving. This is what I must do to prove it will be all right. I want her to go find our family and live the life she deserves. I know the four men with her will make sure that happens.

Holding on to the knowledge that I've done the right thing, I quicken my pace until I can no longer hear River's cries. I stop at the point where we discarded our weapons and pick them up. Heavily armed, I continue toward the city infested with the Afflicted.

A mixture of emotions overwhelms me when the end of the bridge comes into view. The carnage in front of me conjures a feeling I've never felt before. No longer will I have the safety net of knowing someone always has my back, I'm left to face the Afflicted and this decaying land alone.

I scan the city beyond the bridge. The Afflicted

scurry from building to building, slowly making their way back to where I stand. I square my shoulders and exhale every ounce of air from my lungs. I'm bound to lose the battle with them, but all the same, I won't let them take me without a fight. And maybe if I'm clever enough... fast enough... I'll make it somewhere safe. Perhaps the Sanctuary does exist, and I can live out the rest of my days inside of its walls.

"How can you walk away without so much as a goodbye?"

My stomach comes alive with butterflies and at the same time sinks. I slowly turn around and say, "What are you doing?"

Ryland doesn't bother to answer my question but carries on with his train of thought. "Because since the moment you came into my life, I've dreaded the day I would have to say those words to you. I've fought and bled to keep you with me. I'm haunted by the very thought of letting you go."

"Everything comes to an end, it's a hard lesson we were forced to learn through all of this," I say.

He steps closer to me, touching a strand of my hair that has escaped the bun on top of my head. He tucks the rogue piece behind my ear and softly says, "That's not the lesson I learned."

I swallow down the emotion building inside of me and ask, "What lesson did you learn?"

"That no matter what I have to face, I don't want to do it without you. I *can't* do it without you."

Tears sting my eyes as I half-heartedly push him away. "You promised to take care of River. You can't stay. I won't let you break that promise to me again."

"You're seriously the most stubborn woman I have ever met. I promised you I'd protect her just as I would one of my friends. I never promised to place her above you."

I shake my head, trying again to shove him back toward the border. "No, please don't do this. You have to go home."

His hand wraps around the back of my neck, and his eyes close tightly as his forehead drops to mine. "I don't have a home without you. I love you, Quinnten."

My knees weaken at his words, and his arm encircles my waist, holding me to him.

This isn't the way it ends for him. He's supposed to return home to his family and piece together the life he left behind, staying here with me is not a future.

"Go home," I beg him, tears streaming down my face.

"No."

"Please go home, Ryland." I don't want to be the reason he stays here. There's nothing but death and heartache in this place. He's done his time, and now he needs to leave.

"Nothing you can say will make me leave you, even if you don't love me in return."

I lift my head from his and grasp his face with both of my hands. "I do love you. I'm so madly in love with you, and it's why it kills me to think you're destined to live out your days here."

"With you," he adds.

I shake my head.

"With you, the woman I love."

"No," I whisper.

"Yes." His fingers dig into my hips, pulling me closer before his mouth covers mine. His tongue brushes against my lower lip, urging me to open to him and mirror the pace he sets. I let go of the last of my resolve and give in to his silent request. I savor the taste of him as I tangle my fingers in his hair, gripping it tightly.

Ryland kisses me with more than passion—it's an all-consuming, unconditional love. His love for me is sacrificial and limitless. It perfectly reflects mine for him. I don't ever want to let him go.

I catch my breath as Ryland plants soft pecks on my face and dries my tears.

"So, we're out of explosives and wondering how the two of you plan on getting us back to the boat," Wes interrupts.

"You do have another plan, right, Quinn?" Aiden asks.

I reluctantly pull my gaze from Ryland and look over his shoulder to see not only the three men I've come to consider my friends but my cousin as well.

My stomach sinks at the sight of them. "Why— How did you get back over the border?" I ask.

Noah shrugs and with a smirk says, "It turns out the guards know what to do when someone wants out of Stern, but they're clueless when people want back in. I think they were in a bit of shock as we ran back this way."

River walks away from the supportive arms of her boyfriend, her face streaked with tears. I swallow under the pure rage in her eyes. I wouldn't be surprised if she lodges one of her arrows into me, but instead, she goes for the less harmful and more immature approach of punching me in the shoulder.

"What the hell, Riv?" I whine, rubbing my arm.

"That's for scheming with my boyfriend behind my back and trying to abandon me." She pulls me from Ryland's arms, folding me into her own. "This is also for scheming with my boyfriend behind my back and trying to save me. Don't do that again, okay?"

I hug her back tightly and choke, "You should've gone and lived your life with Noah and found your parents."

"I don't think that's such a good idea right now. I'm pissed at him for plotting with you. I could use the time to cool down." She pulls away from me and flashes a sad smile. "Besides, we all leave, or none of us leave."

As much as I wish at least she and Noah would've continued to Giran, I'm glad I still have her with me. I know it's selfish, but I can't imagine surviving without her.

After I release River, Ryland steps back to my side, taking my hand into his. "So, what's the plan, love?"

I blow out a puff of air, the weight of the question pressing down on me. "I'm still working that out. But for now, it's to stay alive and hope the Sanctuary truly does exist."

He shakes his head. "It's an asinine idea, but I'm behind you if you think it's what we should do. In fact, I'll let you lead the way."

There's a total shift between us. I no longer feel the need to prove myself and fight for my place. He has accepted me as I am and trusts me as I trust him. We're better and stronger together.

I smile and marvel at the clarity of his green eyes as I say, "We stick together and do this as a team, Ry."

THE AFFLICTION TRILOGY BOOK TWO

READ IT NOW ON
KINDLE UNLIMITED

Acknowledgments

This book is almost ten years in the making. I've spent countless hours refining it to be the book you just read. I couldn't have done it without the amazing support system I have behind me. Living my dream of writing stories would not be possible without each and every one of these people.

Tony: I could not ask for a better husband. You work your ass off so I can do what I love. I'm so thankful for your listening ear and the hours long drives you take me on. Thank you for being my rock and audiobook listening partner.

Aidyn: Let's face it, it's a good feeling knowing my kid thinks I'm cool for writing books. Thank you for always coming into my office and giving me hugs, laughs, and snacks.

Rachel: Not everyone is as lucky as I am to find a best friend who you can do it all with. You not only make me a better person, but you push me to be a better writer. Here's to many more years of doing what we love.

Sam: What would we do without you? You make it possible for us to reach new readers by sharing our books on social media. Thank you for everything you do that takes the strain off us so we can write all the stories to our little hearts' content.

Tiffany: You are the reason that I knew this book could be something more. If my dark-romance-mafia-loving friend could fall in love with it, then so could the rest of the world. Thank you for giving me the courage to move forward with publishing it.

Ashlee: Every day you are a source of happiness. I love our group conversations and that you have a tendency of getting a little silly. Thank you so much for always being a joyful break in my day.

Heather: Your love for this story and your excitement to share it have motivated me through the editing and promotion of *Affliction*. Thank you for every post, every encouraging word, and for all the amazing pictures you take as Quinn.

Isabella: Thank you so much for helping me refine my book. Your talent for proofreading is amazing. And I'll always love your laugh.

The Wattpad Readers: Many of you have watched the evolution of this story from the very beginning. I'm so grateful for every comment and like. A special thank you to those brave enough to share their thoughts when it wasn't always positive feedback. You helped to make this story something I'm very proud of.

The Beta and ARC Readers: Thank you to each and every one of you that took the time to help me perfect this story. It is so amazing that so many of you fell in love with Quinn and Ryland.

About the Author

Crystal J. Johnson is a bestselling and award-winning author. Her works include the Affliction Trilogy, the Crown Trilogy and Staged. She is a Wattpad Creator and Featured Author, with almost a million reads on the publishing platform.

Along with Felicity Vaughn, Crystal is one half of the writing duo, Crystal and Felicity. Together they are the bestselling authors of KEPT IN THE DARK, EDGE OF THE VEIL and SPELLBOUND. Their third traditionally published novel, UNLEASHING CHAOS will be released by Anna Todd's Frayed Pages x Wattpad Books in June 2024.

To learn more about Crystal J. Johnson visit www.CrystalJJohnson.com.

More Books
From Crystal & Felicity

Made in the USA
Monee, IL
02 September 2024

64473570R00184